THE EAST PARK SYNDICATE

INSPECTOR WEST

PETER MULRANEY

ISBN: 978-0-6482661-9-8

Cover image from photo by Keenan Constance on Unsplash

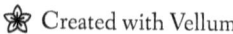 Created with Vellum

for Tess

MAJOR CRIMES TEAM

DCI Rankin (Chief)
DI West (Carl)
DS Fuller (Harry)
DC Beard (Nigel)
DC Paterson (Wayne)
DC Templar (Lisa)

Supporting Officers

Dr Jonas (Mike) Pathologist
Dr Worthington (Emma) Pathologist
Sgt Lang (Dean) Forensics
SC Head (Charlie) Uniform
PC Chan (Lily) Uniform
PC Monks (Adam) Uniform
PC Highland Community Liaison

CHAPTER ONE

Joanna Clarke looked at her watch, and then across the table at her older son, Justin, who was on his phone.

'He's still not answering, Mum,' said Justin. 'I hope he's on his way.'

It was ten minutes to two. Joanna didn't know what to think. It wasn't like Doug to be late, especially when it came to being in the spotlight, and today he was supposed to be introducing the Premier to launch Justin's election campaign.

She looked across the restaurant. People were eating and drinking at every table. The air vibrated with the sounds of clinking cutlery and excited voices. She felt an inner glow of pride. Justin had certainly attracted a large crowd of supporters to launch his campaign to become their local member.

She looked at her watch again, and then towards the foyer, expecting to see Doug striding across it to make a grand entrance. But there was no sign of him, and the Premier was due to arrive in less than ten minutes.

Not wanting to show her concern, Joanna took a deep breath and set her smile, although she knew something had to be wrong.

This launch meant as much to Doug as it did to Justin. He'd worked for years to get Justin selected as the party's candidate, and she knew there was no way he'd be missing the launch of his campaign if he could help it. What worried her was she hadn't heard from him since he'd left the house that morning to keep some appointment before joining them at the restaurant, and Doug was a stickler for letting her know when he was running late.

She looked at her watch again and turned to her younger son, Richard, sitting on her left with his wife, Kathy. 'You'd better think of a few words to introduce the Premier. It doesn't look like your father is going to make it in time.'

Richard, who was president of the local branch of the Liberal Party, smiled at her. 'He's sure cutting it fine.'

'Something unexpected must have come up,' said Joanna, 'but I'm surprised he hasn't called.'

Richard placed his hand on his mother's. 'I've got it covered, Mum. I've got a copy of Dad's speech in my pocket. I wrote this one.'

Joanna cocked an eyebrow. She'd always believed Doug wrote his own speeches.

'He didn't have time,' said Richard, 'besides, the Premier's office sent us the text, so it's not as if he could have ad-libbed much in any case.'

A white car with a state flag fluttering from a short staff at its front end pulled up outside the restaurant and all heads turned to watch the Premier and his minders make their way inside.

Richard stood, walked out to the foyer to greet the Premier, and then escorted him to the microphone set up in front of the bar.

The noise level abated as the serious part of the campaign launch got under way. Richard introduced the Premier using the glowing words of the text the Premier's office had sent him. The

Premier spoke for ten minutes outlining the party's policy platform and then introduced Justin Clarke as their local candidate.

Justin spoke to loud applause and answered several questions from the floor.

The Premier shook hands and posed for photographs with the party faithful who had come out to support their candidate. Then, he waved to the crowd and left with his minders to return to the never-ending list of duties that came with his office.

Joanna allowed herself to be swept up in the euphoria of the moment but, when it was over, she reached into her handbag and pulled out her phone. There was still no message from Doug.

Richard sat down beside her. 'Dad's going to be disappointed he missed this.'

'I can't believe he didn't turn up,' said Joanna.

'Why don't you try calling him again, Mum?' said Kathy.

Joanna picked up her phone and pressed the button to call Doug's number. She listened until his voicemail message came on.

'He's still not answering.'

'Something must have happened to him,' said Kathy.

'I'm going home,' said Joanna, gathering her things. 'If something's happened to him, that's where people will come looking for me.'

'Do you want me to come with you?' said Kathy.

'I should be okay,' said Joanna.

'Might be a good idea,' said Richard, 'especially if something has happened to Dad.'

Joanna didn't want to go there but the sinking feeling in her stomach told her Richard was probably right. 'Thank you.'

'I'll drop round when we finish up here,' said Richard.

CHAPTER TWO

Detective Inspector Carl West gazed at the mansions, set in extensive gardens and shielded from prying eyes by high fences and hedges, as Detective Sergeant Harry Fuller drove them deeper into East Park. The ambience of the suburb, created by galleries of overhanging street trees and the foliage of the urban forest growing in the park that gave the area its name, did nothing to lift Carl's sense of unease. He'd never enjoyed dealing with the self-important people that lived in East Park and wasn't looking forward to having to do it again.

Harry turned their silver Ford onto the roadway leading into the park and drove between the trees. After a few minutes, they came to a parking area next to one of the playing fields hidden within the forest, where several police vehicles and the coroner's grey van were parked.

'Ever been in here before, Boss?' said Harry, as he parked next to the patrol cars.

'Not for a long time,' said Carl. 'Not since I played football for the academy.'

'That sounds like ancient history,' said Harry.

'I'm not that old,' said Carl, 'but, to be honest, I don't remember the trees being this big.'

Harry laughed as they got out and walked around to the rear of the car to slip on their protective clothing.

'Sure is quiet in here,' said Carl.

'Hard to believe the city's just out there,' said Harry, pointing back towards the road they'd followed into the depth of the forest.

They walked over to the constable controlling access to the crime scene and signed themselves in.

'Who's in charge?' said Carl.

'Senior Constable Head, Inspector,' said the constable, lifting the crime scene tape for them.

They walked across the vacant parking area beyond the tape to where the scene of crime team had erected their blue tent.

Carl looked through the open side of the tent pitched in the grass on the edge of the parking area. The lifeless blue eyes of a white-haired man, dressed in a dark grey suit, soft pink tie, and a torn white bloodstained shirt, stared back at him. He wondered what a man dressed in a suit and expensive looking black shoes was doing in the middle of the East Park forest on a Saturday morning.

Harry squatted and studied the wound in the man's chest.

'Not much blood here, Boss,' said Harry, pointing to the ground next to the body.

Carl turned to SC Head, who was standing near the entrance of the tent.

'What do we know, Charlie?'

'Body was found about an hour ago by a couple of boys walking their dog.'

'How old?' said Carl.

'The older one is thirteen,' said Charlie. 'His little brother's a ten-year-old.'

'They okay?' said Carl.

'Seemed okay. Their father was here when we arrived,' said Charlie. 'The boys had a mobile phone and called their father. He's the one who called us.'

'Get a statement?' said Carl.

SC Head nodded. 'Yeah, but nothing useful from the boys. They didn't see anyone or hear anything but we know who the victim is, Inspector. The father recognized him as the local mayor. A man named Doug Clarke.'

The name didn't mean anything to Carl. 'Have you been able to confirm that?'

'Did a quick check on the council website. Looks like him.'

At least that would give them somewhere to start, thought Carl. 'Get an address, Harry.' He turned back to SC Head. 'Anything found on the body?'

'Nothing in his pockets, Inspector,' said Charlie.

Carl wondered why someone would remove the victim's ID and then dump his body in the middle of the suburb where he was the mayor.

'Anybody else in the vicinity?'

'We haven't seen anyone,' said Charlie, 'not even any spectators.'

'Thanks, Charlie.' Carl walked over to where Dr Mike Jonas, the police pathologist, was packing up his equipment.

'Nice place for a picnic,' said Mike.

'Or for boys to walk their dog,' said Carl.

'Yeah, but I guess stumbling across this might have ruined their day,' said Mike.

'Be something to tell their mates at school on Monday,' said Carl. 'What can you tell me about our friend here?'

'Someone stuck a knife into him, right up under his ribcage.'

'Doesn't seem to be much blood on the ground here,' said Carl.

'Can't argue with that,' said Mike.

'How long do you think he's been dead?' said Carl.

'Not long, Carl. Probably only a matter of hours.'

Sgt Lang from the scene of crime team came over to join them.

'What do you think, Dean?'

'I'd say the body was dumped here, Inspector.'

'What makes you think that?'

'There's bugger all blood on the ground where the body is or anywhere else in the immediate vicinity and, if you look there,' said Dean, pointing at the ground between the shoes of the victim and the edge of the parking area, 'you can see the body was dragged into the grass from the car park.'

Carl looked where Dean was pointing. There were two faint lines of depressed grass that ended at the heels of the victim's shoes. 'Any other footprints?'

'Only impressions in the grass,' said Dean. 'Nothing conclusive.'

'Anything in the car park?' said Carl.

'Nothing we can use,' said Dean. 'I guess it's fair to assume whoever left him here drove in and out in a vehicle but this uneven surface makes it difficult to pick up any tread marks.'

'Any sign of a murder weapon?'

'We're still searching the area, Inspector, but it might take a while. Could be anywhere along the length of the road into here, if it's here at all.'

'Let me know if you find it,' said Carl.

———

The house at 14 Orange Drive was set well back from the street behind a high stone wall but, to Carl's surprise, the gate giving access to the driveway was open. They drove in and parked behind the Mercedes sedan at the top of the driveway.

'Nice house,' said Harry, as they got out of the car.

'Must cost a fortune to maintain a place like this,' said Carl, admiring the stonework adorning the front of the two-storey dwelling.

'You'd definitely want someone to cut the grass,' said Harry, pointing towards the sweep of lawn in front of the house.

'Even I have someone come in and mow the lawns,' said Carl. 'Can't see the point of wasting my free time walking around behind a lawnmower.'

Harry pushed the doorbell and they waited on the veranda until the door was opened by a woman Carl decided was too young to be the victim's wife.

'Detective Inspector West, City Police,' said Carl, showing her his ID. 'We're looking for Mrs Clarke.'

'I'm Kathy Clarke. I'm married to Richard, but I guess you're looking for my mother-in-law if you're here.'

'Is she home?' said Carl. 'I need to speak to her.'

'Something's happened to Dad, hasn't it?'

'Why would you think that?' said Carl.

'He didn't show up for the launch and we can't get him to answer his phone.'

'Who is it?' said Joanna, walking up behind Kathy.

'The police, Mum. They're here about Dad,' said Kathy.

Carl wondered if she'd read his body language or knew more than she was letting on.

'Has he been in an accident?'

'Might be best if we come in, Mrs Clarke,' said Carl. 'I'm afraid it's a bit more serious than that.'

The color faded in the older Mrs Clarke's face and Carl thought that she, at least, appeared surprised.

'He's dead, isn't he?'

'We need to make a positive identification before I can confirm that, Mrs Clarke, but we have a body that's been tentatively identified as being your husband. I'm sorry.'

'What was your name again?' said Joanna.

'Detective Inspector West.'

'You'd better come in and give us the details, Inspector' said Joanna, 'in case it is him. We can go into the library.'

Joanna led them into the first room on the left off the entrance hall. The walls were lined with shelves holding the Clarke's extensive collection of books. She invited them to sit in the comfortable looking armchairs occupying the space between the bookcases.

'Where was this body found, Inspector?' said Joanna.

'Near the playing fields in East Park.'

'What would Doug be doing in the park?' said Joanna. 'He never goes in there.' She looked at Carl. 'What makes you think it's Doug?'

'The father of the boys that found the body told us he recognized him,' said Carl. 'Do you have a recent photograph of your husband, Mrs Clarke?'

'I've got one on my phone,' said Kathy. 'I took one of him with Dougie the other day.'

They waited while she scrolled through her photos. 'Here, this was taken last weekend.'

Carl took her phone and looked at the image of a smiling Doug Clarke holding his grandson. The man in the photograph had the same blue eyes that had stared back at him in the park.

'Show them the photo, Sergeant.'

Harry opened his tablet and showed Joanna the head and shoulders shot the police photographer had sent him.

'That's Doug,' said Joanna, sinking back into her armchair.

Harry turned the tablet so Kathy could see the image. She took one look and raised her hands to her face.

Carl waited. Mrs Clarke did not appear to be going to pieces on him.

'What happens now?' said Joanna.

'I'll need to ask you some questions,' said Carl, 'and we'll need to arrange for a family member to formally identify the body.'

'One of the boys can do that,' said Joanna.

'How many sons do you have?' said Carl.

'Just the two. Justin and Richard.'

'Richard should be here soon,' said Kathy. 'I'm sure he'll do that for you.'

Carl waited for Harry to take out his notebook.

'When was the last time you saw your husband, Mrs Clarke?'

'This morning. He left around ten. He was supposed to meet up with us at the restaurant.'

'A special occasion?' said Carl, taking in the attire of the women he was interviewing and thinking of the grey suit and pink tie the victim had been wearing.

'The launch of our son's election campaign, Inspector. Justin's standing to be the local member. Doug was meant to be introducing the Premier but Richard had to do it.'

Carl glanced at Kathy. She was sitting with her arms wrapped around each other. For the moment, now that he understood the context of her earlier statement, he was prepared to give her the benefit of the doubt.

'Where was your husband going when he left this morning?' said Carl, wondering how extensive Doug Clarke's network was if he knew the Premier and his son was running for parliament.

'Said he had a meeting.'

'Did he say who he was meeting?'

'Doug was the mayor, Inspector. He was always going to

meetings.' Joanna shrugged her shoulders. 'I have no idea who he was meeting this morning.'

'Did he keep a diary?'

'Be on his phone.'

'Do you have the code for opening his phone?'

'It will be in his little black book in the study,' said Joanna, making no move to retrieve it.

'Did he have his phone with him when he left this morning?' said Carl.

'He didn't go anywhere without it. Wasn't it in his car?'

'What was he driving?'

'A Mercedes like the one outside,' said Joanna, looking from Carl to Harry and back again. 'Wasn't it where you found the body?'

'No,' said Carl. 'Did Doug normally carry a wallet?'

'Is that missing as well?' said Joanna.

'Yes,' said Carl. 'You'll need to contact your bank to get a stop on his accounts.'

The sound of the front door closing, followed by the tapping of footsteps in the hallway outside the library, interrupted Carl's train of thought.

'In here, Richard,' said Kathy.

A man Carl immediately recognized as a son of the victim appeared in the library doorway.

'Who are you?' said Richard.

'They're the police, honey. Dad's dead.'

Richard stepped into the room and stood behind his mother's armchair. 'What happened?'

'We're treating it as a homicide,' said Carl.

'And, you are?'

'Detective Inspector West,' said Carl, showing Richard his ID, 'and this is Detective Sergeant Fuller.'

'Homicide? You mean you think somebody killed him?' said Richard.

'Yes.'

'How?'

'I'd prefer not to go into details at this stage, Mr Clarke,' said Carl. 'Perhaps you could each tell me where you were this morning between say ten and noon. Mr Clarke?'

'Are we suspects now, Inspector?'

'Everybody who knew your father in any way is a suspect, Mr Clarke, until we can eliminate them from the list.'

'I was at home with Kathy until eleven,' said Richard, 'then we took our son to Kathy's parents' place. We were at the restaurant by twelve. I had to help set up.' He looked at his wife.

'That sounds about right,' said Kathy.

'And you, Mrs Clarke?'

'I was here on my own after Doug left,' said Joanna. 'I left for the restaurant just before twelve thirty.'

'Thank you,' said Carl.

'When can we see the body?' said Richard.

'We'll need someone to make a formal identification,' said Carl. 'Could you do that when we finish here?'

'Can I bring my brother?' said Richard.

'By all means,' said Carl, passing him a card. 'The address you'll need to come to is on here.'

'I can't believe this is happening,' said Richard.

'I'm sorry,' said Carl. 'Believe me, I wish it wasn't either but it's a reality you're going to have to deal with.'

'Where do you start?' said Joanna. 'How do you find his killer?'

'Did your husband mention anything about being threatened by anyone?'

'Doug was everybody's friend, Inspector. That's why he'd been elected mayor three times. He didn't have enemies.'

Carl doubted that was true. He turned to Richard. 'Did he say anything to you?'

'Nothing,' said Richard.

Carl pushed himself up from the armchair. 'Can you give me your husband's mobile phone number, Mrs Clarke? It might help us trace his last movements.'

'I'll give you one of his business cards.'

Carl waited while Mrs Clarke retrieved a business card from her husband's study.

'When you contact the bank, Mrs Clarke, ask them if anyone has used your husband's accounts today?' said Carl. 'It may help us identify the killer.'

'And how will I tell you about that?' said Joanna.

Carl handed her one of his business cards. 'My contact details are on here if you need them.' He turned to leave and then stopped. 'By the way, is your husband's car registered in his name?'

'No. It's registered in the name of Doug Clarke Real Estate,' said Richard. 'All our cars are, but Mum and Dad's are the only Mercedes we have on the books.'

———

Carl kept his eyes on Richard and Kathy Clarke standing on the veranda as Harry reversed their car out of the driveway into Orange Drive.

'What did you make of that, Harry?'

'They didn't seem all that shocked when you told them he was dead. It was almost as if they'd been expecting it.'

'They must have known, at least suspected, something had happened to him,' said Carl. 'After all, he hadn't turned up for what sounds like an important event or answered his phone.'

'But they hadn't reported him as missing either, Boss.'

'Maybe they were hoping he'd turn up,' said Carl.

'Wonder how connected these Clarkes are to the Premier, Boss. That could be a problem.'

'I'll let the chief deal with that. Let's see if we can trace his movements through this phone number and get an APB out on his vehicle. We might get lucky if we find his car.'

'Or if the killer uses his credit cards,' said Harry.

CHAPTER THREE

Carl felt a nudge in his side. He opened his eyes and looked at the screen of the baby monitor on the bedside cabinet. Sophie was standing in her cot and calling out to him, which meant she was ready to get up and start her day. He glanced at their alarm clock. It was five fifty-nine. He hit the off button, slipped out of bed, and went into the nursery.

'How's my little princess this morning?'

'Daddy! Daddy!'

Sophie stretched her arms out to him and he lifted her out of the cot. He kissed her on the cheek. She pulled his hair and grinned at him

'Drink!' She pointed to her water bottle on the cupboard next to the change table.

Carl handed Sophie the bottle, and she sucked on its tube as he placed her on the table and exchanged her wet nappy for a fresh one.

'Come on, let's go and see what Mummy is doing,' said Carl, lifting Sophie from the change table and taking her into the kitchen where Nina was preparing breakfast.

'Mummy! Mummy!' said Sophie.

Carl held Sophie close to Nina. She kissed her mother on the cheek and pulled her hair.

'Hello, pumpkin,' said Nina, as she gently extracted her hair from Sophie's grasp. 'Mummy's making your breakfast.'

Carl put Sophie into her high chair and slipped on her bib.

'Your eggs are ready,' said Nina, placing a bowl of soggy cornflakes and a spoon on the tray of the high chair.

Carl ate his breakfast while Sophie spooned most of the cornflakes into her mouth, then went to the bathroom for a quick shave before changing into the suit he wore to work. He looked at his watch as he walked back into the kitchen. It was five to seven. His train left the platform at seven ten.

He kissed his wife and daughter, who tried to wipe her sticky hands on the sleeve of his jacket. 'I'll see you when I get home, Sophie. Be good for Mummy.'

'Let me know if you're going to be late,' said Nina. 'Harry and Jessika are coming for tea tonight.'

'Shouldn't be a problem,' said Carl, giving Nina a hug. 'Gotta go or I'll miss my train.'

———

Carl stood in front of the whiteboard mounted on the wall outside his office. He placed the head and shoulders photograph of Doug Clarke that the crime scene investigators had given them on the whiteboard and turned to face the team.

Wayne looked like he'd had a heavy Saturday night but knowing Wayne's wife of twenty-six years had left him, Carl knew better than to say anything. He knew Wayne was struggling to accept his new reality, despite it being one many officers experienced. And, he knew how difficult the early days were from his own painful experience when Virginia had walked out on him. He hoped their new case would be enough to distract Wayne from his personal problems. He was a good detective. Carl didn't want to lose him.

He cast his eye over the rest of the team assembled before him. Harry looked like he'd had a good night's sleep, but Lisa and Nigel were both a little bleary eyed. He hoped their coffees would kick in soon.

'Doug Clarke,' said Carl, pointing to the photograph on the whiteboard. 'Found dead next to the playing fields inside the East Park forest yesterday morning. He was stabbed in the chest but the cause of death won't be official until after this morning's post mortem.'

'Isn't he the mayor of East Park?' said Wayne.

'You know him?'

'Know of him. Seen his mug on poles during council elections.'

'Apparently been elected mayor three times,' said Carl. 'At least, that's what his wife told us.'

'But you don't live in East Park,' said Harry, turning to face Wayne.

'Doesn't mean I don't go there, Sarge. Besides, we've got history. He sold me my first house.'

'Know anything else about him?' said Carl.

'I hear he's in the Premier's inner circle, one of his trusted advisors, apparently.'

'How do you know all this?' said Harry.

'I'm a member of the party. In fact, I heard last week that one of his sons had been preselected for Lidall, one of the safest seats in the state.'

'Justin,' said Carl. 'We met him yesterday when he came in with his brother to identify the body.'

'Hope this isn't going to be difficult,' said Wayne. 'Don't think I'd like to be in the Commissioner's shoes if this drags on.'

'Well, we're starting behind the eight ball,' said Carl. 'Sgt Lang thinks he was killed elsewhere and his body dumped in the forest. So, I guess we can expect a bit of heat from upstairs until we get this sorted.'

'Who found the body?' said Lisa.

'A couple of boys out walking their dog, and they seem to have been the only people in the East Park forest at the time.'

'Did they see anyone?'

'Apparently not.'

'Do we have a murder weapon?' said Nigel.

'Not yet,' said Carl, turning to Harry. 'Any luck with that mobile phone number?'

'It's been turned off since nine forty-five yesterday morning. So, I'd say he switched it off before he left home, if what his wife told us is correct.'

'Do we know what he was supposed to be doing yesterday?' said Lisa.

'He told his wife he was going to a meeting and that he'd meet her at the restaurant where their son was launching his election campaign. He was supposed to be introducing the Premier,' said Carl.

'Pretty cloak and dagger,' said Wayne, 'a mayor not wanting anybody to know who he was meeting or where.'

'Hopefully we'll find that out when we recover his phone,' said Carl. 'Apparently he used it as his diary.'

'We might be able to work that out from his call log,' said Harry. 'They've promised me an annotated log first thing this morning.'

'Any news on his car, Sergeant?'

'Not yet, Boss. Anything from his wife on his bank accounts?'

'No sign anyone's tried to access them,' said Carl, 'which suggests theft wasn't the motive.'

'So, who would want to kill him?' said Wayne.

'That's where we come in,' said Carl. 'We need to start talking to people who knew him. DS Fuller and I will speak to the family, but I'll need you to speak to members of the East Park Council and members of the Liberal Party, starting with the Lidall branch. Perhaps you can use your connections there, Wayne, and Nigel and Lisa can tackle the members of the council.'

'Could take a while,' said Nigel.

'Start with the council website, Nigel. It should list the councillors and give you some way to contact them. You can always follow up at the City of East Park on Monday if you need to. Besides, it might be a good idea to get an insight from East Park's CEO as well.'

As the detectives started on their assigned tasks, Carl headed for the elevator to go down to the police morgue under the building. 'I'll catch you after the autopsy, Harry.'

———

Mike Jonas was on the telephone in his office when Carl arrived in the morgue. Carl slipped into the green gown that would protect his suit during the autopsy and waited for Mike to emerge from his office.

'Bloody politicians,' said Mike. 'That was the Premier's office wanting to know how our friend here had been killed.'

'What did you tell them?' said Carl, wondering who would be at work in the Premier's office on a Sunday morning.

'That they'd find out in due course like everybody else,' said Mike, pulling on his gloves. 'Wasn't this guy the mayor of East Park?'

Carl nodded.

'How does that make him important enough for the Premier to want to know how he was killed?'

'I gather he was one of the Premier's inner circle of advisors,' said Carl, 'but I'm surprised the Premier's office called you, given he has a direct line to the Commissioner.'

'Hmmm. Maybe it's not the Premier but someone in his office that wants to know,' said Mike.

'Who called?'

'Someone called John Jeffries.'

'I'll have a word with him,' said Carl, writing the name in his notebook. 'Be interesting to find out why he's poking his nose into our business behind the Premier's back.'

'Ready?' said Mike. 'This shouldn't take long. Looks pretty straight forward.'

Carl watched as Mike examined the surface of the body.

'There's a wound to the back of the head consistent with a blunt force trauma, possibly caused by the victim falling backwards and hitting his head,' said Mike. 'There are traces of what looks like sand in the dried blood around the wound.' Mike used a swab on a stick to remove some of the dried blood for analysis. 'Should be able to tell you the color of the sand, at least.'

Carl made himself a note to look out for that in Mike's report.

Mike examined the victim's fingernails. 'Nothing under the nails. It looks like he didn't get a chance to fight back.' The pathologist moved his attention to the wound in the victim's chest. 'This is a pretty clean cut, Carl. Looks like your killer knew what he was doing.'

'What do you think he used?' said Carl.

'Probably a long-bladed hunting knife or something similar.'

'Ruptured lungs?'

'We'd see blood around the mouth and nose if that were the case,' said Mike. 'I suspect he's pierced the heart. I'll have a better idea when I open him up.'

Carl wondered whether the murderer was a trained killer or

someone who'd simply got lucky when he stuck the knife in. He watched Mike open the victim's ribcage and examine his heart.

Mike lifted the heart out of the victim's body. 'Deep gash across the ventricles. He would have bled out pretty quickly, Carl.'

'What do you think, Mike? Frontal attack or stabbed from behind?'

'Hard to tell, Carl, but it looks like an upward motion to me. It's not like the knife went in horizontally. Your killer's picked the centre of the diaphragm and pushed the knife up into the heart. As I said, I reckon he knew what he was doing.'

Carl waited while Mike completed the steps required to write up his autopsy report.

'Nothing out of the ordinary, health wise, for a man in his early seventies,' said Mike. 'I think we can assign the cause of death to the knife wound to the heart without fear of contradiction.'

'Find anything on his clothes?'

'Some dark fibres, similar to those you'd find in the matting in the trunk of a car,' said Mike, 'but nothing to help you identify the killer, I'm afraid.'

'That lines up with Dean's theory,' said Carl.

'Sorry I can't give you anything else, Carl.'

'Perhaps we'll get something when we find his car.'

———

Harry was staring at the screen of his computer when Carl returned from the autopsy.

'Get that call log yet, Harry?'

'He sure talked to a lot of people,' said Harry, pointing to his screen.

'What details have they given you?'

'Names and addresses. I just have to work out who's who in the zoo.'

'Did he talk to anyone Saturday morning?'

'Not on this phone.'

'Anyone try to call him after he turned it off?'

'Only members of his family,' said Harry, 'and that doesn't start until twelve forty-five.'

'What about text messages?'

'Nothing on Saturday but it looks like most of his text messages are between him and his wife, and occasionally with Justin's number.'

'So, anything standing out?'

'There's more than a hundred calls in the week leading up to his death, and that looks fairly average.'

'Didn't realize a mayor's life was so hectic,' said Carl. 'Is there a pattern?'

'There are some numbers that appear quite often. I'm just trying to figure out who the people are and where they might fit into his life. Find out anything from Mike?'

'Nothing we didn't know,' said Carl, 'although, Mike thinks the killer knew what he was doing. Knife went straight into the heart.'

'Could have been a lucky stab,' said Harry.

'Or we're dealing with a trained killer,' said Carl. 'Maybe our victim had some enemies after all.'

'He's had a lot of calls from someone called Howard Stenhouse,' said Harry. 'Spoke to him three times on Friday.'

'Find out who he is. Might be someone worth having a chat with.'

———

The foreshore playground was deserted. The families that had enjoyed the sunshine of the warm spring Sunday he had spent at work had headed home by the time Carl arrived at the playground with Sophie.

He unclipped Sophie from the safety harness of her stroller, pulled her hat down over her ears, and lifted her onto the grass.

'Swing!' said Sophie, as soon as her shoes touched the grass.

She ran over to the swing and waited for Carl to lift her in and do up the chain.

'Hold on,' said Carl, as he pushed her away from him. He watched a grin spread across her face as the swing rose into the air.

'More!' said Sophie, as the swing brought her back to him.

He gave her another gentle push.

After another few pushes she stopped asking for more and lifted her hands in the air. It was time for something else. Carl lifted her out of the swing and followed her to the slide, where he helped her climb the short ladder up to the top. When she was seated, he let her go and stepped to the bottom of the slide to catch her before she hit the ground.

'Again!' said Sophie.

They repeated the routine until Sophie had had enough of the slide and wanted to crawl through the tunnels and climb on the tower.

When the street lights came on, Carl bundled Sophie back into her stroller and headed for home, happy he'd spent half an hour in the playground with her, far away from the cares of his job. Life would be so much easier if people didn't kill each other, he thought, as he pushed her along in the stroller.

———

It was eight-thirty by the time Carl finally settled Sophie into her cot. As he checked the baby monitor and quietly closed the door to the nursery, he wondered if they should go ahead and try for another child. He knew Nina was nearing the age where they'd have to make that decision soon or resign themselves to being parents of an only child.

He went into the dining room and joined the others at the table.

'She's asleep,' said Carl, as he sat down.

'How long will she sleep for?' said Jessika.

'Until about six in the morning,' said Nina.

'That's good, isn't it?' said Harry. 'Has she always slept right through?'

'I wish,' said Carl, 'but she's been a lot better since her last lot of teeth came through.'

'Still enjoying being a dad?' said Jessika.

'She's the best thing that's ever happened to me,' said Carl, 'after Nina, of course.'

Nina blew him a kiss across the table. 'Make sure you remember that, mate.'

Harry laughed and topped up Carl's glass from the bottle of shiraz on the table.

Carl noticed Harry didn't offer any red wine to Jessika after he topped up Nina's glass. 'Not having any wine, Jessika?'

'Not for the next few months,' said Jessika. 'We're pregnant.'

Carl slapped Harry on the back. 'Congratulations!'

'Be a playmate for Sophie,' said Jessika, as she returned Nina's hug.

'I was hoping to talk Carl into having another child myself,' said Nina, 'before he gets too old.'

'Me?' said Carl. 'I'm not the one with a time limit on my eggs.'

'I've got a few more years yet,' said Nina.

'Perhaps we could do this together,' said Jessika, winking at Carl.

'At least Harry won't have to worry about being mistaken as the grandfather,' said Nina.

'I'm learning to take it graciously,' said Carl.

CHAPTER FOUR

With the team waiting outside his office, Carl listened to Chief Inspector Rankin's voice sounding in his right ear.

'If there's anything political about this, Carl, the Commissioner wants to know before we take it to the media.'

'No problem with that, Chief, but I think we're a long way from knowing if that's even on the cards at the moment.'

'Maybe,' said Chief Inspector Rankin, 'but, given Doug Clarke's connections, you might want to keep it in mind as a possibility.'

The chief inspector ended the call. Carl returned the handset of his desk telephone to its cradle and left his office to start the business of the day.

'How are we going with our interviews?' said Carl.

'I've got a long list,' said DC Paterson. 'Might need some help.'

'Make a start, Wayne. Nigel and Lisa can help you when they're finished with the councillors,' said Carl. 'How's that looking, Nigel?'

'We're doing six each, Inspector. Most of them today, and I'm speaking with the CEO tomorrow morning. He's interstate.'

'Anything from Forensics?' said DS Fuller.

'They've drawn a blank,' said Carl. 'What about that call log?'

'Still working on it,' said DS Fuller.

'This might get easier if we can narrow down who he could have been meeting with on Saturday morning, so make that a focus of your questioning,' said Carl.

'Wouldn't the mayor have an office in the East Park Council Chambers?' said DC Templar. 'We might find a copy of his diary there.'

'Check it out,' said Carl. 'And, folks, the Commissioner doesn't want any of us talking to the media, especially about anything connected to a sitting politician, so be discreet.'

———

The first thing Carl noticed when they arrived at Justin Clarke's house was that it was nothing like the home of his parents. Justin lived in a new but modest dwelling, by East Park standards, located in a zone of the city undergoing transformation through the process of urban renewal. The house was one of those modern buildings he'd heard Nina describe as boxes. All straight lines with no character. Carl could hear her disparaging assessment of such houses as 'functional but lacking in aesthetics' as he waited with Harry on the tiny front porch for someone to answer the door.

They were shown into the study, where they met with Justin and his brother.

'Any idea why your father would have turned off his mobile phone?' said Carl.

'No wonder we couldn't reach him,' said Richard.

'Are you sure it was turned off?' said Justin. 'That doesn't sound like Dad.'

'Your mother told us he left the house around ten on Saturday morning,' said Carl. 'His provider has advised they haven't had a signal from his device since nine forty-five Saturday, which suggests he turned it off or its battery was flat.'

'Dad would have plugged it into the charging port in his car if the battery was low,' said Justin. 'He had a policy of being contactable at all hours. Drove Mum nuts at times, but that's how it was. Something's not right here, Inspector.'

'Any idea who he might have been meeting?' said Carl.

'He hadn't told us he was meeting with anybody,' said Richard, shaking his head. 'I still can't believe he'd scheduled a meeting before the launch. He'd been working on Justin's preselection for years, building up the numbers we'd need when the time arrived. Dad was pretty excited we'd pulled it off.' Richard looked at Carl. 'We hadn't expected Ross Whitaker to step down until the next election.'

'What made Whitaker resign early?' said Carl, wondering if he'd been pushed.

'It's all a bit sad, really,' said Justin. 'Ross' wife has been diagnosed with early onset dementia and he's resigning to look after her.'

Carl shuddered. He didn't want to think about dementia; the thought of losing his mind as he got older was one he preferred to avoid.

'How was your Dad's relationship with Ross Whitaker? Could he have been meeting with him?' said Carl.

'Ross was at the launch,' said Justin, 'with his wife.'

'Had your father fallen out with anybody in the party?' said Carl.

'I'm sure there are people he had differences of opinion with,' said Justin, 'but that's the nature of politics. But I can't say I'm aware of anyone we'd see as an enemy, at least not anyone who'd go as far as killing Dad to shut him up.'

'Where do you fit into this political game?' said Carl, turning to face Richard.

'I'm president of the local branch. I took over the role when Dad became mayor.'

'What does that involve?' said Carl.

'Fundraising and networking, mainly.'

'So, you're the man behind your brother's preselection?'

Richard smiled and shook his head. 'Dad did most of the networking.'

'So, your father knew a lot of people, then?'

'That's an understatement, Inspector,' said Justin. 'Dad knew just about everybody who was anybody on our side of politics. We're going to have to bury him from the cathedral, and even that might not be big enough to hold the crowd.'

'And there's all the people in real estate he knew,' said Richard. 'You're going to have to talk to a hell of a lot of people to find out who he was meeting with yesterday, Inspector, if you don't find his phone.'

'Was your father still involved in the business?'

'Not officially,' said Justin. 'He retired and handed the running of the business over to us when he decided to run for mayor. That was about ten years ago. He was halfway through his third term as mayor.'

'How did he get on with the City Council?'

'Pretty well as far as I know,' said Justin. 'He'd been on the council for years before he decided to have a go at becoming mayor.'

'Is there any family besides you?'

'Dad has a younger brother, Robert. He runs the family farm, which is just out of North Summit. He has three sons around our age,' said Justin. 'They're all on the land up at North Summit. We get together a few times a year but Dad wasn't all that keen on going up to the farm. We had to pester him when we were kids. Things changed a bit after his father died. He seemed more relaxed about visiting after that.'

'Had he had a fallout with his father?'

Justin shrugged his shoulders. 'You'll have to ask Mum about that, Inspector. He never said anything to us about it.'

'If anyone comes to mind or you hear anything, give me a call,' said Carl, standing.

'Where do you go from here, Inspector? It doesn't seem like you have much to go on,' said Richard.

'We've asked the public to help us locate your father's car,' said Carl. 'Hopefully, we'll get a picture of his movements from what they tell us.'

———

As they drove into the car park at Police Headquarters, Carl remembered he hadn't called John Jeffries.

'Someone claiming to be from the Premier's office called Mike before the autopsy, yesterday,' said Carl. 'Someone fishing for information.'

'Could be anybody,' said Harry.

When they reached the third floor, Carl went into his office and looked up the number for the Premier's office. When he found it, he punched the digits into the keypad of the telephone on his desk.

'Detective Inspector West from City Police. I'd like to speak to John Jeffries, please.'

'There's no-one here by that name, Inspector. Is there anyone else who can help you?'

'Looks like I've been given the wrong number.'

'Would you like me to check the public service directory for you, Inspector?'

'If you don't mind,' said Carl.

'Just a minute.'

Carl waited and wondered if Mike had received a prank call.

'I'm sorry, Inspector, there's no-one by that name listed in the directory.'

'Thanks,' said Carl. 'Sorry to have troubled you.'

He ended the call and keyed in Mike' s number.

'What's up?' said Mike.

'Any numbers on your call log I need to know about?'

'I have a mobile for those calls, Carl. Why do you ask?'

'There's no-one called John Jeffries working in the Premier's office.'

'Could be someone from the media,' said Mike. 'Wouldn't be the first time one of them has pulled a stunt like that.'

'Well, let's see if we can find out who wanted to know,' said Carl.

He ended the call and rang Dean Lang.

'Dean, get one of your technicians to retrieve the incoming call log on Mike Jonas' office line. I want to know who called him just before nine on Sunday morning.'

As he replaced the handset, Carl's mobile phone started ringing.

'Operations, Inspector. Your Mercedes has turned up.'

'Where?'

'About fifteen kilometres this side of North Summit.'

'What condition is it in?'

'It's intact, Inspector. One of the local boys is sitting with it until you arrive. I'll send you the map reference.'

When the email arrived, Carl forwarded it to Dean Lang and then called him.

'Sent you an email, Dean. Need a team to retrieve Doug Clarke's car and go over the spot where it was found.'

'On my way, Inspector.'

'Meet you there,' said Carl. He slipped his mobile phone into his pocket and walked out to Harry's desk. 'Get your coat, Harry. Uniform have located the victim's car outside North Summit.'

'Just let me get the contact details for his brother, Boss. Perhaps we can kill two birds with one stone while we're up there.'

————

Harry pulled in behind the Highway Patrol car parked on the shoulder of the road leading to North Summit. Carl eased out of the car and stretched in an effort to overcome the effects of two hours of sitting. The wind stung his face and messed with his hair.

Carl glanced around. There was no sign of the Mercedes. He assumed it was somewhere behind the trees that lined the road. Then he spotted the dirt side road in front of the patrol car and wondered if they'd actually arrived or still had some way to travel.

The constable sitting in the Highway Patrol car got out of the vehicle as they approached.

'DI West,' said Carl, showing him his ID.

'Bill Amberton. I'm from Ashcroft, Inspector.'

'Your sergeant told us we'd find you here, Bill. Where's the car?'

'There's a parking spot used by the local kids behind those trees,' said the constable, pointing to the scrub on the other side of the dirt road. 'This is where they catch the school bus.'

'Who called it in?'

'The Mercedes was here when the Richmond kids came

down to catch the bus this morning. Young Simon recognized it from the Sunday paper and called us.'

'Did you speak to him?'

'No, Sgt Snow took the call. Gary, that's Simon's father, was here when I arrived. Said he'd come down to keep an eye on things until I got here,' said PC Amberton. 'Gary reckons the car wasn't here Sunday morning when they drove past on their way home from Church, around eleven.'

Carl wondered where the Mercedes had been between the time Doug Clarke had left home on Saturday and someone had abandoned it here after eleven on Sunday morning. 'Anyone been near the vehicle?'

'Not since I got here, Inspector, and I heard Sgt Snow telling Simon not to touch anything.'

'Double check with the boy to make sure they didn't touch anything before he called, and let me know,' said Carl, turning to Harry. 'Any word from Dean?'

'Be here in about five.'

'Guess you can be on your way, Bill, when they arrive,' said Carl.

'Let me give Sgt Snow a call, Inspector. He was going to interview Simon when he got to school.'

Carl took the opportunity to relieve his bladder in among the trees while PC Amberton checked with Sgt Snow, and was making his way back to the patrol car when a white van and a flatbed tow truck pulled in behind their Ford.

'Sgt Snow says Simon told him they didn't go near the car,' said PC Amberton. 'Seems the kids these days watch enough crime shows to know not to contaminate the evidence.'

'Thanks, Bill.'

PC Amberton drove off as Carl and Harry slipped on their scene of crime suits, before joining the team from Forensics to examine the Mercedes, which was parked between the trees lining the road and the fence of a paddock in which two older model cars were parked.

Carl watched as Sgt Lang tried the driver's side door. It opened. Sgt Lang looked inside, then walked around to the trunk, pushed the release, and lifted the lid. He stepped back from the car and turned his head away.

'Better take a look in here, Inspector.'

Carl smelt it before he saw it. The matting was covered in dried blood.

'Smelt it as soon as I opened the door,' said Sgt Lang.

'If he's this careless, we might get lucky, Dean.'

'We'll give it the treatment, Inspector. If he's left anything inside, we'll find it.'

'Wonder why he left it here.'

'Key fob's inside,' said Sgt Lang, walking back to the driver's door.

Carl waited. Sgt Lang checked the shift was in park and then pushed the button to bring the instrument panel to life.

'Fuel gauge is on empty, Inspector.'

'Let's have a look around before you load it up.'

They searched the area around the Mercedes without finding anything, apart from numerous footprints between where the Mercedes was parked and the spot where the school bus stopped on the main road.

Carl walked along the roadway in the direction of North Summit, beyond the tyre tracks left by the school bus pulling back onto the road, and looked at the compacted gravel along the shoulder of the highway. There were no footprints in the gravel, suggesting to Carl the driver had either walked on the bitumen or been picked up.

CHAPTER FIVE

Sitting in the manager's office at Doug Clarke Real Estate, Justin Clarke turned his attention to the month's figures. After spending half an hour wading through the sea of condolence emails in his inbox, he felt the tension in his shoulders release as he focussed on the numbers.

It looked like they'd make budget, despite the continued decline in property sales across the eastern suburbs they serviced. Justin wondered how long they'd manage to keep their heads above water if things didn't improve. He didn't relish the idea of having to let go any of his sales agents but he didn't have any new developments coming onto the market in the foreseeable future. They were relying on the sale of existing properties but, according to the spreadsheet in front of him, their stock of houses to sell was shrinking, not expanding. Something would have to give soon.

He looked at the property management figures. Richard, at least, looked safe. His portfolio of rental properties was showing no signs of stress. In fact, Richard had added another ten properties to the portfolio since he'd last checked. They'd have to recruit another property manager if the number of properties they were managing continued to climb.

He realized they'd have to do that in any case when he was elected to the State Legislature, as Richard would have to take on the role of general manager. Justin hoped his younger brother was up to the task, but he didn't have the same confidence in Richard their father had had in him. At least he'd be assured of a regular income while he held the seat, and since it was regarded as a safe seat for the party, he'd knew he'd be set for life as long as he performed. Any dividend he received from the business would be a bonus.

Justin knew Richard was good at property management. He was good at administration and working with like-minded people, but managing or motivating sales agents was not his forte. Neither was he much good at attracting the property developers that were the lifeblood of the firm. That had been their father's strength, and although he'd mentored them in the years before he'd transitioned to being the mayor of East Park, Richard hadn't taken to the task. Perhaps Richard would persuade Kathy to come back into the office. She'd been one of their best sales agents before young Dougie had come along, and she knew how to lead a sales team.

Justin made himself a note to speak to Richard about getting Kathy back into the office. Keeping it in the family was the best way to go, in his opinion. Besides, once he'd been elected, Amy would be too busy as the wife of the local member to work in the firm.

The telephone on his desk rang.

'Howard Stenhouse for you, Justin.'

Justin took a deep breath. Howard Stenhouse was one of the firm's most significant clients. They had handled the sale of his property developments for as long as Justin could remember.

'Put him through, Josie.'

'Sorry to hear about your father, Justin. He's going to be missed.'

'Thank you, Howard.'

Justin waited. Howard never called to make polite social conversation.

'Now, my boy, your father promised me he'd get the Union Street development approved. I'm relying on you to make sure that still happens.'

Justin knew his father had always gone in to bat for Howard's developments and had worked closely with him to make sure his big ideas aligned with the council's vision of urban renewal, but he had no idea how much support his father had garnered for the Union Street project.

'I don't have any say in council approvals, Howard,' said Justin. 'Unlike Dad, I'm not the mayor, and I doubt they'd take much notice of what I want.'

'You've got strings to pull, thanks to Doug. I suggest you use your political influence to get that approval for me, Justin. I will be very disappointed if that project doesn't go ahead,' said Howard. 'Get me that approval if you want my support for your campaign.'

The line went dead.

Justin wasn't sure he needed Howard's support to be elected but his father had warned him never to cross Howard Stenhouse. He wished his father was still alive to keep the promises he'd made to Howard and didn't think it was fair for Howard to hold him accountable for his father's failure to deliver, given the manner of his demise.

Justin turned back to his computer and brought up the council's website. It didn't take him long to find out that Howard's development application was on the agenda for the next council meeting. He picked up his mobile phone and called Trevor Jones, a member of his father's faction on the council.

'Trevor, Justin.'

'What can I do for you, mate?'

'I see the development application for Union Street is on this week's agenda. What are its chances?'

'Stenhouse been on your back, too. I don't know why he's bothering you about it. I told him to leave you out if it,' said Trevor.

'You know what he's like,' said Justin. 'Pushes all bases. Probably thinks I can work magic for him because I'm running for parliament. Anyway, do you have the numbers?'

'Now that your father's out of the picture, it looks like the deputy mayor is siding with the Union Ward Residents Association, and that could influence the outcome. I told Howard he's probably going to have to scale it back and resubmit, unless he wants to appeal to the State Planning Authority, and you know how long that could take. You'll probably be a sitting member before they make a decision.' Trevor laughed.

Justin didn't want to think about the pressure Howard would apply to get him to influence the outcome of the State Planning Authority. He knew enough about the rules of the game to know he wouldn't last long in parliament if he agreed to do Howard's bidding once he'd been elected. 'Nothing you can do to shore it up?'

'I'm doing what I can, mate, but there's a bit of a power struggle going on now that your Dad's left us, and we've lost a couple of our votes to the other camp.'

CHAPTER SIX

Carl keyed the name of the road Robert Clarke had given them into the satnav. The system recalibrated and refreshed the map on its display.

'It's only five ks from here,' said Carl.

'Let's hope it's a sealed road,' said Harry, pulling onto the highway and heading in the direction of North Summit.

'Prepare to turn left after eight hundred metres.'

Harry slowed to turn.

'Turn left at the cross road.'

Harry turned onto an unsealed road leading across the face of the foothills below North Summit.

'You have reached your destination.'

'Another ten ks and we should come across a white drum on the right,' said Carl. 'Turn in there.'

Ten minutes later, the white drum came into view and Harry turned onto the gravelled driveway that led up to the Clarke farmhouse.

'Looks like they've had a good season,' said Carl, taking in the green pastures and the number of sheep he could see as they approached the house.

A man Carl immediately recognized as Doug Clarke's brother strode across from the shearing shed as they got out of the car.

'I see you didn't have any trouble finding us, Inspector.'

'No, your instructions were spot on, Mr Clarke,' said Carl. 'This is Detective Sergeant Fuller.'

Robert Clarke shook their hands. 'Come up into the house. Beth's got afternoon tea ready for us.'

They followed Robert into the sunroom on the northern side of the house and sat in the warmth of the spring sun streaming through the floor-to-ceiling windows of the room.

Robert's wife served them afternoon tea and then withdrew to her kitchen.

'When was the last time you saw Doug?' said Carl.

'Couple of months ago. He was up for a funeral.'

'Family friend?'

'A woman we went to school with,' said Robert. 'Starts to happen when you get to our age.'

'Did you have much contact with your brother?'

'Pretty much every week.'

'Did he ever express any concerns for his life?' said Carl.

Robert shook his head. 'No, Inspector. Mostly we talked farm business. This is a family operation. Doug's always had a say in what we do and it was his money that helped us expand. We have three properties now.'

'I understand Doug was a couple of years older than you. Any reason why you stayed on the farm and he didn't?'

Robert looked at his hands. 'I guess it will all come out at some stage, now that he's been murdered.'

'Yes, I'm afraid murder investigations tend to do that,' said Carl.

'Doug was meant to take over the farm but things didn't work out that way. He was pretty bright. He wanted to go to uni and make something of himself and, as you know, he did.' Robert leant back in his armchair. 'He'd intended to come back and run the place when Dad was ready to retire, but then he did something we'd all take in our stride these days. Unfortunately, it was a big deal in these parts fifty years ago.' Robert smiled. 'When he came home that first summer, he got his girlfriend pregnant.'

'Why was that such a big deal?'

'Her family owns half the district, Inspector. They didn't know she was seeing Doug. We weren't in their social class.' Robert paused and picked up his cup of tea. 'Her parents isolated her. There was no talk of them getting married. Doug wasn't allowed anywhere near her or to see the child, his own daughter, after she was born.'

'How did your parents react?'

'Dad wasn't very happy with Doug,' said Robert. 'He forgave him, eventually, but he never recovered from the shame of being told his son wasn't good enough to marry a Richmond.'

'Is that the same Richmond family that owns the place between here and Ashcroft?' said Carl.

'They're a branch of the family. Old man Richmond, Melanie's father, owned all the land in the next valley, right up to the summit.'

'Do you know if your brother had any contact with her later in life?'

'I don't know, to be honest, but it was her funeral he was last up here for, so someone must have told him about it.'

'Did you go?' said Carl.

'I didn't even know she was dead. Doug dropped in on his way home from her funeral. That's when he told me she'd died.'

'Do you know anything about the daughter?'

'Only that Melanie had a daughter. Heard that through

mutual friends. I'm afraid I don't know anything about her, not even her name. Doug never said anything about her, but I guess she would have been at the funeral if she's still alive.'

'Does Doug's wife know about this?' said Carl.

'You'll have to ask her,' said Robert. 'It was never discussed while Dad was alive.'

'We found Doug's car abandoned not far from here, near the turn off from the highway to the Richmond place. Any idea who from around these parts would want to kill him?'

Robert shook his head. 'This is a pretty peaceful community, Inspector. Not even old man Richmond wanted to kill him. Just didn't want him as a son-in-law.'

———

Harry turned the car onto the highway and headed in the direction of Ashcroft. A bright yellow school bus was stopped on the side of the road when they passed the spot where Doug Clarke's car had been found.

Carl took out his mobile phone and called Nina. 'We're just leaving North Summit, honey. I probably won't be home before Sophie goes to bed.'

'Is Harry with you?'

'He's driving.'

'Does he want me to let Jessika know?'

'It's OK. He'll call her when we get to Ashcroft. We have to stop there before we head back.'

'I'll see you when you get here.'

Carl slipped his mobile into his jacket pocket, thankful that, as an ex-detective sergeant, Nina understood the vagaries of the job, and wondered how Jessika was coping.

'How's Jessika handling being married to a detective?'

'She keeps some pretty weird hours herself,' said Harry, 'especially when she's on the legal aid roster. I think the test will be when she stops work to have the baby.'

'It can be a tough gig for wives,' said Carl. 'I didn't get it right the first time. You need to make the effort to be there for her whenever you can, and always keep her in the loop so she isn't waiting up worrying about whether you're coming home or not.'

'Jessika and I had that conversation after Wayne told me about his situation,' said Harry. 'How do you think he's doing?'

'He looked like he'd at least had a sleep this morning,' said Carl. 'We're going to have to keep an eye on him. I'd hate to lose him.'

'Might pay to pair him up with Lisa and let Nigel go solo for a change. Does she know the score?'

'I think Wayne's told everyone on the team.'

They drove in silence for a couple of minutes.

'What do you think about this case, Harry?'

'I'm wondering if the car was planted up here, like the body was in East Park. Someone could be leading us up the garden path, you know, making us think the killer's from up here.'

'That someone would have to know this part of the world is connected to our victim.'

'Or be from around here,' said Harry, 'someone like the victim, someone that no longer lives here but knows he's from here.'

Carl looked out at the passing fields. 'We still need a motive, Harry. When we work out why someone wanted him dead, we should be able to narrow down our search.'

'We're going to have to consider it could be connected to someone up here,' said Harry. 'It could be unfinished business from him getting that girl pregnant.'

Carl thought fifty years was a long time to wait to get even but he'd come across stranger tales. 'Better see what we can find out about this Melanie Richmond and who was at her funeral.'

'We might want to look into the Clarke family as well, Boss, and see who stands to gain from his death.'

'You've got a suspicious mind there, Harry.'

'That's why I'm a detective, isn't it?'

Carl laughed.

———

The Ashcroft police station was in the main street, located on the western edge of the commercial zone. Harry parked in front of the stone building, next to the patrol car standing in the street. Carl got out of the car and went into the station while Harry called Jessika.

Sergeant Snow was waiting for him behind the counter that divided the operational from the public side of the station.

'Any sightings of a hitch-hiker between here and North Summit on Sunday?' said Carl.

'Bill's been asking around,' said Sgt Snow. 'Nothing yet.'

Carl folded his arms on the counter between him and Sgt Snow. 'Do you know of a woman named Melanie Richmond from North Summit?'

'There's plenty of people named Richmond over there,' said Sgt Snow. 'In fact, the lad that found the car's one of them. What's so special about this Melanie?'

'Seems she had a relationship with our victim, years ago. Probably before either of us was born,' said Carl. 'Robert Clarke told me his brother had last been up here for her funeral, a couple of months ago.'

'So, she'd be a woman in her sixties, then?'

'Probably late sixties.'

'Most local funerals are covered by the Ashcroft Times. There might even be a photograph,' said Sgt Snow. 'They're open tomorrow. I'll pay them a visit. Anything in particular you want me to look for?'

'See if you can find out who was at that funeral.'

'If there's a photo, I should be able to track down any locals in it,' said Sgt Snow. 'There might even be one of those signed registers that seem to be popular these days.'

'Heard any rumours about Robert Clarke or his sons?'

'What sort of rumours do you have in mind, Inspector?'

'Financial problems,' said Carl. 'People tend to do things you wouldn't expect when they're in financial difficulty.'

Sgt Snow screwed up his face. 'Not many farmers with financial problems up here, Inspector. They call this God's backyard. It's the poor buggers on the other side of the ranges in the rain shadow that are doing it tough.'

'It's not always the weather that causes financial hardship, Sergeant. There are plenty of families that go under thanks to gambling or bad business decisions.'

'I suppose you're right, Inspector, but if the Clarke's have any financial issues, they've kept it to themselves. To be honest, I haven't heard a bad word about Robert Clarke or his sons in all the years I've been here.'

———

Sophie was asleep when Carl got home.

'Don't you go waking her up,' said Nina, as he crept into the nursery to look at her.

Carl spent a minute watching her sleep and then quietly closed the door to her room and made his way back to the kitchen, where Nina was making him something to eat.

'How was your day?' said Nina, as he took off his suit coat and sat down at the table.

'Spent a fair part of it in the car. That Mercedes we were looking for turned up just out of North Summit.'

'Wondered why you were up there.'

'Our victim was born there,' said Carl. 'Interviewed his brother while we were there.'

Nina took his bowl of soup out of the microwave and placed it on the table. 'Could your killer be from there?'

'Hard to say. Harry thinks the car may have been planted to throw us off the scent.'

'I guess that's possible. You wouldn't have to be a genius to know we'd look into the victim's background.'

Carl tried the soup. 'This is good.'

'Evelyn was here today. She made it.'

'No wonder the chief's putting on weight,' said Carl, 'if she's feeding him like this every day.'

'You won't have to worry, then, will you?'

'Not unless you start making soups like this.'

'Don't hold your breath.' Nina laughed, as she placed a pot of water onto the cooktop to cook Carl's pasta.

'Still haven't got a motive,' said Carl.

'Something will turn up. It always does. Anything in the car?'

'Dried blood in the trunk. Dean's people are going over the interior. We could get lucky.'

'Evelyn said the chief is thinking about retiring,' said Nina.

'He hasn't said anything to me.'

'I think he has now.'

Carl put down his spoon. 'You think he sent Evelyn with the message?'

'There's no I think about it. She told me he'd asked her to pass on the message so you wouldn't be surprised when the news gets out.'

'Wonder why he hasn't told me himself,' said Carl.

'I don't think he wants to admit he's getting old,' said Nina, 'and he doesn't want to be seen to be playing favourites.'

'Well, he's not the only one with grey hair.'

Nina sat down beside him. 'Might be time you thought about applying for his job. It would be nice if I didn't have to worry about you being in the field.'

Carl leant back in his chair. 'My name's already on the list but, as you know, it won't be my call. That's up to the Commissioner.'

'I reckon you stand a good chance,' said Nina.

'You're biased,' said Carl. 'Besides, the chief hasn't resigned yet.'

CHAPTER SEVEN

The team gathered around the whiteboard with their morning coffees. Carl attached a photograph of Doug Clarke's car onto the board.

'This is the victim's car,' said Carl. 'It was located fifteen kilometres south of North Summit early yesterday morning. Forensics have retrieved it and will examine it today. Hopefully, we'll get something that might help us identify the driver.'

'Surprised it wasn't torched,' said DC Paterson.

'Maybe someone wanted us to find it,' said DS Fuller.

'Or we're dealing with someone who either doesn't know what he's doing or doesn't care enough to hide his tracks,' said Carl. 'Anyway, DS Fuller and I went up to have a look and speak to the locals. The car was concealed from the highway but left next to a spot where some farm kids catch the school bus.'

'That doesn't sound all that clever,' said DC Beard.

'Looks like he ran out of gas and did his best to hide it. Guess he was lucky to come across a side road when he did.'

'Or he knew that spot was there,' said DS Fuller, 'and ran down the tank.'

'We'll have to consider both possibilities.'

'Does Ashcroft have anything?' said DC Templar.

'We've made a request to the public for information on anyone seen hitch-hiking or walking along that stretch of highway on Sunday.'

'Why not Saturday as well?' said DC Paterson.

'We have a statement from a farmer who uses the road next to where the car was found. Says it wasn't there on Sunday morning, when he was coming home from church.'

'Any idea why someone would leave it there?' said DC Templar. 'North Summit is a long way from East Park. Is there any connection?'

'Our victim grew up in North Summit,' said Carl, 'and was apparently still involved with the running of the family farm.'

'So, our killer could be someone from there?' said DC Beard.

'Or someone who wants us to think that,' said DS Fuller.

'Do we know if Clarke visited the area?' said DC Paterson.

'Not often, but apparently he went to the funeral of an old girlfriend up there a couple of months back. Sgt Snow from Ashcroft is finding out who else was at that funeral. Might lead nowhere, but it will give us people to talk to. We still need a motive.' Carl took a sip of his coffee. 'How did you go yesterday, Wayne?'

'I talked to some people at party headquarters, Inspector. I got the feeling they were closing ranks. Nothing but he was a great fellow bullshit.'

'What makes you think it was bullshit?'

'You can't operate the way Clarke did and not make a few enemies, Inspector. The guy engineered the removal of a sitting member to get his son preselected, for starters.'

'Thought the sitting member's wife was on the sick list. That's what Clarke's sons told us, wasn't it?' Carl looked at DS Fuller.

DS Fuller flipped through his notes. 'Ross Whitaker's the sitting member. Justin told us he was resigning because his wife has early onset dementia.'

'From what I hear,' said DC Paterson, 'Whitaker's resigning because Clarke took over his branch and stacked the numbers against him. The wife thing's a convenient cover story to save face. She's had a carer for years.'

Carl listed Ross Whitaker on the whiteboard as a person of interest.

'Anything else, Wayne?'

'I got more people to talk to.'

'What about you, Lisa?'

'I've interviewed my six councillors, Inspector. I gather the council is divided into pro and anti-mayor groups. A couple of the councillors I spoke to were happy to see the back of him.'

'Any particular reason?'

'They claimed he was too close to some of the property developers,' said DC Templar.

'Any names?'

'Howard Stenhouse came up a few times, and a Rory McLaren.'

'Stenhouse is one of the names from the call log,' said DS Fuller.

'Guess we'd better speak to him,' said Carl. 'What about you, Nigel? How did you go yesterday?'

'I got the same story as Lisa, Inspector. I gather the deputy mayor is moving swiftly to consolidate his position, and according to Councillor Jones, he's anti-development.'

'Who's the deputy mayor?' said Carl.

'Someone called David Callinan.'

'I spoke to him yesterday,' said DC Templar. 'He was one of the ones who told me Clarke was too close to the developers I named.'

'Sounds like someone who had something to gain from our victim's demise,' said DS Fuller.

Carl added the name of the deputy mayor to the list of persons of interest.

'Wayne, take Lisa with you today and introduce her to a few of your friends in the party,' said Carl. 'By the way, Lisa, did you get a look at the mayor's diary?'

'He didn't have any official appointments over the weekend, Inspector.'

———

Stenhouse Construction was housed in a small brick building three streets away from the East Park Council Chambers. Carl showed his ID to the receptionist. 'Detective Inspector West to see Mr Stenhouse.'

'Just a moment, Inspector,' said the receptionist, without looking at his ID. 'I'll tell Mr Stenhouse you're here.'

Carl looked around the office. It was functional, with faded architectural drawings on the walls of the waiting area.

A door opened in the wall behind the receptionist and a giant of a man, well into his fifties by Carl's estimation, stepped into the waiting area. 'Inspector West?' Howard Stenhouse extended his hand and crushed Carl's as they shook hands.

'This is Detective Sergeant Fuller,' said Carl, wriggling the fingers of his right hand to restart the circulation.

Howard squeezed the life out of Harry's hand and invited them into his office.

'What can I do for you, boys?'

'I understand you knew Doug Clarke,' said Carl.

'Who didn't?' said Howard. 'He didn't deserve to be killed like that.'

'Nobody does,' said Carl. 'How well did you know him?'

'He helped me get started. Lent me some money and sold my early projects.'

'How long ago was that?'

'Be close to thirty years,' said Howard. 'We've done a lot of projects together over the years.'

'What about in recent years, since Doug became mayor?' said Carl, thinking there would have to be some conflict of interests between a mayor and a developer doing business together.

Howard smiled. 'Well, we've done some developments in Northfield over that time. You should check out what we're doing out there in Ryan Street, but nothing here in East Park. When Doug joined the council, he stopped investing in developments within the city limits. Not kosher, you know, him being mayor and all that.' Howard grinned. 'Didn't stop him helping me prepare development applications to meet council guidelines, though. He was a good mate.'

'When was the last time you saw him?'

'Monday, last week. We had lunch at Vinnie's.'

'Any reason?'

'Our regular monthly catch up.'

'You were in frequent telephone contact in the days leading up to his death,' said Carl. He watched as Howard's eyebrows twitched. 'What was that about?'

'I've got an application for a group of townhouses in with council,' said Howard. 'Doug didn't think we'd get this one through without some changes. I was trying to persuade him otherwise.'

'Where's that development?'

'Union Street.'

'What are your chances now?'

'Guess we'll find out at this week's council meeting, Inspector, but I don't like my chances with Callinan in charge. That man wants to keep East Park in the dark ages.'

'Doug didn't happen to mention who he was meeting last Saturday morning by any chance, did he?' said Carl.

'The only thing he had on I'm aware of was the launch of Justin's election campaign,' said Howard. 'He wouldn't stop talking about it. You'd think he'd won the lottery the way he was going on about it.'

'Did you attend the launch?'

Howard shook his head. 'I'm not a member of the party, Inspector. I'm not even allowed to contribute to the party. Can't be seen to be corrupting our precious politicians, not that any of the bastards would need any help from me.'

Carl stood up. 'Mind telling me where you were Saturday morning, Mr Stenhouse?'

Howard glared at Carl. 'You don't honestly think I had anything to do with it, do you?'

Carl smiled. 'To be honest, Mr Stenhouse, I don't know what to think or who may have killed your friend, but I need to know where you were on Saturday morning.'

'I was playing golf, Inspector.'

'Who with?'

'Rory McLaren. He's in the game like me. We played a round and then had lunch in the clubhouse. I would have been at the course from eight until around two, maybe later,' said Howard. 'I don't really recall when I left.'

'Which club?'

'East Park,' said Howard. 'It's on the western side of the park, on the edge of the forest.'

Carl recalled the greens he'd spotted on the way to Howard's office.

'Do you have a contact number for Rory McLaren?'

'He's easy to find, Inspector. Just look up McLaren Construction.'

———

Harry pulled into the car park of the East Park Golf Club and they went into the clubhouse.

Carl flashed his ID and asked to see the manager.

'How can I help you, Inspector?'

'I'd like to confirm that a couple of your members were here on Saturday.'

'Who would that be?'

'Howard Stenhouse and Rory McLaren.'

'Let me check for you, Inspector.'

Carl waited while Harry went to speak to the manager of the restaurant.

'Ah, they teed off at eight, Inspector. It's a regular booking.'

'Is there any way of confirming they were actually here?' said Carl.

'Members swipe their cards to access the course, Inspector. If you look here,' he turned the monitor towards Carl, 'you can see they swiped at five to eight.'

Anyone could swipe a card, thought Carl. 'Do you have CCTV anywhere?'

The manager smiled. 'Our members prefer their privacy.'

Carl thanked him and walked out to the car park to wait for Harry. While he waited, he examined the map of the course he'd picked up inside the clubhouse. The front nine holes skirted the western edge of the forest, but the back nine were well inside the tree line. The green of the fifteenth was only a few hundred metres from the car park where Doug Clarke's body had been found.

Carl wondered if Doug Clarke had come into the forest to meet with Stenhouse and McLaren away from the public gaze. But that didn't make any sense to Carl, since everything was pointing to Doug Clarke having been killed someplace else.

Neither could he fathom why Clarke would want to meet Howard in secret, when they met openly every month for lunch, unless it had something to do with McLaren.

Carl's train of thought was interrupted by Harry coming out of the clubhouse and walking over to where he was standing.

'Stenhouse paid for their meal at two twenty-eight,' said Harry. 'He's not the sort of bloke that's easy to forget, given the size of him.'

'This course passes fairly close to where Clarke's body was found,' said Carl. 'They would have been on the back nine by ten.'

'There would have been a few people here on Saturday, Boss. I doubt they would have been able to meet up with Clarke and not be seen.'

'I suppose you're right,' said Carl. 'Let's set up a meeting with McLaren.'

'Still, if they had set up a meeting, Boss, it'd be a good spot to have someone waiting to take him out.'

'But why?' said Carl. 'He was helping them get things through council.'

'Maybe there's more to our man than being mayor,' said Harry.

———

Sgt Lang's report was waiting in Carl's inbox when they returned to the office, along with an email informing him they'd traced the number used to call Mike Jonas prior to the post mortem to a payphone on North Terrace.

Had to be someone in the media trying to get a jump on the rest of the pack, thought Carl. He opened the attachment containing Forensics' report on their examination of the victim's car and scanned its contents.

The blood type of the blood in the trunk matched that of the victim, suggesting he'd been transported in the car after being stabbed, and that perhaps he'd died in the trunk of his car.

Not a pleasant way to go, thought Carl.

Forensics had lifted several fingerprints from both the body-work and interior of the car that did not match the victim's, but they didn't match anybody on the national database either. They were yet to crosscheck with fingerprints from members of the victim's family, but the fact some of them were bloodstained suggested to Carl they belonged to whoever had moved the body.

A small breakthrough, thought Carl, as long as they could find someone with prints to match.

He walked out to Harry's desk.

'Get Nigel onto seeing if he can find Clarke's car in the traffic recordings, Harry.'

'That could be like finding a needle in a haystack, Boss.'

'At least we know what the needle looks like and when it was on the move, and where it ended up. Nigel's good with that stuff.'

CHAPTER EIGHT

Carl was reading Nigel's report on his interview with the CEO of East Park Council when his mobile phone rang.

'Sgt Snow, from Ashcroft, Inspector.'

'How'd you get on?' said Carl.

'I've got a list of the people that attended Melanie Richmond's funeral, Inspector, and I've had a chat with the paper's photographer. She took a few more photos than the one that's in the paper.'

'Anything interesting?'

'Your man was definitely there, Inspector. Seemed pretty chummy with Gary Richmond, according to the photographer.'

'Isn't that the farmer whose son found his car?'

'That's him,' said Sgt Snow.

'Any sightings of a hitch-hiker?'

'No, but Gary Richmond has a twenty-three-year-old son, Greg, at university in the city. He was home for the weekend, apparently. Was seen at church with his folks on Sunday morning. He doesn't have a car at the moment, Inspector. Wrote it off after a wild weekend a couple of months back. Could be coincidence him being here, but we've had no other reports of strangers in the district, especially not anyone walking along the highway between here and North Summit.'

Carl wondered whether Greg Richmond had driven Clarke's car home or perhaps seen it on the way up.

'Find out where young Richmond lives, Sergeant. Might be worth having a chat with him. He may have seen the car on the road. And send me your list.'

'I can email you the photos if you like. She gave me copies, and the names of the people she could identify in each photograph,' said Sgt Snow. 'Young Greg's in one standing next to Doug Clarke and his father.'

'That would be good.'

Carl ended the call and made a note to follow up Greg Richmond and his father. Then he turned his attention back to Nigel's report.

Nigel had highlighted a line towards the bottom of the first page, where he'd noted that the CEO had advised him the deputy mayor had reported the mayor to the Local Government Authority for not divulging his interest in several properties developed by McLaren Construction.

Carl wondered why David Callinan hadn't divulged that information to Lisa when she'd interviewed him the previous day.

He showed the report to Harry. 'What do you think of this?'

Harry read the highlighted paragraph. 'Might give Clarke a reason to bump off Callinan. Can't see it working the other way around.'

'Might give McLaren a motive,' said Carl. 'When's his interview?'

'Can't get in to see him until tomorrow afternoon at two,' said Harry.

'Had a call from Sgt Snow from Ashcroft,' said Carl.

'Anything interesting?'

'Seems our victim was friendly with the farmer whose son found his car.'

Harry cocked an eyebrow.

'And, the farmer has a son going to uni here in the city who was home over the weekend. At least, he was seen at church on the Sunday,' said Carl, 'and, according to Sgt Snow, he doesn't have a car at the moment.'

'That raises a few questions,' said Harry.

'We'll need to speak to him when we find out where he lives,' said Carl. 'Would appear he was acquainted with Clarke. Was photographed standing next to him at the funeral.'

'Got a name?'

'Greg.'

'Let me check Registrations.'

'Sgt Snow is asking his father,' said Carl.

'Won't that tip him off?'

'Only if he's got something to hide.'

———

Harry parked in front of the Lidall Electorate Office, a short walk from the East Park Council Chambers.

'This would have been convenient for Clarke,' said Carl, 'especially if he'd lived to see his son elected.'

'Would have given him easy access to the local member,' said Harry. 'I wonder if he used it or preferred backroom deals with the Premier and his people.'

Carl showed his ID to the receptionist.

'Mr Whitaker is expecting you, Inspector. You can go straight in.' She pointed to the open door on her left.

Carl stepped through the doorway. Ross Whitaker was sitting at his desk reading.

'Mr Whitaker?'

Ross looked up from the paper on his desk.

'Detective Inspector West, City Police,' said Carl, showing him is ID. 'This is Detective Sergeant Fuller.'

Ross stood and shook hands. 'Ah, you want to talk about Doug Clarke. Is that right?'

'Yes.'

'Man was a ruthless bastard. Had to win at any cost.'

'I gather you weren't friends, then,' said Carl.

'We were once,' said Ross. 'We started in the party together.'

'When was that?'

'We met at uni. We were both doing law.' He sat down. 'Take a seat. Can I get you a coffee or something?'

Carl looked at Harry, who nodded slightly.

'Coffee would be good. White, no sugar.'

Ross looked at Harry.

'The same,' said Harry.

Ross walked to the door of his office. 'Trish, can you make us three white coffees, please?'

'So, you've known Doug Clarke for around fifty years,' said Carl.

'Give or take.'

'When did you go into politics?'

'About twenty-five years ago.'

'Did you practice law before that?'

'Yes. I worked for my father's firm until he died. That's when I went into politics. I'd had enough of the law by then.'

'Whitaker and Walsh?' said Harry.

Ross looked at Harry. 'You don't look old enough to know that, young man.'

'Max Walsh is my father-in-law.'

'Ah, I remember young Max. He's got his own firm these days, hasn't he? How is he?'

'Walsh and Garcia,' said Harry. 'He's fine, thank you.'

The receptionist came in with their coffees on a tray.

'Thanks, Trish,' said Ross.

She handed each of them a coffee and left, closing the door behind her.

'Don't know what I'd do without her,' said Ross.

Carl took a sip of the coffee in his cup. 'I understand you're retiring at the next election.'

'My wife is ill,' said Ross. 'She has dementia. I need to take care of her.'

Carl placed his coffee cup on the desk in front of him. 'Is that the real reason?'

Ross sank back into his seat. 'What do you mean, Inspector?'

'As you would appreciate, Mr Whitaker, in a murder investigation we talk to a lot of people, and they tell us things that are, shall we say, not common knowledge.'

'Oh. What have you heard?'

'That your wife has been ill for some time, Mr Whitaker, and that Doug Clarke organized a coup against you in favour of his son.'

Ross took a sip of his coffee. 'You're fairly well informed, Inspector, but I don't bear any grudges. Now that I've had time to think about it, I know I should have resigned at the last election.' He shook his head slowly. 'It's too late now in any case. I'm going to have to put Mary into a home. She doesn't know where she is.'

Carl took a sip of his coffee and waited while Ross regained his composure.

'When was the last time you saw Doug Clarke?'

'Couple of weeks ago. Would have been at the last State

Council meeting. Doug was no longer a delegate but he was always there, keeping an eye on things for the Premier.'

'Is that a government or party thing?' said Carl.

'Party's governing body,' said Ross, 'not that the Premier takes much notice of what the rank and file want.'

'Would you say Doug had enemies in the party?'

'Oh, he had plenty of enemies, Inspector, but we're politicians, not gangsters. You can't seriously think anybody in the party had him killed.'

Interesting turn of phrase, thought Carl, wondering if assassination was the way a politician would do it.

'I need to keep an open mind on that question, I'm afraid,' said Carl. 'Is there a possibility he could have stumbled across something others wouldn't have wanted him to know about?'

Ross looked at Carl. 'Are you suggesting someone in government could be corrupt, Inspector?'

'I'm not suggesting anything, Mr Whitaker. I'm trying to work out why someone killed him.'

'You mean you're looking for a motive?'

Carl nodded.

'Not sure I can help you there, Inspector.'

'Do you know anything about his involvement with property developers?'

'That's where Doug made his money. His real estate business was basically a front for his property development interests. Mind you, he never put his name on projects. He was a behind the scenes broker for private investors,' said Ross. 'I put money in with him before I became the local member. Got a good return, too. If you want to know about his investments, I suggest you talk to Howard Stenhouse and Rory McLaren. Doug was their major backer.'

'Do you know if Doug's sons are involved in property development as well?'

'They might be nice boys, Inspector, and young Justin will probably make a good local member, but Doug told me those boys are clueless when it comes to making money. He set up a separate business to support himself and Joanna before he gave the real estate business to the boys. He didn't want to have to rely on them making a go of it.' Ross shrugged his shoulders. 'I'm surprised they've lasted as long as they have. Maybe Doug underestimated them.'

————

After leaving Ross Whitaker, Carl and Harry went into a nearby cafe to get something for lunch.

'What did you make of that?' said Carl, as they sat at an outside table in the sunshine.

'He could be lying about not bearing a grudge,' said Harry. 'I know I'd be pissed off if someone I thought of as a friend organized a coup against me.'

'Not sure Whitaker's our man, Harry, but I'm not buying that bit about politicians not being gangsters.'

Harry laughed. 'Think we'd be better off looking into Clarke's investment business, Boss. People are more likely to do dastardly things when money is involved.'

'When's his funeral?' said Carl.

'Friday.'

The waitress delivered their lunch. Carl unwrapped the sandwich he'd ordered and took a bite.

'Let's talk to his wife again after the funeral. I want to know more about this investing business Whitaker mentioned.'

'Do you think his sons know about it?'

'Guess we'll find out soon enough,' said Carl, looking at his watch. 'Where are we meeting McLaren?'

'His office is only ten minutes from here. We've still got plenty of time.'

Carl's mobile phone pinged. He looked at the text message from Sgt Snow. 'Greg Richmond lives around here with his aunt and uncle.' Carl looked up. 'Guess who they are?'

'Anyone we know?'

'Clare and Rory McLaren.'

CHAPTER NINE

Carl and Harry walked into the light-filled reception area of the offices of McLaren Construction, located in a modern two storey building on the edge of the East Park central business district, at three minutes to two.

'Detective Inspector West to see Mr McLaren,' said Carl, showing the receptionist his ID.

'Take a seat please, Inspector. I'll let Mr McLaren know you're here.'

As Carl and Harry were sitting down, a red Mercedes SUV turned in off the street and pulled into the car park. A middle-aged man dressed in a suit emerged from the vehicle and walked in through the automatic doors, looking at his watch. The receptionist pointed towards the waiting area and he walked over to where Carl and Harry were sitting.

'Hi, I'm Rory.' He extended his hand. 'Hope I haven't kept you waiting, Inspector.'

'No, we've just arrived,' said Carl. 'This is Detective Sergeant Fuller.'

Rory shook hands with Harry. 'Come into my office. It's a bit more private in there.'

A lot of money on show here, thought Carl, recalling the dated interior of Howard Stenhouse's premises as they entered Rory's office.

'Can I get you anything?'

'We've just had lunch,' said Carl. 'Perhaps we can get to the point of our visit.'

'Sure.'

'Tell us about your relationship with Doug Clarke,' said Carl, settling into a chair opposite Rory.

'It's a little complicated. My brother is married to Doug's daughter, Sonya.'

'I wasn't aware Doug had a daughter,' said Carl.

'Well, Joanna isn't her mother,' said Rory. 'She's Melanie and Doug's daughter. That's Melanie Richmond. It's a long story.'

Harry coughed.

'Ah, I think we've heard it,' said Carl. 'So, Sonya would be the child born out of wedlock Doug's brother mentioned?'

'Yeah, that's right.'

'Would I be right in assuming you're from North Summit, Mr McLaren?'

Rory nodded. 'We went to school with Doug's nephews.'

'Well, that's very interesting, Mr McLaren, but I'm particularly interested in your business relationship with Doug Clarke.'

'Oh. That sort of relationship,' said Rory. 'Sorry, I misunderstood your question.'

'How did that work?'

'That was pretty straight forward. Doug organized the finance for us and we paid him a fee.'

'You don't use bank finance?'

'It's a lot easier getting money from private investors, especially when you have to wait for properties to sell to see a positive cash flow. They have more patience than the banks.'

'Do you use Doug's real estate firm to sell your properties?'

'Some of them, but we prefer to sell off the plan.'

'So, is Doug's death going to cause you any problems?' said Carl.

'Not with our current projects, but we might have to find another broker going forward. Depends on whether Joanna wants to continue with the operation on her own.'

'Mrs Clarke's involved in this as well, then?'

'To be honest, Inspector, I think she's the brains. She had her own accountancy practice until a few years ago,' said Rory. 'Doug was good with people, but she's great with numbers.'

'Who manages the disbursement of funds back to Doug's investors?' said Carl.

'That's all managed by Doug and Joanna. I deposit funds to their trust account. I'm assuming Joanna will continue to take care of it unless I hear otherwise.'

'Do you know who any of these investors are?'

'Not personally, Inspector. Our funding contract is with Doug and Joanna. You'll have to speak to her if you want to know who their investors are.'

Carl wondered if the Clarke's investment fund was being used to launder money, and whether Doug had double-crossed someone.

'When was the last time you saw Doug Clarke?'

Rory leant back in his chair. 'I saw him on Friday afternoon. He told me it looked like the Union Street project wasn't going to get council approval in its current form.'

'Is this the same Union Street project Howard Stenhouse is involved with?' said Carl.

'Joint venture,' said Rory. 'One of our bigger projects.'

'Was Doug organizing the finance for that one?'

'He would have,' said Rory, 'but that step doesn't usually start until we've got council approval.'

Carl nodded. 'I understand you played golf with Howard on Saturday.'

'We play every week, and then have lunch.'

'Did Doug mention to you who he was meeting on Saturday morning?'

'The only thing he said about Saturday was he was attending Justin's campaign launch.'

Carl stood. He was ready to leave. 'By the way, I understand Greg Richmond lives with you.'

'Yeah, he's one of my sister's boys.'

Carl handed Rory a business card. 'Can you ask him to give me a call? I understand he was in North Summit over the weekend.'

'He came up with us Saturday, after golf. It was my mother's birthday on Sunday.'

'You didn't happen to see Doug's car on the drive up or back by any chance?'

'I don't think so,' said Rory. 'You don't see many cars on that road after Ashcroft.'

———

Carl gazed at the East Park forest as Harry negotiated the traffic on their way back to Police Headquarters. He wondered if Doug Clarke had been the financial wizard Rory McLaren had described or someone who had cheated his investors and paid for it with his life.

'We're going to have to go through Clarke's investor accounts,' said Carl.

'Wayne will love that,' said Harry.

'We need to find out where his money was coming from, and

if he'd owed anyone a substantial amount,' said Carl. 'Politicians might not be gangsters, but investing in real estate through this sort of back door would be one way of laundering ill-gotten gains.'

'You thinking Clarke could have short-changed the wrong type of investor?'

'It's a possibility.'

Harry waited for the lights to change. 'Guess there'd be no reason for Stenhouse or McLaren to have him killed, Boss. Sounds like they depended on him.'

'Unless it wasn't related to money.'

'He wouldn't be the first rich old man caught up in a love triangle,' said Harry.

'Hmmm. That's something else to think about. Wonder if any of those meetings his wife mentioned were a cover for seeing someone else.'

'Be a good reason for turning off your mobile,' said Harry, 'or having more than one of them.'

'See what his provider can tell us about when his mobile was offline. See if there is a pattern.'

'Let's hope Nigel can spot his car in all that traffic camera footage,' said Harry.

'Or a member of the public calls in with a sighting of his car. Get onto Crime Stoppers and see what they have.'

———

When he arrived home from work, Carl took Sophie to the playground in her stroller. It was a ten-minute walk to the seaside park and she talked for the entire time.

He enjoyed spending time with Sophie when he got home early enough to play with her. Having to keep an eye on her every move in the playground was a welcome distraction from whatever case he was working on.

He released her from the straps keeping her in the stroller and helped her clamber over the equipment, pushed her on the swing, and listened to her squeals as she slid down the slide.

As he secured her into the stroller for the trip home, he thought about what becoming chief inspector could mean for his work life balance. A chief inspector worked more regular hours than his investigators, and rarely worked weekends. It would certainly mean having more time with Sophie, and he knew Nina wanted him home every night.

He pushed the stroller out of the playground onto the foot-path for the walk home, and hoped he'd cope with becoming a cog in middle-management if he won the promotion.

CHAPTER TEN

When Carl and Harry arrived at the Clarke house for their appointment with Joanna, there was a black BMW parked in the driveway.

'Did she say anything about someone being here when you made the appointment, Boss?'

'No,' said Carl, wondering whether Joanna Clarke had called in a friend for moral support or a lawyer to protect her interests.

Harry rang the bell. The door was opened by a middle-aged man dressed in a dark suit offset by a white shirt and sky-blue tie.

'Inspector West?'

'Yes,' said Carl.

'Philip Carol. I represent Mrs Clarke. Please, come in. Mrs Clarke is waiting for us in the library.'

They crossed the entrance hall and entered the library.

'I hope you don't mind Philip being here, Inspector,' said Joanna, 'but I thought it best to have someone witness our conversation.'

'No problem,' said Carl, wondering why she was worried about talking to them.

They sat in four armchairs facing each other across the coffee table in the centre of the room.

'What did you want talk about?' said Joanna.

'Two things,' said Carl. 'Let's start with your husband's business. I understand that, in addition to selling real estate, he arranged finance for property developers.'

'Yes,' said Joanna.

'How precisely does that work?'

Joanna looked at Philip Carol.

'Mr Clarke was a registered finance broker, Inspector. He acted as a middleman between private investors and property developers. It's a fairly common arrangement in the industry.'

'How many property developers did he work with?'

'Quite a few over the years,' said Joanna, 'but over the last ten years, since we passed the real estate business to the boys, we've worked with the Yorke Group, Howard Stenhouse, and Rory McLaren.'

'You're involved in the business, Mrs Clarke?'

Joanna leant back in her chair and smiled. 'Doug was the one with his name up in lights, Inspector. He was the one everybody wanted to do business with but he relied on me to manage it all.' She paused. 'Doug might have known how to make money, Inspector, but he wasn't what you'd call good with figures.'

'How much money are we talking about for a property development?'

'Millions of dollars, Inspector. We finance multi-dwelling projects.'

'How do you attract private investors for a property development?' said Carl. 'Do you have to advertise?'

'Yes, but not to the public,' said Joanna. 'We pool funds from a network of accountants with clients looking for places to invest their money. We let them know when we have a project on the go.'

'So, you don't know who the individual investors are, then?'

'Makes it a lot easier to manage, Inspector. This way, I only have to deal with five or six accountants. They manage their individual investors.'

'Do the investors know which developments they've invested in?'

'You'd have to ask their accountants,' said Joanna.

'I'll need the details of those accountants, Mrs Clarke.'

Joanna looked at her lawyer.

'Where are we going with this, Inspector. That is confidential information,' said Philip.

Carl crossed his arms and leant back into his armchair. 'This is a homicide investigation, Mr Carol. There is no confidential information when it comes to murder. Either your client supplies what I've asked for voluntarily or we use a warrant. The outcome will be the same.'

'Is that all you want?' said Joanna.

'We'll need access to your accounts.'

'Why's that?'

'So we can trace the money trail, Mrs Clarke.'

'That won't tell you who killed Doug,' said Joanna. 'I do all the accounts.'

'It might,' said Carl, 'especially if someone thinks they've been cheated.'

'But I'd have to be the one doing that,' said Joanna.

'Do your investors know that?'

'Oh, I see what you mean.'

'Is there anything you want to tell me about that?' said Carl.

Philip Carol stood up.

'It's alright, Philip,' said Joanna. 'I've got nothing to hide. You'll find the accounts are in order, Inspector.'

'Are you involved in any current development projects?' said Carl.

'We were winding down the business, Inspector. Doug wanted to retire when his term as mayor was up. I'm in the final phase of directing funds back to investors from our latest project. That should be all over in the next couple of months.'

'Were you planning to finance the Union Street project?'

'That will be our last project, if it gets approved.'

'You're going ahead with it on your own?'

'If I get my registration,' said Joanna. 'Should be a formality, given my qualifications.'

'When can you hand over what I've asked for?' said Carl.

Joanna stood. 'Give me a few minutes. I'll print the details for you.'

———

'Was there something else, Inspector? I thought I heard you say you had two things to ask me about?' said Joanna, as she handed Carl a copy of the information he'd requested.

'There is one other question,' said Carl.

Joanna smiled. 'Do you want to know if Doug had a girl-friend, Inspector?'

'That's one way of putting it.'

'Doug and I were married for forty years, Inspector. Why would you think he had a girl on the side?'

'Your son told us your husband always had his mobile phone on so he could be contacted twenty-four-seven. Is that right?'

Joanna nodded. 'Doug was a people pleaser, Inspector.'

'What do you usually do on a Saturday morning, Mrs Clarke?'

'I visit my mother. She's in a nursing home,' said Joanna. 'I take her out for lunch somewhere most weeks.'

'So, you'd have no reason to call your husband most Saturday mornings?'

'Doug was always at some meeting. He didn't like me interrupting him when he was meeting someone.'

'So, the day he was killed would have been one of the few Saturdays you'd tried to call him?'

Joanna looked at Carl. He watched her eyes widen and her smile fade.

'What are you trying to tell me, Inspector?'

'We've looked at his telephone records, Mrs Clarke. It appears your husband's mobile phone was always switched off for several hours on Saturday mornings.'

'How can you possibly know that?' said Philip.

'No signal picked up by phone towers in the network.'

'That doesn't make sense,' said Joanna.

'It does if your husband didn't want anyone to track his movements,' said Carl.

'What are you suggesting?' said Philip.

'That wherever Mr Clarke went on the morning he was killed, it's possible it was a place he went every Saturday,' said Carl.

'Surely you have enough traffic cameras to track his car,' said Philip.

'We're looking at that,' said Carl, 'but we're assuming he was driving the car we know about.'

'What else would he have been driving?' said Joanna. 'That was the only car he used.'

'Are you sure?' said Carl.

Joanna sat down and put her head in her hands. 'I'm not sure of anything anymore.'

———

Carl read the list of names Joanna Clarke had given him as Harry drove them back to Police Headquarters.

'There's one here from Ashcroft,' said Carl.

'Where are the others?' said Harry.

'Here, in the city. Perhaps we can speak to them first.'

'Let's take a look at the accounts first, Boss. Be helpful to know where most of the money comes from.'

Carl smiled. He liked the way Harry's brain worked. 'Why do you think our friend Carol was there?'

'Moral support,' said Harry, checking the rear-view mirror before changing into the left lane.

'You could be right, Harry, but you'd think she'd have one of her sons for that, not her lawyer.'

'Maybe she doesn't trust her sons, Boss.'

CHAPTER ELEVEN

Carl looked up from his case notes when DC Beard knocked on the door of his office.

'What's up, Nigel?'

DC Beard stepped into the office. 'Came across an interesting call to Crime Stoppers, Inspector. Someone reported they'd seen Clarke's car the Saturday before he was murdered.'

Carl put down the pen he'd been using to update his notes. 'Where?'

'Outside a block of apartments in Portside.'

'That's a bit of a drive from East Park,' said Carl. 'Have you spoken to this person?'

'Took a statement from Mr Rehn yesterday, who reckons he'd seen Clarke's car parked in the street outside his apartment more than once. Apparently, Clarke was a regular visitor to the woman in number eight.'

'How did he know it was Clarke?'

'Identified him from his photograph in the paper,' said DC Beard. 'That's what prompted him to call Crime Stoppers.'

'Have you spoken to the woman?'

'Not yet, Inspector. She wasn't home when I called, and Mr Rehn couldn't recall seeing her since the weekend he'd heard about the murder.'

Carl wondered if the woman had done a runner after hearing about Clarke's murder. 'Did you get a name?'

'Gail Swan,' said DC Beard. 'According to Mr Rehn, she's about forty, maybe younger.'

Sounds like the girlfriend Mrs Clarke had been so dismissive of, thought Carl. 'Track her down, Nigel. Speak to the property manager and run her details through Registrations. She's definitely a person of interest.'

As soon as DC Beard had left his office, Carl called Joanna Clarke.

'Does the name Gail Swan mean anything to you, Mrs Clarke?'

'In what context, Inspector?'

'Someone your husband may have mentioned.'

'I don't think so, Inspector. The only Gail I remember him talking about was Gail Rowan. She's on the council. Who's this other Gail?'

'I'm not sure yet. It's a name that's been given to us by someone who says he saw your husband in Portside a couple of Saturdays ago.'

'Might be someone connected to the party, Inspector. Doug was always out talking politics. Maybe someone in the Premier's office will know who she is.'

'Thanks,' said Carl. 'I'll be in touch.'

Carl decided he'd let Nigel have a go at finding out who Gail Swan was before he started asking questions of the Premier's office, and drawing unnecessary attention to his investigation.

———

After lunch, Carl sat down with Harry and Wayne to discuss their initial analysis of the Clarke's accounts.

'Most of the money going to Stenhouse and McLaren projects comes through Richmond and Wells Accounting in Ashcroft,' said Harry.

'How much money are we talking about?' said Carl.

'Clarke put four million into the last project he did with Stenhouse and around two into his current project with McLaren,' said Wayne.

'What about the other accountants on the list?' said Carl.

'Looks like Clarke used them to fund projects by the Yorke Group, and we're talking twenty to thirty million dollars with some of them,' said Wayne. 'The last project he funded was the extension of the Portside Shopping Centre last year. He put twenty-five million into that one.'

'See any irregularities in the accounts?' said Carl.

'Nothing that stands out,' said Wayne, 'but we'd need to talk to all parties to confirm that.'

'This network of accountants has access to some serious amounts of cash,' said Harry. 'Controlling access to that would be worth a bit, don't you think?'

'Be worth selling if he wanted to retire,' said Carl.

'Maybe that's what his mysterious Saturday meetings were about,' said Harry.

'According to Nigel's witness, some of those meetings were with a woman in Portside called Gail Swan,' said Carl.

'What do we know about her?' said Harry.

'Not much,' said Carl. 'Nigel's looking into her background, and I guess we'll know more when he gets to speak to her.'

'Where do you want to go with this?' said Harry.

'Speak to the accountants and find out if they have any concerns about the way things have been handled by the Clarkes, and then have a chat with someone at the Yorke Group. Clarke may have mentioned his intention to retire to them.'

———

Carl was thinking about going home when his mobile phone rang.

'Justin Clarke, Inspector.'

'What can I do for you, Mr Clarke?'

'My mother said you asked if she knew someone called Gail Swan.'

'Do you know who she is?'

'She's a finance broker. I remember Dad telling me she wanted to buy his broking business.'

'Was he interested in selling?'

'I think so, Inspector. He wanted to retire and enjoy his grandkids, but I don't think he'd told Mum. He was a bit old-fashioned like that.'

'Do you know if he had been meeting with this Gail Swan?'

'I got the impression they'd only talked on the phone and Dad was still thinking about her offer. I'm sure he would have said something if he'd decided to go ahead.'

Carl wondered just how close Justin Clarke had been with his father, since he seemed to know a few things his mother wasn't aware of.

'How long ago did he mention it?' said Carl.

'Three, maybe four months.'

'Sounds like your father may have met with her since then,' said Carl. 'We have a statement from a witness saying he'd seen your father visit Gail Swan's apartment on several occasions in the weeks leading up to his death.'

'News to me,' said Justin, 'but it wouldn't be the first time my father had visited a woman without any of us knowing.'

'Like to elaborate?'

'My father wasn't exactly what you'd call a saint, Inspector. In fact, I'm surprised my mother stayed with him. He certainly wasn't as faithful to her as she's been to him.'

'That puts a different light on things.'

'Don't go jumping to conclusions, Inspector. I don't think Mum had anything to do with his death. She's not that sort of person.'

'I hope you're right, Mr Clarke.'

Carl ended the call and made a note of what Justin had told him. Then he called Harry.

'Justin Clarke's just told me Gail Swan is a finance broker who wanted to buy his father's business.'

'That might explain the meetings, Boss.'

'He also let slip his father was a bit of a womanizer, so he may have been seeing her for other reasons.'

'That would give the wife a motive.'

'Possibly,' said Carl. 'Anyway, the reason I called was to get you to ask the accountants if they'd been contacted by this Gail Swan now that Clarke's dead.'

'Want me to ask Yorke as well?'

'May as well. She'd have to work both ends.'

Carl ended the call, shut down his computer, and prepared to leave for the day.

As he walked towards the elevators, he realized Mrs Clarke didn't have an alibi for the Saturday morning her husband had been killed, which, in light of what her son had told him, was a bit of a problem.

He spent the time on the train going home thinking through how Joanna Clarke could have killed her husband at home, and dumped his body in the forest before going to her son's campaign launch. She could have had the opportunity, since they only had her word that he'd left home at ten. But where had she hidden the car, and how did she get it to North Summit? Was she strong enough to drag his body into and out of the trunk of his car? Carl didn't think so. And, what about those bloodstained fingerprints they'd lifted from the car? They didn't match hers.

By the time the train pulled into Morton Sands, he'd decided if Joanna Clarke was behind the murder, someone must have helped her. He couldn't see how she could have pulled it off herself.

As he got off the train, he decided he'd talk it through with Nina. She always had a more objective perspective on his cases than he did.

———

The next morning, Carl met with Chief Inspector Rankin.

'I think we need to search the Clarke house, Chief.'

Chief Inspector Rankin leant back in his chair. 'You think she did it?'

'It's a possibility.'

'What makes you think that, Carl?'

'Clarke's son told me his father was a bit of a womanizer. That could give her a motive.'

'Bit far-fetched after forty years, don't you think?'

'Possibly,' said Carl, 'but she doesn't have an alibi for the morning of his death. And, we've only got her word that he left the house at all.'

'Well, he must have left at some time to end up dead in the park,' said Chief Inspector Rankin.

'That park's only a five-minute drive from their house, Chief.' She could have dumped him in the park before she went to the campaign launch. She had plenty of time. The body wasn't found until after midday.'

'What about his car?'

'Could have been in their garage the whole time,' said Carl. 'We didn't check.'

'How do you explain the car ending up in North Summit? And those fingerprints?'

'She must have had an accomplice. I can't image someone her age moving the body on her own.'

'You're going to need a more solid case against her before I can agree to accusing her of involvement,' said the chief inspector. 'The Commissioner would have my guts for garters if I let you search her house based on what you've just told me. Do some more background work on her and her sons. If we're going to move in that direction, we need to know who her probable accomplices are, and what we're going to find before we search her house.'

'They could destroy the evidence, Chief.'

'It's almost impossible to get rid of blood stains, Carl. They'll still be there no matter how much they scrub. Go and get some evidence you can use to justify searching the place that even the Commissioner can't argue against.'

CHAPTER TWELVE

DC Nigel Beard pressed the button on the intercom for apartment eight at 23 Highland Street, Portside and announced himself. There was no response. He made his way around to the parking spaces behind the building. There was a green Mazda 3 parked in the bay for apartment eight. Nigel checked the registration number with the one he'd recorded on his phone. It was Gail Swan's car. He kicked himself for not checking the parking space to see if there'd been a car in bay eight when he'd tried her door on the day he'd spoken to Mr Rehn.

He went back to the front of the building and tried the button for number seven.

'Police! Is anyone home?'

'What do you want?' said a male voice.

'Have you seen the woman that lives in number eight?' said Nigel.

'Gail?' said the voice.

'When was the last time you saw her?'

'Isn't she home?' said the voice. 'Her car's out the back. She never walks anywhere.'

'She's not answering,' said Nigel. 'This is the second time I've been here.'

'Just a minute. I'll come down.'

Nigel waited until a young man opened the door that let people into the lobby for apartments five to eight.

'You the police?' said the man.

Nigel showed him his ID. 'And, your name is?'

'Sam Green.'

'So, when was the last time you saw Gail, Sam?'

'She in trouble, then?'

'I just want to ask her a few questions about a case I'm working on.'

'I thought she was home,' said Sam. 'Have you got her mobile number?'

'I've tried it. Goes through to voicemail.'

'I thought I heard it ringing half an hour ago.'

'That would have been me,' said Nigel. 'Can you take me up to her apartment?'

'Okay.'

They climbed the stairs to the second level landing that apartments seven and eight opened on to. Nigel called Gail's number.

'Hear that?' said Sam. 'That's her ringtone.'

'When was the last time you saw her?'

'Be at least a week ago,' said Sam.

Nigel squatted by the door and breathed in, and wished he hadn't.

'Can you smell that?' said Nigel.

Sam walked over to the door of apartment eight and copied Nigel's action.

'That's gross. What is it?'

'That's what death smells like.'

Sam stepped away from the door and stared wide-eyed at Nigel. 'You think she's dead in there?'

'Smells like it.'

'Shit!'

'You okay?' said Nigel. 'Come on, take a couple of slow breaths.'

'Can we sit down?' said Sam, opening the door to his apartment.

Nigel followed him into his apartment. 'Do you know if she owns the place or rents?'

'Most of these apartments are rentals.'

'Do you have the number of the property manager?' said Nigel.

While they waited for the property manager to arrive, Nigel showed Sam his photograph of Doug Clarke. 'Ever seen this guy here?'

'Couple of times,' said Sam. 'Isn't he the bloke that was found dead in East Park?'

'Doug Clarke,' said Nigel. 'I'm investigating his murder.'

'You think Gail had something to do with it?'

'Don't know,' said Nigel. 'I was hoping to ask her but it looks like I might be a bit late.'

———

The smell of something dead hit him when the property manager opened the door to Gail Swan's apartment. Nigel stepped inside with his fingers over his nose and looked around.

There was a mobile phone plugged into a charger on the kitchen bench, a handbag hanging on the back of a chair, and a dead cat in the bathroom. There was no sign of Gail Swan.

Nigel walked back to the door. 'It's alright, Sam. It's a dead cat.'

'She loved that cat,' said Sam. 'Something must have happened to her.'

Nigel turned to the property manager. 'I'll have to get this place checked over in case a crime's been committed here.'

'Suit yourself, mate. Just make sure you lock up when you're finished, and get rid of that bloody dead cat.'

Nigel went back into the apartment and opened a window. He found a garbage bag in the kitchen and wrapped up the dead cat. It looked like it had died from dehydration but he decided he'd let Forensics work that out. He called Inspector West.

'I'm in Swan's apartment, Inspector. She's not here, and she hasn't been here for some time.'

'How can you tell?'

'Dead cat in the bathroom next to an empty water bowl.'

'Sounds pleasant, Nigel. Anything else?'

'Her car's downstairs and her mobile's on the bench in the kitchen along with her handbag. Doesn't look like she was planning on going anywhere. Her keys and her purse are still in the handbag.'

'Any sign of a struggle?'

'Nothing obvious, Inspector, and I had to get the property manager to let me in.'

'What about the neighbours?'

'The guy in number seven reckons he hasn't seen her for at least a week. I haven't spoken to any of the others yet, apart from Mr Rehn, of course, and he told me he hadn't seen her since the day Clarke was killed.'

'Sit tight. I'll get Forensics to send someone out to check the place over. Then you'd better interview the neighbours. I'll send Lisa out to help you.'

CHAPTER THIRTEEN

The team gathered around the whiteboard with their notebooks and morning coffees. Carl printed the report he'd received from Forensics and joined them.

He waved the pages of the report in the air. 'We've got something from Swan's apartment.'

The social chatter stopped.

'Forensics have identified several distinct sets of fingerprints. For the moment, we're presuming the most prolific set belongs to Swan. What's interesting, though, is one set matches Clarke's and one of the others matches the bloodied prints lifted from his car.'

'That confirms Mr Rehn's statement, then,' said DC Beard.

'And, it tells us there's a connection between Swan and Clarke's killer,' said DC Paterson.

'Possibly, but it does confirm there's a connection between Swan and whoever drove Clarke's car to North Summit.'

'That lets Mrs Clarke off the hook,' said DS Fuller.

'Unless she's the mastermind,' said DC Paterson.

'That's going to be hard to prove,' said Carl.

'We've got people saying their relationship wasn't all that

great,' said DC Paterson. 'According to a few people I've spoken to, he was a bit of a playboy and there's gossip about her having a lover.'

'Got any of that in writing, Wayne?'

'Only notes from speaking to people I know in the party. No-one's prepared to go on the record.'

'Hmm. His son let slip something along those lines when he told me Gail Swan was looking to buy his father's broking business, so I guess there's something to it,' said Carl. 'How did you get on with your enquiries, Sergeant?'

'No-one's reported any irregularities in their accounts, Boss, and they're all happy to show us their books if we want to identify their clients.'

'Any of them been approached by Gail Swan?'

'No.'

'What about the Yorke Group?'

'They haven't heard of her.'

'She's not registered as a finance broker,' said DC Beard. 'I checked.'

'Her mobile number's on Clarke's call log,' said DC Templar. 'She's been calling him for at least three months.'

'Any calls going the other way?' said Carl.

'No.'

'What else do we know about Gail Swan?' said Carl.

'Not much,' said DC Beard. 'She's forty-three. She told her property manager she worked in public relations. And, she's been at that Portside address for about two years.'

'Do we have a photograph?'

'Only the one from her driver's licence, and that's six years old,' said DC Beard.

'Nothing in the apartment?'

'Not unless there's something on her phone, and that's locked.'

'Okay. Circulate what you have. We need to find her.'

'Anything else in that report, Boss?' said DS Fuller.

'No sign of forced entry,' said Carl.

'If she didn't leave on her own, Inspector, she would have had to go downstairs to let in whoever she went with,' said DC Beard, 'and, going by what she left behind, I'd say she probably wasn't expecting to leave when she did.'

'Abducted?' said DS Fuller.

'Be my guess,' said DC Beard.

'Anyone see her leave?' said Carl.

'No-one,' said DC Templar, 'and we asked everyone living in that street with a view of her building.'

'Dig into her background, Nigel. We need to know more about her if we're going to find out what's she's been up to with Clarke before his murder.'

———

Carl took DC Lisa Templar with him to meet with Joanna Clarke in the offices of her lawyer, Philip Carol.

'Is my client a suspect?' said Philip.

'Not at this point,' said Carl.

'So, why have you asked for me to be present at this interview?'

'We need to clear up a few points with Mrs Clarke, and I think it's better we do that in your presence.'

'What do you want to clear up?' said Joanna.

'The nature of your relationship with your husband,' said Carl. 'And, before you say anything, let me advise you that people are talking to us about things they have seen or heard.'

'Whatever you've been told is gossip.'

'Are you telling me your husband didn't have any affairs, Mrs Clarke, or are you saying you weren't aware of them?'

'How dare you!'

'Sit down, Mrs Clarke.' Carl waited for Joanna to resume her seat. 'Let me remind you, Mrs Clarke, lying to a police officer during the course of a murder investigation is not a good idea. I'm sure Mr Carol can explain the implications of obstructing police if you need him to.'

'What makes you think my client is lying, Inspector?' said Philip.

'An admission from one of her sons and a set of fingerprints in the apartment of a woman named Gail Swan.'

'Whose fingerprints?' said Joanna.

'Your husband's. They were lifted from the bedside table and the wall of the bathroom.' Carl stopped talking and watched Joanna's face for a reaction.

Joanna sighed and leant back into her chair. 'I told him to stay away from her. I knew she'd be nothing but trouble.'

Carl realized she'd lied to him when he'd initially asked her about Gail Swan. 'So, you knew about her?'

'She spun him some cock and bull story about wanting to take over our broking business, but she never came up with the money I told him to ask for,' said Joanna, 'but, that was months ago. She wasn't even registered.'

'Did you ever meet her?'

'No. Doug told me about her proposal for buying us out and I did the sums. We never heard back from her after he'd told her how much she'd have to come up with.'

Carl leant back in his chair. 'According to one of her neighbours, your husband was a frequent visitor to her apartment in recent months.'

'Is she young? Doug couldn't keep his hands off the young ones.'

'Forty-three.'

'I guess that's young these days,' said Joanna.

'How many others were there?'

'I've lost count.' Joanna smiled. 'Some of them were married women. I'm surprised some aggrieved husband didn't kill him sooner.'

'Was he ever threatened?' said Carl.

'Not to my knowledge.'

'What about you? Did you ever want to kill him?'

'That's a leading question, Inspector' said Philip. 'I can't let my client answer that one.'

Joanna smiled and dropped her hands into her lap.

'Why did you stay with him?' said Carl.

'We came to an arrangement, Inspector. I don't expect you to understand, but there were some things we were good at as a team. We just weren't good lovers. We found a way to make it work for the kids and the business.' Joanna paused and looked down at her hands. 'And to answer your question. No, I never wanted to kill him. We were friends, Inspector.'

'We found a second set of prints in the woman's apartment,' said Carl, 'and they match the unidentified prints found in your husband's car.'

'Have you arrested this woman?' said Philip Carol.

'She's disappeared. We're looking for her.'

'I hope you find her, Inspector,' said Joanna. 'She might know who killed Doug.'

'You don't think she could have killed him?'

Joanna smiled. 'She was a gold digger, Inspector. You need to keep your sugar daddy alive to win at that game.'

Carl stood and gathered his things. 'Has anybody else approached you about buying the business?'

'It's not on the market,' said Joanna.

'But has anyone asked about buying it?' said Carl. 'It must be a tempting opportunity.'

'I suspect there'll be those who'll try to muscle in and push me out,' said Joanna, 'but they don't know who they're up against.'

'Thank you for your time, Mrs Clarke. I'll be in touch.'

———

Nigel came to speak to Carl as soon as he'd returned to Police Headquarters after interviewing Joanna Clarke.

'We have several recent pictures of Gail Swan, Inspector.'

'Do we?'

'She's in several of the photos taken at that funeral Clarke attended in North Summit.' Nigel handed a print to Carl. 'She's the one with the short dark hair standing next to Clarke.'

Carl looked at the photograph. He could see why a man like Doug Clarke would have been attracted to her.

'What made you look at this, Nigel?'

'Swan's her married name, Inspector, but she's divorced. I traced her back through Registrations. Her maiden name is Richmond and she was born in North Summit.'

'How is she related to the Richmond woman that died?'

'Haven't worked that bit out, yet, Inspector. There are quite a few Richmond families up there. I'm waiting on details from Births, Deaths and Marriages.'

'Get this photo out and let's start looking for associates. Someone must know her and what she's been up to.'

'She was living in Ashcroft until a couple of years ago,' said Nigel.

'Was that before or after her divorce?'

'After. She lived at an address in Northfield before then, but she's been divorced for twelve years.'

'Have a chat with her ex. He might have an axe to grind.' Carl smiled. 'Take Lisa with you. Men like talking to her.'

'That's because she's a good listener,' said Nigel.

'By the way, how's Lily?'

'She's good,' said Nigel, 'but now she's been promoted to senior constable, she wants us to get married.'

'How do you feel about that?'

'I don't know to be honest, especially after what's happened to Wayne.'

'Don't let that put you off. She's a terrific girl and she knows the job. And, take my word for it. That makes a big difference.'

Nigel smiled.

'I wouldn't let her get away, Nigel.'

———

Carl rang Sgt Snow from Ashcroft.

'What can I do for you, Inspector?'

'One of the people in those photos you sent me is a woman named Gail Swan. She's become a person of interest in the Clarke investigation,' said Carl. 'She lived in Ashcroft until a couple of years ago after her divorce.'

'Is Swan her maiden name?'

'No. Swan's her married name. She was Gail Richmond.'

'Oh, that Gail. She calls herself Richmond up here and, as far as I know, she still lives here. She's got a house on Carey Road.'

'She's been living in an apartment in Portside.'

'You sure we're talking about the same person, Inspector?'

'You still got those images from the funeral?'

'Yeah.'

'Have a look at image 0358. She's the woman standing to the right of Doug Clarke.'

Carl waited.

'That's Gail Richmond,' said Sgt Snow.

'She's still using Swan on her driver's licence and registration,' said Carl, 'and she's changed her address to the apartment in Portside.'

'Do you want me to speak to her?'

'She's disappeared in what looks like suspicious circumstances, and we lifted some prints from her apartment that match the prints found in Clarke's car. Check out that house you mentioned and ask around. If you find her, hold her.'

'Anything else, Inspector?'

'Any idea what she was doing in Ashcroft?'

'Working for her uncle. He's an accountant.'

'Richmond and Wells?' said Carl.

'Yeah. They're the biggest firm in town.'

'Find out what she was doing there.'

CHAPTER FOURTEEN

Richard Clarke pulled the envelope out from under the windscreen wiper of his BMW and flipped it over. There was no writing on either side. He looked around. There was no-one in the car park behind the offices of Doug Clarke Real Estate, and he knew there was no security camera covering the area.

He held the envelope in his hands and turned it over several times. It felt like it contained nothing but paper. He used his pocket knife to slit open the sealed end and extracted the single sheet of paper from inside the envelope. He opened the page and read the neatly typed message: Go to Appleby lookout. We are watching you.

Richard folded the page and slid it back into the envelope. Then, he got into his car and sat for a long time. He had a decision to make but he didn't like either of the options available to him.

He knew it had been a mistake to agree to play their game. Hindsight told him he should have stopped playing when he'd lost the first time but he'd given in to the enticing possibility of winning it back in the next game, and that decision had drawn him into a downward spiral of ever increasing losses.

He'd had some wins but not enough to pay back what he'd borrowed, and no-one would lend him a cent. He'd asked, but he was mortgaged to the hilt, and there were some people he just couldn't ask. He'd be able to pay them back if they'd give him more time. He had about half the amount he owed them. But, they'd stopped him playing and started putting the pressure on after his father's death.

The debt had been a mistake, but he'd been desperate to keep the bank off his back and to hide his shame from Kathy. It was black money, which meant his assets were safe, even if he wasn't. At least Kathy would have somewhere to live if the worst happened.

It had been fun when it started, and a way to earn back the money he'd lost. They'd paid him to play with their money. When he lost, it was to them, and when he won he handed it over to them and they still paid him for playing. But, he'd made that one mistake and hadn't been able to repay what he'd borrowed without their consent.

He wondered what would happen if he went to the police. A lot of people in high places had shares in the casino. No doubt, they'd be affronted if he exposed their dirty little secret, and Justin's political career would probably be over before it even got started. And, there was a fair chance he'd still end up dead.

Their price for forgiving the debt had been access to his father's property finance business but his father had wanted more than they were prepared to pay, despite the efforts of their negotiator, who'd gone beyond what he'd expected of her to win over his father. She'd told him they were almost there, but clearly something had gone wrong. His father was dead and she wasn't answering his calls.

Following his father's death, they'd approached his mother

but she had refused to sell to them or accept their money for investment. She'd told him, when he'd asked, she'd sell when it suited her and that she had access to more than enough money to fund the projects she had in the pipeline.

He'd been too ashamed to tell her what he had done and what was likely to happen to him if she didn't agree to their terms. Now, it was too late and there weren't many options left to him.

He decided to face the music and see if he could talk them into giving him more time. If that didn't work, there was always the other option if they didn't kill him first.

He started the car and drove out of the car park onto the street, turned left, and headed towards the hills. He hoped Kathy would forgive him if he had to take the second option.

He didn't notice the dark-colored Mercedes glide out from the shadows and follow him as he drove into the failing light of dusk, but he knew they'd be there.

———

Richard hadn't expected there to be as much traffic as there was as he drove into the hills on the eastern edge of the metropolitan area. He'd forgotten about the people who commuted daily from the towns and villages scattered through the hills to work in the city.

As he climbed further into the hills closer to his destination, Richard noticed fewer and fewer cars in his rear-view mirror until there was only one set of headlights on the road behind him. That had to be them.

He pulled into the parking spot where he'd been told to take the money, a car park that serviced a lookout with a scenic view over the river valley below. It was a popular place for tourists to stop and take photographs. At this hour, it was deserted. The car travelling behind him pulled in alongside his BMW.

Richard killed the lights and waited. The passenger side door of the Mercedes opened and a man dressed in a suit was illuminated by the interior light as he climbed out of the car. Richard didn't recognize him.

The man tapped on the window above Richard's shoulder. Richard pushed the button and waited while the window slid down inside the door.

'You got the money?'

'I need more time,' said Richard.

The man opened the door of the BMW. 'Get out, Mr Clarke.'

Richard looked at the man standing above him illuminated by the car's interior light, expecting to be threatened, maybe beaten up a little. He was prepared for that. He didn't think they'd hurt him that much if they wanted him to come good with the money.

He was about to turn off the ignition and unbuckle his seat-belt when he saw the pistol in his assailant's hand. Instead of complying, he took his foot off the brake pedal, which reignited the engine from its automated shutdown, slipped the shift into reverse and stomped on the accelerator. The BMW shot backwards, its open door forcing his assailant to jump back so quickly he stumbled and fell to the ground. Richard swung the car round in an arc and shifted the selector to drive. His door slammed shut as he fishtailed back onto the road, spraying gravel behind him.

Richard switched on the headlights, turned left and headed further into the hills, hoping to outrun them.

Within minutes, they were behind him. He heard a sharp popping sound. The rear window of the BMW shattered. Then, the interior was flooded in light as the driver of the Mercedes switched its lights to high beam.

The BMW slid sideways as Richard entered the approaching bend at speed. He struggled to correct and keep the car on the road as the rear end headed towards the trees. He pulled the front end back into alignment with his intended direction of travel, but the car swerved sharply as the rim of the front right-side wheel dug into the bitumen. The BMW flipped, crashed through the guard rail, and plunged into the darkness of the valley below.

The pursuing Mercedes screeched to a halt.

Two men got out and peered into the darkness beyond the edge of the twisted guard rail. A bright flash pierced the blackness of the abyss as the fuel tank of the BMW exploded on the rocks below. They turned away, got back into the Mercedes, and drove into the night.

CHAPTER FIFTEEN

DC Templar waved Carl over to her desk as he made his way through the squad room to his office. 'Take a look at this, Inspector.' She pointed to her screen.

'What have you got?'

'Richard Clarke's number is in Gail Swan's call log. They were exchanging calls months before she started calling his father.'

'That's interesting.'

'Do you think he could have been having an affair with her as well?' said DC Templar.

'Don't know,' said Carl. 'See what he has to say about it. What about his brother? Is his number on her call log?'

'No, Justin's number isn't listed.'

'How did you and Nigel get on with her ex?'

'Claims he hasn't seen her since their divorce,' said DC Templar, 'and his number's not in her call log.'

'What did he have to say about her?'

'Nothing flattering, but it turns out her ex has form. He's

been inside for extortion. Worked as a standover merchant for the Rileys.'

'That before or after their divorce?'

'Before. She divorced him when he was inside.'

'What's he doing now?'

'Works as a gardener for the City of East Park,' said DC Templar. 'Did a course when he was inside. Spends his days maintaining the playing fields in the urban forest.'

Carl looked at the whiteboard. Someone looking after the playing fields would know when they were not being used on a weekend. 'Are his prints on file?'

'Yes. But, there's no match with the prints from the victim's car. I checked.'

Carl smiled. Lisa had beaten him to that thought. 'Where was he on the day Clarke was killed?'

'Home with his wife and kids.'

Carl wondered how watertight that alibi might be. 'Do you believe him?'

'No reason not to, Inspector. She didn't seem under pressure to me.'

'Did he say what Gail was doing when they were married?'

'Said she worked for some accounting firm. He couldn't remember what it was called.'

'That gels,' said Carl. 'Sgt Snow from Ashcroft said she was working for her uncle's accounting firm up there.' Carl stroked his chin. 'Sgt Snow thought she was still living in Ashcroft.'

'She's changed her address with Registrations,' said DC Templar.

'When did she do that?'

'February last year.'

'Any luck with her bank accounts?'

'First National said we'd have them today.'

'Follow them up, and then have a chat with Richard Clarke. There's obviously more to this than the Clarke's have let on.'

———

Twenty minutes later, DC Templar came into Carl's office.

'We could have a problem, Inspector. No-one's seen Richard Clarke since yesterday afternoon.'

'Who have you spoken to?' said Carl.

'His brother and his wife. She said he didn't come home last night.'

'What about his mother?'

'His brother said she didn't know where he was either.'

'Do any of them sound worried?'

'His wife sounded distraught,' said DC Templar.

'Distraught enough to file a missing person's report?'

'Not yet.'

'Go and see her,' said Carl. 'Find out what she knows about Gail Swan. Take Nigel with you.'

———

Ten minutes after DC Templar left to interview Kathy Clarke, Carl's phone rang.

'DI West.'

'Dean Lang, Inspector. I'm at a crash site in the hills at the bottom of Appleby Gorge. A car came off the road here sometime last night but it wasn't spotted until this morning. Driver's deceased. Burnt beyond recognition. The car's registered to Doug Clarke Real Estate. Thought you might be interested.'

'Anything suspicious?'

'Looks like he hit the guard rail at speed and flipped over the top,' said Dean, 'but there's a set of skid marks up there close to where he went over that didn't come from his car.'

'So, someone must have seen him go over,' said Carl, wondering why they hadn't called it in.

'Could have been racing,' said Dean, 'or chasing him.'

Carl didn't think Richard Clarke was the type who'd engage in racing through the hills. 'Who's examining the body?'

'Dr Worthington.'

'Tell her it's probably Richard Clarke. He's been missing since last night. And, Dean, have a good look around. Racing doesn't fit his profile.'

Carl ended the call and hit the button for DC Templar. She answered on the second ring.

'Inspector?'

'The wreckage of Richard Clarke's car's been found at the bottom of Appleby Gorge with a badly burnt body inside.'

'Is it Clarke?' said DC Templar.

'Probably,' said Carl, 'but we can't be sure.'

'What do you want me to do?'

'Forget the interview for now, Lisa. I'll get Community Liaison to send someone out to inform her.'

Carl ended the call and arranged for a community liaison officer to break the news to Richard Clarke's wife.

Then he walked to Harry's desk. 'What's left of Richard Clarke's car is at the bottom of Appleby Gorge. Whoever was driving was incinerated.'

'Do they think it's Clarke?'

'He's been missing since last night,' said Carl, 'so, it's probably him.'

'What do they think happened?'

'Dean's not sure but he thinks another car could have been involved. Said there were skid marks on the road that don't appear to have come from Clarke's car.'

'Maybe someone ran him off the road.'

'Guess we'll have a better idea when we see Dean's report,' said Carl. 'What worries me is we now have two dead Clarkes with some connection to Gail Swan. Think we'd better talk to Justin.'

———

When Carl and Harry walked into the offices of Doug Clarke Real Estate, Justin Clarke was standing at the front desk talking to the receptionist.

'Mr Clarke. We need to talk,' said Carl.

'Has something happened to Richard?'

Carl remembered Lisa had spoken to Justin earlier when she'd been looking for his brother.

'Might be best if we talk in your office, Mr Clarke,' said Carl.

Justin ushered them into his office and shut the door.

'The wreckage of your brother's car has been found at the bottom of Appleby Gorge,' said Carl.

'What about Richard?' said Justin. 'Is he alive?'

'I'm sorry,' said Carl. 'The driver was incinerated. We don't know for sure if it is your brother but, until we hear otherwise, it's probably better to assume it is.'

Justin sat behind his desk and let his head drop into his hands.

Carl waited until Justin lifted his head and sat back in his chair. 'Any idea what he would have been doing up in the hills last night?'

Justin shook his head. 'We don't have any listings up there.'

'Did he have any friends living up there?'

'Not that I know of.'

'When was the last time you saw him?'

'He was still here when I went home last night.'

'What time was that?'

'I left at six. I had a meeting with the state office at eight,' said Justin. 'That went until half ten. I went home after that.'

'When did you know your brother was missing?'

'When he didn't turn up this morning. I called Kathy. She said he hadn't come home.'

'Was that unusual?'

'It wasn't the first time he'd stayed out all night,' said Justin, 'if that's what you mean.'

'Marital problems?'

'I don't know,' said Justin. 'He always told me to mind my own business whenever I asked him about it.'

Carl didn't have any experience with being or having a brother but thought he'd be concerned if his brother had been cheating on his spouse.

'You didn't push him?'

'I knew what he was like,' said Justin, 'besides, I had to work with him.'

Carl decided it was time to change tack. 'Were you and your brother involved in the finance side of the business?'

'No. We only worked in the real estate side. The finance side was done through Mum's accounting office. Not here.'

'Have you met Gail Swan, the woman who was talking to your father about buying that business?'

'I only know about her because Dad told me she'd approached him about buying him out. He was surprised. He hadn't told anyone he wanted to sell at that point.'

'So, you've never met her or spoken to her?

'She's just a name to me, Inspector.'

'Did you know Richard had been in contact with her?'

Justin crossed his arms on the desktop. 'News to me. Perhaps she has a property to let or was looking to rent one. Richard handled the property management side of the business.'

'I don't think she was in the rental market, Mr Clarke, but she'd been exchanging calls with your brother for several months before she called your father.'

'What? Dad said she'd called out of the blue.'

'So, it's possible your brother may have been seeing her for other reasons,' said Carl, 'and maybe he was the one who told her your father was interested in selling his business.'

'I suppose,' said Justin, 'but I guess you'll have to ask her now.'

CHAPTER SIXTEEN

Kathy didn't know what to think. Richard hadn't come home. He hadn't called and he wasn't answering his phone.

Last night, she'd given up waiting at eleven and gone to bed. This morning, when she still hadn't heard from him, she'd called Justin and Joanna. Neither of them had heard from him since Justin had left him in the office at six the previous evening. Then, that female detective Joanna had told her about had called and asked to speak to him. She'd told the detective she didn't know where he was and promised to call her back when she heard from him.

Now, as she watched Dougie playing on the floor with his blocks, she wondered what Richard was up to this time. The last time he'd stayed out all night he'd arrived home from the casino in a taxi, drunk. She'd made him sleep in the spare room for a month. He'd promised he wouldn't do it again and, as far as she knew, he hadn't, until now.

She'd had enough of him running around to meetings to please his father. They'd argued over and over about him standing up for himself, but Richard had never seen it or had the courage to challenge his father in any way.

At least Doug's murder had resolved that issue between them and they'd discussed how they would run things when it was just them operating the real estate business after Justin's election. Richard had seemed relieved when she'd agreed to come back into the business, and she was looking forward to it. She enjoyed being a mother but she couldn't wait to be back in the office and participating in adult conversation, and away from the chaos of living with a determined three-year-old boy.

'Mummy?'

Kathy dragged her awareness back into the room. Dougie had a quizzical look on his face. She wondered if he could read her mind. 'Yes, sweetheart.'

'Where's Daddy?'

I wish I knew, she thought. 'Daddy's at work, sweetheart. Do you want to go to the playground?'

She expected him to say yes. He liked the playground.

'Play with my blocks,' said Dougie.

The doorbell rang before she could respond, and when she opened the door with Dougie hiding behind her legs, there were two police officers standing on the front porch.

'Mrs Clarke?'

'Yes.'

'I'm afraid we have some bad news, Mrs Clarke. May we come in?'

Kathy felt the world slipping away from her. The policeman reached out and caught her as her knees buckled, and then helped her into the lounge and into an armchair.

Dougie started crying. The policewoman scooped him up, closed the front door, and carried him into the lounge.

'What's your name?'

'Dougie.' He looked at her. 'I want Mummy.'

'Mummy's not feeling very well, Dougie. Do you want to sit here next to her?'

Dougie wriggled out of her arms and clambered onto Kathy's lap as she opened her eyes.

'I'm sorry,' said Kathy. 'What were you saying?'

'Your husband's car has been involved in an accident, Mrs Clarke,' said the policeman.

'Is he hurt?'

'Was he driving his car?'

Kathy blinked. 'What?'

'Do you know if your husband was driving his car or had he lent it to someone else?' said the policeman.

'I don't know,' said Kathy. 'He didn't come home last night.'

The policeman looked at his colleague and then back at Kathy. 'The car caught fire, Mrs Clarke. The driver was killed.'

Kathy burst into tears.

'What's wrong, Mummy?'

Kathy hugged Dougie to her chest.

'I'll put the kettle on,' said the policeman.

'I'm sorry, Mrs Clarke. Is there anyone we can call?' said the policewoman.

'Are you sure it's Richard?' said Kathy, catching her breath.

'We'll need access to his dental records to confirm his identity,' said the policewoman, 'but, you need to prepare yourself for the worst. I'm sorry.'

'Can you call my mother for me?'

———

By the time the police called to confirm Richard had died in his car at the bottom of Appleby Gorge, Kathy had resigned herself to hearing that outcome. That hadn't made hearing the news any easier but she knew the outcome fit the facts: Richard hadn't come home or called. The police had simply used his dental records to verify what she knew in her heart to be true.

With Dougie in her parents' care, Kathy went into the room Richard had used as his home office. She needed to get her head around their finances, which Richard had managed ever since they were married. He'd given her a credit card and told her not to worry about how much she spent. She'd restrained herself and trusted him, and they'd never argued over money. There'd always seemed to be enough whenever she'd wanted anything, even after she'd stopped work when Dougie was born.

In their pre-child days, when they were both working, they had earned good money and invested in real estate. They owned five rental properties and, as Kathy logged on to their internet banking portal using Richard's password, she expected to see a healthy balance in their savings account. When the page loaded, she was surprised to see their loan account had an outstanding balance close to two million dollars. She thought they'd payed that down to less than a hundred thousand before she'd stopped work. Their savings account was empty, and the account Richard's pay went into had a balance of just over three thousand dollars, which was close to the amount they owed on their credit cards.

Kathy sat at the computer and stared at the screen. It looked like Richard had withdrawn all the money they'd paid into the loan account. She scrolled through the transactions and realized he'd maxed out the credit line secured by their investment properties six months ago. She drilled down into the transactions. He'd been transferring money to his credit card; ten thousand dollars at a time.

She switched her attention to his credit card account and scrolled back into the history of his spending. There were a lot of cash withdrawals from an ATM on North Terrace. Then, it hit her. Cityscape Casino was on North Terrace. Richard had lied to her. He'd been back to the casino on those nights he'd told her he was at meetings with his father, and he'd gambled away all their money.

'You bastard! You lying bastard!' She stopped and stared at the screen. Her anger moved sideways and opened a window in her mind. 'Oh, Richard, what have you done?'

She couldn't stop the tears. 'Why didn't you tell me? We could have worked this out. Oh, honey, what have you done?'

Kathy took several deep breaths and then reached for her phone. She waited for her father to answer his mobile.

'Dad, I'm going to need some help. Richard's gambled all our money away at the casino.'

'How much?'

'Nearly two million dollars. He's left me nothing to live on.'

'Didn't he say anything?'

Kathy swallowed her pride. 'Dad, I think Richard may have killed himself instead of talking to me.'

'I'll be right over, sweetheart.'

CHAPTER SEVENTEEN

Carl and Harry listened as Sgt Lang walked them through the photographs he'd taken of the roadway leading up to the point where Richard Clarke's car had gone over the guard rail into Appleby Gorge.

'There's no sign he hit the brakes before colliding with the rail,' said Sgt Lang. He pointed to the road next to the mangled guard rail. 'He's come across here but there's no skid marks leading to the point of impact.'

'So, he could have driven into it intentionally,' said Carl.

'I don't think so,' said Sgt Lang. He clicked onto the next image in his presentation. 'If you look at this one, you can see the car slid along the rail before going over the edge. That suggests he was trying to take the bend at speed and lost it. If he'd driven straight into it, the barrier would have given way or buckled in the direction of impact.'

'Tell me about the skid marks,' said Carl.

Sgt Lang clicked onto his next image. 'These skid marks intersect with the path taken by the BMW, Inspector, but they follow the road, not the path taken by the BMW. Whatever created those marks came to a halt, and look at this.' Sgt Lang changed the image. 'Somebody stood on the edge of the road here and looked over the edge.'

'Could that have been the person who reported the crash?' said Harry.

'She was wearing heels, Harry. This was created by someone wearing a size eleven boot who weighs a lot more than she does.' He switched images. 'These are her footprints.'

'So, someone else came across the crash site before she did but failed to report it,' said Harry. 'Perhaps they didn't see the wreck below.'

'Why would someone come to a screaming halt like that to investigate a damaged guard rail?' said Sgt Lang. 'I think you need to consider the possibility your victim was either hoon racing or being chased. Take a look at this.' He changed the image. 'See that indentation there in the road surface? That was made by the edge of a wheel rim cutting into the road. He was either going like the clappers or he'd lost a tyre coming into the bend.'

Carl leant back in his seat. 'What about the wreck? Anything that sheds more light on what happened?'

Sgt Lang changed the image. 'This.'

'What's that?' said Carl.

'One very deformed nine mill slug,' said Sgt Lang. 'Ballistics reckon they look like that after passing through safety glass.'

'Where did you find that?' said Harry.

'Inside the cabin area,' said Sgt Lang.

'So, someone's fired a shot at him,' said Carl.

'Looks like it,' said Sgt Lang. 'No sign of a round in the immediate area, though.'

'Take another look,' said Carl.

Kathy Clarke opened the door with Dougie in her arms.

'We need to talk, Mrs Clarke,' said Carl, 'there are a few things we need to sort out.'

'Can't it wait?' said Kathy.

'Afraid not.'

'Who's your friend?'

'This is Detective Constable Templar,' said Carl.

'Oh, we spoke on the phone,' said Kathy.

'That's right,' said Lisa. 'I'm sorry about your husband.'

'Yeah, well you'd better come in then.'

She led them through the house to the family room, where she deposited Dougie on the floor among his toys. 'What do you want to talk about?'

'We're not convinced Richard's death was accidental,' said Carl. 'There are signs he may have been trying to get away from someone the night he was killed.'

'I think the only one Richard was running away from was himself,' said Kathy.

'What makes you say that?'

Kathy sat at the table and indicated they should do the same. 'He'd gambled away all our money and then some, even though he'd promised me he'd stay away from the casino.'

Carl hadn't expected that answer but it made him think about who Richard Clarke's enemies might be. 'And, you weren't aware of him doing that?'

'I looked after the house, Inspector. Richard handled the finances. I trusted him.' She smiled. 'That was a mistake, wasn't it?'

'I'm not here to pass judgement, Mrs Clarke.'

'So, why are you here?'

'Do you know Gail Swan?'

Kathy shook her head. 'Joanna mentioned that name the

other day. Isn't she the woman Doug was supposed to be having an affair with?'

Carl nodded. 'According to your mother-in-law, she was trying to buy their finance business, but did you know Richard was exchanging phone calls with her?'

'Richard wasn't like his father, Inspector.'

'Her phone records show your husband was talking to her months before she called his father.'

'Perhaps she was looking for a property to rent,' said Kathy, 'or perhaps she's in the party?'

'As far as we know, she was working for an accountant in Ashcroft that supported your in-law's finance business.'

'Richard never mentioned her to me,' said Kathy.

Carl crossed his arms and leant forward on the table. 'Was Richard ever threatened by anyone?'

Dougie came to the table and offered Lisa a block to play with.

'Thank you,' said Lisa, accepting the block and tousling his hair.

Dougie walked around to his mother and held up his arms. Kathy picked him up and placed him on her lap.

'He never said anything if they had,' said Kathy.

'Do you think he might have gambling debts?' said Carl.

'I don't know, to be honest. What I can tell you is he ran out of money six months ago. I don't know if he was still going to the casino after that or not. He was always out at meetings, thanks to Doug and his obsession with getting Justin into parliament.'

Kathy put Dougie back down onto the floor. 'What makes you think he didn't kill himself, Inspector?'

'The marks on the road where he went over the edge.' Carl took out the print of the image of the skid marks on the road and slid it across the table to Kathy. 'Someone stopped in a hell of a hurry and got out to have a look at what had happened.'

'Could just be a sticky beak,' said Kathy.

'And, then there's this.' Carl showed her the image of the deformed nine millimetre bullet.

'What's that?'

'That's the remains of a bullet that was found inside Richard's car,' said Carl. 'It's been fired through one of the windows.'

'Do you think they'll come here?'

'I don't know,' said Carl, handing her his business card, 'but let me know if anyone approaches you for money.'

———

The team sat around in a semicircle of chairs in front of the whiteboard outside Carl's office.

'You've seen Forensics' report,' said Carl. 'I'm not convinced Richard Clarke's death was either suicide or a tragic accident.'

'That bullet's a bit of a worry, Inspector. Makes you wonder who he got tangled up with,' said DC Paterson. 'Must be something beyond politics. I've never heard of anyone being shot at over a pre-selection contest.'

Carl pointed to the photograph of Gail Swan on the whiteboard. 'We know Richard had been in contact with Swan, and whoever drove Doug's car to North Summit has been in her apartment. I want to know who she's connected with and what they wanted from the Clarkes.'

'If she's still alive,' said DC Beard.

'Even if she's not, she's still our way into working out what's going on.'

'She hasn't accessed her bank accounts,' said DC Templar.

'What did the deposits tell you?' said Carl.

'Mostly from Richmond and Wells, but there's also a pattern of monthly deposits from an account at B and A in the name of

Anthony Slade. She was doing pretty well for herself. No debts.'

'We know she worked for Richmond and Wells,' said DS Fuller.

'Pay them a visit, Harry, and talk to anybody that knows her in Ashcroft.'

'Right, Boss. What about the house she was living in up there?'

'Get a warrant and search the place. Take Nigel with you.'

'What about the casino?' said DC Templar.

'I'd like you and Wayne to look into his history with the casino, given what his wife told us. They'll have CCTV coverage of their tables. See what you can find out. He may even have an account with them.'

The team dispersed to their assigned tasks.

Carl went into his office and shut the door. He needed to think. He had two bodies, a father and son, and a missing woman known to both, whose reputed offer to buy Doug's business was intriguing, if true, seeing that she wasn't a registered finance broker. Carl wondered if she'd been the attractive front of an operation to get access to Doug's business, given the discovery of Doug's fingerprints in her bedroom. But, he couldn't see where Richard fit into the picture, unless he'd been having an affair with her as well.

Her disappearance bothered him, since what had been left in her apartment suggested she'd left unexpectedly, and perhaps involuntarily.

The monthly deposits into her bank account was something else that disturbed him. The amounts suggested to Carl she was doing something besides working for her uncle, and that something, whatever it was, paid handsomely. He'd have to find out who this Anthony Slade was and what she'd been doing for him.

CHAPTER EIGHTEEN

Cityscape Casino was located in the middle of the night life district that straddled the eastern end of North Terrace. At night, the area was transformed into a dazzling wonderland of lights but, during the day, it was a row of drab grey buildings.

Lisa and Wayne parked in the underground car park and caught the elevator up to the foyer of the casino. They stepped out into a hall lined with marble tiles and illuminated by several crystal chandeliers.

'Been here before?' said Wayne.

'Only ever been here on business,' said Lisa. 'Gambling's not my thing.'

'It's an interesting place,' said Wayne. 'You see all sorts.'

'You a regular?'

'Not really, but the beer's cheaper here than in most pubs in the city.'

Lisa smiled. 'You guys are all the same.'

'Yeah, you're probably right.'

They walked up to the information desk and presented their ID.

'How can I help you?' said the uniformed guard sitting behind the desk.

'We'd like to speak to the security shift manager,' said Wayne.

'Do you have an appointment?'

'We do now,' said Wayne.

The guard smiled, picked up the handset of the telephone on the desk, and spoke to someone within the building.

As they waited, Lisa watched the continuous lines of people making their way into and out of the gambling hall and wondered if the place was ever empty. The sound of approaching footsteps brought her attention back to why they were there. She turned back towards the desk as a woman in a black uniform with red embellishments approached them.

'Hi, I'm Miriam. How can I help you, Detective?'

Lisa opened the photograph of Richard Clarke on her mobile phone and showed it to her. 'Do you recognize this man?'

Miriam looked at the image. 'He's one of our regulars.'

'How regular?' said Wayne.

'Couple of nights a week, at least, but I haven't seen him for a couple of months.'

'What's he play?' said Wayne.

'Poker.'

'Winner?'

Miriam smiled. 'This is a casino, Detective. Sometimes they win, sometimes they lose.'

'What about this guy in particular?' said Lisa.

'You'd need to talk to the dealers. It's not like we keep a tally.'

'What about CCTV in the gaming area?' said Wayne.

'You might be out of luck with this guy. Our focus is on watching what people do at the tables, to make sure they don't cheat. We don't keep the footage forever, unless we pick something up. What's his name?'

'Richard Clarke,' said Lisa.

'He's not on our watch list,' said Miriam, 'and if he hasn't been in for a month or more, we're not going to have anything.'

'If you're here now,' said Wayne, 'when was the last time you worked a night shift?'

'We rotate shifts every week,' said Miriam. 'That's part of our integrity control system to ensure there's no collusion between staff to cheat the house.' She smiled. 'I was on nights last week, and I don't remember seeing him.'

'Can you get us a list of the dealers working the poker tables?' said Lisa.

'Sure,' said Miriam, 'but that will be a long list. We have twenty tables.'

'That won't be a problem,' said Lisa, handing Miriam her card. 'Send me the details and we'll follow them up.'

'Can you send me a copy of that photograph?' said Miriam. 'It might be easier if I show that to the dealers.'

'Okay,' said Lisa. 'What's your email address?'

———

Over the next few days, Lisa and Wayne interviewed five dealers who'd recognized Richard Clarke from the photo they'd given Miriam. There was a common theme to their stories. Richard had been one of a group of four players who'd always played together, and although he'd lost more times than he'd won, he'd had a big win the last time any of them recalled him being in the casino, around three months prior to his death.

When Wayne asked if they knew the names of the other players, they denied knowing who the players were, but one of the dealers disclosed that the other three were still regulars at the casino and volunteered to point them out.

The dealer arranged for Wayne to view the CCTV footage

of a recent poker game involving the three men he wanted to talk to about Richard Clarke.

As they sat watching the screen in the CCTV control room, the dealer pointed to three men sitting at a poker table under his supervision. 'Those guys always played when your man was at the table.'

'Always?' said Wayne.

'Ever since he started playing with them,' said the dealer. 'Before that, he played with whoever was at the table.'

'When did he start playing with this group?'

'Around the middle of last year.'

'Is that when they started coming to the casino?'

'No, they've been playing here for years.'

Wayne turned to the technician. 'Can you make me a copy of this?'

'No problem, mate.'

'Do they come in every night?' said Wayne.

'Just about,' said the dealer.

'How much money is involved with their games?'

'These boys each bring ten thousand to the table every night.'

Wayne did a quick calculation. If they came in five nights a week, that was two hundred thousand a week or a million dollars every five weeks, assuming they always played as a foursome.

'Anyone taken Richard's place?' said Wayne.

'I don't think so.'

'What time do they usually come in?'

'Around seven thirty,' said the dealer. 'Sometimes later.'

'I reckon you'd find them in the Gamers Bar before that,' said the technician. 'I've seen them there when I work nights.'

Wayne showed them a photograph of Gail Swan. 'Have you seen this woman in the casino?'

'Don't think so,' said the dealer.

'No,' said the technician. 'She's not someone a man would forget, is she?'

———

When Wayne returned to Police Headquarters, he showed Lisa the copy of the video he'd watched at the casino.

'Stop there!' said Lisa. 'Zoom in on that face.'

'Someone you know?' said Wayne.

'That's Jack Swan. I interviewed him with Nigel last week. Didn't think he'd be the sort to spend his nights at the casino playing poker. He's a gardener for the East Park Council. Got a wife and a couple of little kids.'

'Maybe poker's his main source of income,' said Wayne. 'He wouldn't be the first bloke to make a living playing poker.'

'He's not making a fortune whatever he's doing, going by the place he lives in.'

'Bit of a dump, is it?'

'Not exactly a dump but nothing to write home about. A pretty ordinary suburban house in Northfield that could use some money spent on it.'

'Flashy car?'

'Not that I saw, and both he and his missus were home the day we called.'

'Hmm,' said Wayne. 'The dealer reckons he brings ten grand to the table every night.'

'It's got to be someone else's money,' said Lisa.

'If that's the case, Lisa, it looks like Clarke might have been mixed up with washing dirty money through the casino.'

'Guess that's what happens when you're a gambling addict and you blow the family fortune behind the wife's back,' said Lisa.

'What about the others guys?'

'Don't know them,' said Lisa.

'Fancy a night at the casino?'

'Why don't we just speak to Swan? We know where he is.'

'We don't want him tipping off the others,' said Wayne, 'particularly if they're using the casino as a laundromat.'

CHAPTER NINETEEN

It was ten thirty, on a warm spring morning three weeks after Doug Clarke's death, when Harry and Nigel walked into the offices of Richmond and Wells Accounting to interview Samuel Richmond. He was waiting for them.

'We were expecting Gail back from leave two weeks ago, Sergeant.'

'Have you heard from her?' said Harry.

'Well, no, and, as I told John Snow, we can't get her on the phone either.'

'Her mobile phone was found in her Portside apartment.'

'I wasn't aware she had an apartment down in the city until John mentioned it,' said Samuel. 'I thought she was living up here.'

'Has anyone been around to where she was living?'

'I sent my son around to see if she was alright when she didn't come to work,' said Samuel. 'He's been to her house several times, but there's no sign of her or her car.'

'Is that a green Mazda 3?' said Harry.

'Yes.'

'That's parked outside her apartment.'

'I don't understand,' said Samuel. 'What's happened to her?'

Harry looked at the certificates on the wall behind Samuel. 'That's what we're trying to work out, Mr Richmond.'

'How can I help?'

'We're looking for Gail because she was in some sort of relationship with Doug Clarke,' said Harry. 'I understand, from what Mrs Clarke told us, your firm is a source of the funds they use for financing property developments in the city.'

'Yes, a few years ago now, Doug invited me to help a couple of local lads make good.'

'Who'd they be?'

'Rory McLaren and Howard Stenhouse,' said Samuel. 'We had a number of clients looking for places to invest at the time, so it wasn't that big a deal to get them involved. Besides, helping each other is the way we do business up here.'

'Would Gail have known about your arrangement with Doug Clarke?'

'She managed that portfolio as part of her role.'

'So, she would have been in contact with Mrs Clarke, then?'

'Yes, she did all the liaison work,' said Samuel. 'Mind you, most of that would have been by email.'

'Did you know she'd approached Doug about buying him out?'

'Gail?' said Samuel. 'She didn't have that sort of money or the know-how.'

'Could she have been representing someone else?'

'If she was, Sergeant, I assure you, it wasn't me.'

'Anything in her personal life you're aware of that might explain her disappearance?'

Samuel shrugged his shoulders. 'Might be better to ask my son that one, Sergeant.'

'Is he available?'

'How long will you be in town?'

'We'll be here for a couple of days,' said Harry. 'We're staying at the Ashcroft Motel.'

'Neil will be in the office tomorrow, Sergeant.'

———

Nigel pulled up outside the house on Carey Road that Sgt Snow had told them was where Gail lived. It was a low cottage with a garden full of flowering native plants some distance from its nearest neighbour. Harry and Nigel got out of the car and walked down the driveway and around to the back door of the cottage.

'I reckon it'll be this key,' said Harry, holding up the oldest looking key from the keyring left in the Portside apartment. He inserted the key into the lock and turned it. There was an audible click as the ancient lock moved.

They pulled on their gloves. Harry pushed the door inwards.

Nigel took a tentative sniff of the air. 'Thank God she took her cat to Portside. Can you imagine what it'd smell like by now if she'd left it here?'

They were standing in the laundry. Harry walked through the doorway that led to the interior and found himself in the kitchen. He opened the blind and blinked at the sudden influx of light. He looked around. The place was neat and tidy. She obviously hadn't left Ashcroft the same way she'd left Portside.

They walked through the cottage. There were two bedrooms, a living room, a bathroom, and a cellar, accessible through a trapdoor in the living room floor.

'Wonder what she keeps down there?' said Nigel.

They lifted the trapdoor. The smell of damp earth wafted into the room.

'Get a torch,' said Harry.

While Nigel was retrieving a torch from the car, Harry

looked into the second bedroom. It contained a single bed and a freestanding wooden wardrobe. The bed was covered with a patchwork quilt. Harry turned it back. Underneath the quilt the bed was unmade. He replaced the quilt and opened the wardrobe. It was empty. He looked under the bed. Nothing but a fine layer of dust and fluff on the wooden floor.

When Nigel returned, he shone the torch down into the cellar space. 'Doesn't look very big, Sarge.'

'Well, let's see what's down there.'

Harry followed Nigel down into the cellar. They had to crouch to avoid hitting their heads on the floorboards of the living room. Nigel slowly moved the beam of the torch around the dark space. It was empty. They climbed up the steps and dropped the trapdoor back into place.

'There's nothing in the second bedroom,' said Harry. 'Have a look through this room while I search her bedroom.'

Harry walked into the main bedroom and flicked on the light. It was bigger than the tiny second bedroom but most of the space was taken up by a double bed jutting out from the wall opposite the door. There was a woollen rug on the floor between the bed and the wooden wardrobes on the wall opposite the window. Harry opened the doors of the closest wardrobe. It was full of women's clothing. He opened the doors of the second wardrobe. One side held more women's clothing but there were several garments, including a dark grey suit smelling of dry-cleaning fluid, that obviously belonged to a man.

Harry opened the suit coat. There was a dry cleaner's tag pinned to the inside pocket. The tag indicated the suit had last been cleaned at East Park Dry Cleaners. Harry took a photograph of the tag attached to the suit and then detached it and placed it in an evidence bag.

He searched through the clothing hanging in both wardrobes

but nothing further piqued his interest. He went back into the living room to see how Nigel was getting on.

'Anything?'

'Found a little book with what looks like her passwords,' said Nigel. 'Might help us open her phone.'

'Any sign of a laptop?' said Harry.

'Not in here.'

'Check the bathroom while I do the kitchen.'

Harry opened the kitchen cupboards and the refrigerator. They were well stocked with food. He looked around the kitchen. Nothing looked out of place. He went through the doorway into the laundry and lifted the lid on the laundry basket. It was empty. He checked the washing machine and the cupboard under the trough. Nothing. He opened the back door and went out into the yard.

It took him a few moments to locate the rubbish bins hidden behind a lattice work trellis next to the rainwater tank. He lifted the red lid of the nearest bin and peered inside. Resting on top of two small plastic bags of household waste was a pair of rolled up blue jeans. Harry reached in and lifted out the jeans. He closed the bin and unrolled the jeans across the lid. The legs of the jeans and the shirt rolled up inside them were stained with what Harry's training told him was dried blood.

He looked at the shirt in his gloved hand. It was big enough to fit him. He wondered who it belonged to and whose blood had stained it.

'Nigel!'

Nigel appeared in the back doorway. 'What's up, Sarge?'

Harry held up the blood-stained clothing. 'We need to secure this place and get Forensics up here.'

———

Neil Richmond arrived at the Ashcroft Motel as Harry and Nigel were finishing breakfast in the dining room.

'Thanks for dropping in,' said Harry.

'Dad said you wanted to talk to me about Gail,' said Neil.

'We're trying to piece together her social life, you know, who she mixed with here.'

'You know she's from here, don't you?'

'Yes, but I understand she moved down to the city when she got married and didn't come back until after her divorce.'

'Moving down to the city didn't make much difference,' said Neil. 'She was up here most weekends playing sport. In a way, it's like she never left.'

'How long has she lived in the house on Carey Road?'

'Forever,' said Neil. 'That was her mother's place. They moved there after Gail's father died when she was little. He was killed in an accident on the farm. Tractor rollover, I think. I was a kid like Gail when it happened.'

'Are you close to Gail?' said Harry.

'We're cousins. We know a lot of the same people.'

'What are people saying now she's missing?'

'Wondering where she is, mostly.'

'Have you heard from her?'

Neil shook his head. 'I wish I had.'

'Any idea where she might be?'

'Told me she was going to be spending time with her new boyfriend.'

'Who's that?'

'Someone called Joe,' said Neil. 'He's been up a few times but he's one of those city slickers. Doesn't like it up here, from what I hear.'

'Have you met this Joe?'

'Just the once. Tall guy with dark hair. Be in his early forties, I'd say. Looks like he spends a bit of time in the gym.'

'Talk to him?'

'Yeah. He's some sort of business consultant. Gail was talking about going into business with him.'

'What type of business?'

'I think she wanted to set up her own practice. She doesn't have much of a future here, unless she wants to work for me when I take over from Dad.'

'Did she ever mention meeting Doug Clarke to you?' said Harry.

'Doug was always a talking point, Sergeant. Gail's father was one of Aunty Melanie's brothers, like my dad. I assume you know about her and Doug.'

'Yes,' said Harry. 'Did she ever mention wanting to buy Doug's business?'

'She told me she liked his business model and wanted to copy it, but I've never heard her say she wanted to buy him out. Frankly, I don't think she'd have the money.'

'Perhaps this Joe has money,' said Harry.

Neil shrugged his shoulders. 'I don't really know anything about that.'

'Did you know about the Portside apartment?'

'I thought that was Joe's place. At least, that's what she told me.'

'Were you aware she'd changed her address to the apartment in Portside in February last year?'

'If that's true, that's almost a year before this Joe came onto the scene. She was seeing some bloke called David back then.'

'Do you recall his full name by any chance?' said Harry.

Neil stroked his chin. 'Callinan. That's it. David Callinan. He's an older bloke. I didn't like him much. Thought he was a sleaze.'

'Do you know what he does?'

'Hate to admit it, Sergeant, but he's an accountant.'

'Every profession has its rogues, Mr Richmond.' Harry laughed. 'Is there anyone you know that Gail may have confided in?'

'Talk to my wife,' said Neil. 'They've been friends since they started school. I'll give Lori a call and let her know you'll be dropping by. She should be home just after nine, after she's dropped the kids off at school.'

———

After Neil Richmond excused himself, Harry turned to Nigel. 'Didn't we interview someone called David Callinan?'

'That's the name of the deputy mayor,' said Nigel.

'Does he fit the description?'

'You'll have to ask Lisa, Sarge. She interviewed him.'

Harry looked at his notes. 'Too bad Richmond couldn't tell us more about this Joe character.'

'Swan's neighbours might know more about him.'

'Let's hope so,' said Harry.

They checked out of the motel and drove around to the address Neil Richmond had given them. Neil's home was a substantial stone house located in what Harry decided was the better part of town. Lori Richmond was waiting for them.

'When was the last time you saw Gail,' said Harry, once they'd settled into the chairs under the pergola.

'She was here the weekend Doug Clarke was killed. We had coffee that Saturday morning.'

'Early or late morning?' said Harry.

'Early. We caught up for breakfast. I had to be home by eleven so Neil could go to golf with his father.'

'Did she seem at all concerned about anything?'

Lori shook her head. 'She seemed pretty happy to me.'

'What did you talk about?'

'Oh, the usual things. The kids. The weather. Other people.'

'Did she happen to mention that she was planning to go away?'

'No.'

'Did you know she was renting an apartment in the city?' said Harry.

'I knew she was spending a lot of time down there,' said Lori. 'She had a new man in her life.'

'Would this be the Joe your husband mentioned?'

'Yes.'

'Do you know his last name?'

'She only ever talked about him as Joe,' said Lori. 'He was better for her than the David she had been seeing.'

'You wouldn't happen to have any photos of her with either of them, would you?'

'I don't think so.'

Nigel showed her an image of David Callinan from the City of East Park's website.

'That's David,' said Lori.

'What's Joe look like?' said Harry.

'He's tall, well built, sort of handsome with dark hair. About forty, I'd say.'

'When was the last time you saw him?'

'The Monday morning after that weekend,' said Lori. 'He was driving Gail's car.'

'Was she in it?'

'Yes, she waved to me when they went past. I thought they were going back to the city.'

'Did she look okay?' said Harry.

'Hard to tell through those tinted windows.'

'Had Joe come up with her?'

'I didn't know he was here until I saw them leaving,' said Lori. 'Joe usually comes up in his Mercedes but I guess they must have come up together, seeing how she'd been down in the city at his place.'

'Would that be the apartment in Portside?' said Harry.

'Portside?' said Lori. 'She told me Joe lived in East Park.'

Harry looked at Nigel, who shrugged. Then he remembered the dry cleaner's tag from the suit hanging in Gail's wardrobe that he'd collected and her comment made sense.

'Any idea where Gail would go if she was in trouble?' said Harry.

'I'd expect her to come back here if she was in trouble,' said Lori. 'I'm really worried about her. I haven't heard from her since that Monday morning, and we generally speak every couple of days.'

'Did she say anything to you about Doug Clarke or buying his business?'

'Doug was here for Melanie's funeral,' said Lori. 'We talked about him quite a bit after that, especially when Gail told me how he'd helped the McLarens.'

'Why was that of interest?'

'Doug and Melanie's daughter is married to one of the McLaren boys,' said Lori. 'You do know about them, don't you?'

'Yes, Doug's brother explained the relationship to us,' said Harry. 'Is that why Gail wanted to buy his business?'

'She never told me she wanted to buy it,' said Lori, 'I was under the impression she was thinking about going into business with Joe.'

CHAPTER TWENTY

The Gamers Bar is a quiet corner of the casino where players retire to enjoy a drink and watch whatever's on the Sports Channel with the volume turned down. Half the tables in the bar were unoccupied when Wayne and Lisa walked in and looked around.

The three men they were looking for were seated at a table watching the English Premier League football.

'Evening, Gents,' said Wayne, showing them his ID. 'Can we have a word?'

'What's this about?' said the man closest to Wayne.

'I know you,' said Jack Swan, pointing at Lisa.

'Hello, Mr Swan,' said Lisa.

'Mr Swan now, is it?' The man sitting next to Jack laughed at his own jibe.

'Knock it off, Pete! They're looking for my ex.'

'Not tonight,' said Wayne. 'We'd like to ask you a few questions about this bloke.' He showed them a photo of Richard Clarke.

'You'd better sit down,' said Jack.

'You know him, then?' said Wayne, pulling a chair over from the next table.

'Richard,' said Jack.

'I understand he played poker with you boys.'

'A couple of times a week,' said Jack.

'When was the last time he played?'

Jack looked at Pete. 'What'd you reckon? Couple of months?'

'Be more like three', said Pete.

'Didn't I see something about him being killed in a car crash?' said the third man.

'Yes,' said Wayne. 'His car ended up at the bottom of Appleby Gorge.'

'Where's that?' said Pete.

'Up in the hills.'

'Nothing to do with us,' said the third man.

Interesting comment, thought Wayne. 'Was Richard winning money off you guys?'

'He cleaned us out the last time he played,' said Pete. 'I was pretty pissed off when I heard he'd been killed.'

'Why's that?'

Pete grinned. 'No chance of getting me money back.'

'I understand you boys bring ten grand to the table each night?'

The three exchanged what Wayne thought were nervous glances and he wondered about the effectiveness of their poker faces.

'Been checking up on us?' said the man nearest to Wayne.

'Been asking around about Richard,' said Wayne, 'which is why we're here.'

'Playing with ten grand is not a crime,' said Jack. 'Besides, it adds to the excitement.'

Wayne noticed beads of sweat forming on the forehead of the man sitting next to him, who stole a quick glance at the exit.

'I was just wondering where you boys got that sort of money.'

'What's it to you?' said Pete.

'Well, it appears Richard didn't have that sort of money to play with,' said Wayne.

'We didn't ask him where he got his money,' said Jack, 'as long as he had ten grand when he sat down to play, he was in.'

'And where do you get yours from, Jack? Didn't think council gardeners earned that much.'

'From my winnings over the years.'

'You must be good at poker.'

'I have my days,' said Jack.

'What about you, Pete?' said Wayne.

'Like Jack, I started small and built up my kitty.'

'And, you?' said Wayne to the man next to him.

'My old man left me twenty grand. I've been lucky.'

'How long have you been playing poker here?'

'Long enough,' said the man.

'Let's see your ID,' said Wayne, holding out his hand to the man sitting next to him.

The man reached into his suit coat, pulled out his wallet, and extracted his driver's licence.

Wayne read the licence. 'Nice to meet you James Weir. Is this East Park address still current?'

'Yeah. That's where I live.'

'And, what do you do for a living, James?'

'I'm a courier.'

'Been doing that for long?' said Wayne, thinking he didn't know any couriers that made good money unless they were drug runners.

'About fifteen years.'

Wayne handed James' licence to Lisa, who used the camera in her phone to capture the details, before passing the licence back to its owner.

'What about yours, Pete?' said Wayne.

Pete extracted his driver's licence from his wallet.

'Nice to meet you Peter Thompson,' said Wayne. 'This your current address?'

'Yep.'

'And, what do you do when you're not playing poker, Pete?'

'I work with Jack.'

'Ah, another gardener,' said Wayne, handing Pete's licence to Lisa.

He waited while Lisa snapped a photo of the licence and passed it back to Pete.

'Not asking Jack for his ID?' said Pete.

'We've spoken to Jack about another matter,' said Wayne.

'Told you they were looking for my ex,' said Jack.

Wayne took out his business cards and gave one to each of the men. 'If you hear anything about Richard, give me a call.'

'Why all the interest in Richard after his death?' said James. 'Didn't he top himself driving over the edge?'

'We have to look into these things for the coroner,' said Wayne, standing and returning his chair to the neighbouring table. 'Thanks for your time, boys. Enjoy your game.'

CHAPTER TWENTY-ONE

On the Friday morning four weeks after Doug Clarke's murder, the team gathered in the squad room to discuss the case and map out their next steps.

'I want you to dig into the background of the poker players, Wayne,' said Carl. 'We need to know who they're working for. Someone's got to be giving them the cash and they must be funnelling it back somehow.'

'No sign of them at the casino last night,' said DC Paterson. 'We must have spooked them.'

'Find out who they're talking to,' said Carl. 'Get their call logs, Lisa.'

'Right, Inspector.'

'Gail Swan appears to be connected to whoever killed Doug Clarke,' said Carl. 'The blood on the clothing found at her place in Ashcroft is Clarke's, and Forensics have a DNA profile of the male person who was wearing the shirt prior to its disposal.'

'We have to allow for the possibility that shirt was planted,' said DC Beard. 'That bin's out in the open behind her house. Anybody could have dropped those clothes into it.'

Carl smiled. He liked how his team covered all angles. 'There's also the match between the prints in her Portside apartment, the bloodstained prints found in Clarke's car, and prints lifted from Ashcroft.'

DC Beard nodded. 'I'm not saying you're wrong, Inspector.'

'Even if you're right, Nigel, we now have a DNA profile we can link to the killer,' said Carl. 'Now, all we have to do is find him.'

'We might have a lead, Boss.'

'What have you got?'

'According to her friend, Lori Richmond, Gail's latest boyfriend is a bloke named Joe.' DS Fuller looked at his notes. 'About forty, tall, well built, sort of handsome with dark hair is how she described him, and she thinks he lives in East Park.'

'What does he do?' said DC Paterson.

'Supposed to be some sort of business consultant, but that's only hearsay.'

'Have a look through her call log again, Lisa. If he's supposed to be the boyfriend he should be in that list somewhere,' said Carl.

'And, we got another name from the Richmonds as well, Boss. David Callinan, described as an older man and a bit of a sleaze. An accountant. Apparently, he and Swan were an item before this Joe came on the scene.'

'Sounds like the David Callinan I interviewed,' said DC Templar. 'The new mayor of East Park.'

'Yes, Lori Richmond identified him from his photo on the council's website,' said DS Fuller. 'Isn't he the guy who reported Clarke to the Local Government Authority?'

'Yes,' said DC Templar. 'Reckoned Clarke had a conflict of interest.'

'Maybe you and I should pay him a visit, Harry,' said Carl.

'Okay, Boss. I'll give him a call and make a time.'

———

Carl was never impressed by people who thought it was a good idea to keep the police waiting, and David Callinan was testing his patience. He looked at Harry, who was reading one of the accounting magazines from the pile on the table in the waiting area.

'Didn't know you were into that stuff,' said Carl. 'Thought law was your area.'

'Got to keep your options open, Boss. Besides, this article's on wine from the Southern Vales.'

Carl laughed. 'And there I was thinking you were reading up on investment advice.'

'Get enough of that from Max. He's always telling me I need to build up my portfolio.'

'Inspector, Mr Callinan will see you now.'

The receptionist ushered them into David Callinan's office and shut the door.

'Have you found Doug's killer yet, Inspector?'

'Working on it,' said Carl.

'Take a seat.' David Callinan came out from behind his desk and joined them at the meeting table. 'What can I help you with?'

'We're looking for a woman named Gail Swan, also known as Gail Richmond.'

'Yes, saw something about that in the paper.'

'I understand you know her.'

'Who told you that?'

'Her cousin's wife,' said Harry. 'Lori.'

'Ah,' said David. 'Yes, we had dinner at their place in Ashcroft a couple of times.'

'How did you meet her?' said Carl.

'I suppose you're wondering what she was doing with an old fart like me.'

'I'm not here to judge anyone, Mr Callinan. I simply want to know how she came to be in a relationship with you.'

'I met her at a workshop. She introduced herself.'

'What was the workshop about?' said Carl.

'Setting up your own accounting practice. I was the presenter. Gail was one of the students.'

'So, she was interested in setting up her own business?'

'She was looking into it,' said David.

'Did she tell you who she was working for at the time?'

'Her uncle. In fact, she introduced me to him. Nice chap, but she wanted to get away from Ashcroft and start a practice here in the city.'

'I assume she'd need funds to do that.'

'That, and a client base.'

'So, you were acting as some type of mentor.'

'You could say that,' said David, 'but, for a while it was a mentorship with benefits.'

Carl smiled and wondered whether Gail had played him for information.

'Did she ever mention Doug Clarke to you?'

David looked at his hands, then crossed his arms on his chest and leant back in his chair. 'She was the one who told me he was funding developments for Stenhouse and McLaren. She was impressed he'd made a business out of helping a couple of lads from his home town.'

'I take it you weren't as impressed as she was.'

'What do you mean?'

'I understand you lodged a formal complaint with the Local Government Authority.'

'Clear conflict of interest, Inspector. Doug was the mayor,

and he was benefiting from getting his development applications through council, right here in East Park.'

'Are you aware Gail had approached Doug to buy out his funding business?'

David uncrossed his arms and leant on the table with his elbows, resting his chin on his hands. 'Did she, now?' He lowered his arms onto the table. 'I admit we had discussed his business model as one way to supplement the income of an accounting practice but I had no idea she had access to the sort of money you'd need to buy Doug's operation. He was funding more than those two I mentioned, you know.'

'How much do you think she would have needed to buy him out?'

'Probably close to a million dollars.'

'Do you think it's possible she told you about Doug supporting developers in East Park so you'd report him and put him under some pressure to sell?'

David screwed up his face and pouted. 'She could have easily found out I was the deputy mayor, I suppose.'

'When was the last time you had contact with her?' said Carl.

'I haven't spoken to her since she broke it off late last year.'

'Any idea where she'd go if she was in trouble?'

'Most of her close friends are in Ashcroft.'

'Do you know anything about her latest boyfriend?'

David shook his head.

'Did you know she was seeing Richard Clarke when she was with you?'

'Richard? I knew Doug was a bit of a playboy but I thought young Richard was happily married.'

'Well, we don't know the exact nature of their relationship to be honest, Mr Callinan, but it would appear she was in a relationship with Doug in the weeks prior to his death.'

'That doesn't surprise me, Inspector. She's very persuasive.'

Carl stood and handed David a business card. 'If Gail contacts you, Mr Callinan, please let me know.'

———

David Callinan stood at the window and watched the two detectives get into their car and drive away. As their car disappeared from view, he took his mobile phone out of his pocket and made a call.

'Phil, it's me. Inspector West has just been here.'

'What did he want?'

'To talk about Gail.'

'What did you tell him?'

'Didn't really have to tell him anything. He's got it all arse about. They think she's behind whatever is going on.'

'Let's keep it that way, shall we?'

David wasn't about to argue with that logic. 'What are we going to do about the casino operation?'

'Leave it on ice, for now. We'll need some new players in any case, besides, I think Joanna might be reconsidering now Richard's gone.'

David liked the sound of that. 'Should we up the offer?'

'Don't think that'll be necessary, Dave. She's looking for a way out.'

David ended the call and poured himself a drink from the bottle of cognac he kept in his credenza. Giving Joanna what she wanted would give them a way out of the casino operation, and a way into a legitimate business aligned with their goal of servicing their most important client's requirements.

———

Chief Inspector Rankin summoned Carl to his office.

'It's been four weeks, Carl. Are we any closer to knowing who killed Doug Clarke?'

'We've got the clothing the killer was wearing when he stabbed him,' said Carl, 'but we still have no real idea who he is.'

'What about this Swan woman?'

'Looks like she's connected to the killer, going by the prints and the clothes being found in her rubbish.'

'Any idea where she is?'

'Still no sightings, Chief. I'm starting to think she's been taken out of circulation.'

The chief inspector leant back in his chair and rubbed the left side of his head with the palm of his hand. 'Do you think someone else is behind this?'

'She doesn't have the money to buy out Clarke. I've just spoken to David Callinan. He told me she'd need around a million dollars. I'm guessing someone with money put her up to negotiating with him.'

'Is that what they call it now? I thought she was screwing him.'

'That too, apparently.'

'Maybe Clarke wasn't meant to get killed,' said Chief Inspector Rankin. 'How did this Callinan fellow know how much Clarke's business would be worth?'

'He's an accountant, and he was Clarke's deputy on the East Park Council. Maybe they'd discussed Doug's business or he's looked into it, seeing as he's lodged a complaint about it citing conflict of interest.'

'Sounds like he's someone who wanted Clarke put out of business.'

'I gather he wanted him sanctioned so he'd stand down as mayor.'

'What about this money laundering at the casino?'

'That's an interesting series of dots, Chief. You've got Gail

Swan talking to Richard Clarke, the financial hole Clarke kept secret from his wife, Swan's ex and a mate, who both work for East Park, and a lot of cash. Far more cash than any of them can explain without an excursion into fantasy land.'

'And, you've got a spent bullet inside the wreckage of young Clarke's car,' said Chief Inspector Rankin.

'I think it's all connected, Chief, but I need to find Swan to pull it all together.'

'You'll be stuffed if you're right about her being taken out of circulation.'

'Thanks, Chief.'

Chief Inspector Rankin massaged his temples and closed his eyes.

'You okay, Chief?' Carl got out of his chair.

Chief Inspector Rankin fell forward onto his desk, scattering papers onto the floor.

Carl rushed to the desk. He confirmed Chief Inspector Rankin was still breathing, before lowering him onto the floor in the coma position. Then, he opened the door separating the chief inspector's office from his personal assistant.

'Mandy! Call an ambulance! I think the chief's had a stroke.'

CHAPTER TWENTY-TWO

Carl sat at the dining table with Sophie in his lap while Nina dished up his evening meal. His thoughts drifted to the scene he'd left at the hospital. The chief was the closest thing Sophie had to a grandfather, and he'd been like a father to Carl ever since he'd joined the force. He hoped the chief would survive without too much damage.

'You okay?' said Nina, placing his food in front of him and extending her arms to lift Sophie out of his lap. 'You look like you're somewhere else.'

Carl held Sophie up for Nina to take. 'It's not me I'm worried about.'

'Want Daddy,' said Sophie, wrapping her arms around Carl's neck.

'Daddy has to eat his tea,' said Nina.

'I'll read you a story after,' said Carl, unwrapping her arms and kissing her on the cheek.

Nina lifted Sophie out of his arms and placed her on her hip. 'Lucky you were there when it happened. Just imagine what would have happened if he'd been on his own.' She walked over to where Sophie's toys were stored in the corner and let her down onto the floor. 'Play here while Daddy has his tea, sweetheart.'

Sophie rummaged in her box of household objects and scattered them over the floor, then she sat on the floor and started placing the smaller objects inside a large blue plastic ice cream bucket.

'He's not out of the woods yet,' said Carl. 'They won't know how bad it is until he regains consciousness.'

'If he does,' said Nina. 'Might be better if he doesn't.'

Carl picked up his knife and fork and started eating. 'A lot of people survive a stroke, you know.'

'Maybe, honey, but would you want to survive if there was no quality of life?'

'I suppose not.'

'Anyway, we don't know how bad it is yet, do we?'

Carl chewed the piece of steak he'd put into his mouth. 'The paramedics said he was lucky we'd called them straight away. Quick action is better than waiting, apparently.'

'I'm sure it is, honey. Did you get a chance to speak to Evelyn?'

'Yes,' said Carl. 'I waited at the hospital until she got there.'

'How is she?'

'You know what she's like. She told me to go home and let her worry about the chief.'

Carl put down his utensils and used his fingertips to wipe away the moisture in his eyes. He took a deep breath and blew his nose in a tissue. He pushed the plate of half-eaten food away from him. 'Come on, Sophie. Time for bed.'

'Story,' said Sophie.

'Daddy will read you a story in bed.'

'She needs to clean her teeth,' said Nina.

'Let's pack up these things,' said Carl, squatting down beside

Sophie and collecting the objects she'd strewn over the floor of the family room. 'Then, we'll brush your teeth and read a story.'

———

Nina snuggled up to Carl on the sofa as he watched the late news.

'Do you think they'll ask you to act as chief inspector?'

'Fair chance, I suppose,' said Carl. 'They'll have to ask one of us.'

'Think you're ready?'

Carl pulled her closer and kissed her. 'Guess this will be one way of finding out.'

'Could be a bit hectic, don't you think?' said Nina. 'Do you think they'll put someone in your position?'

'Probably not,' said Carl, 'at least not until they know what's happening with the chief.'

'That's not really fair on you, is it?'

'What's fairness got to do with it? Anyway, Harry's perfectly capable of taking control of the Clarke investigation. It's not like I'll be out of the loop.'

'I hope Evelyn's alright,' said Nina.

'Give her a call,' said Carl. 'I'm sure she'd appreciate it.'

———

Carl's mobile phone pinged as he walked into Police Headquarters. He looked at the text message and pressed the button for the tenth floor. Assistant Commissioner Thaler was waiting for him in his office.

'Morning, Sir.'

'Take a seat, Inspector. I understand you're aware of Chief Inspector Rankin's situation.'

'I was there when it happened.'

Assistant Commissioner Thaler shuffled the papers on his desk until he found the one he was looking for. 'Sounds like the chief inspector will not be returning to work any time soon, if at all.'

'Thought that would be the case, Sir. He still hadn't regained consciousness when I spoke to Mrs Rankin this morning.'

'How is she? I haven't had a chance to catch up with her yet.'

'She's a strong woman, Sir. I'm sure she'll cope,' said Carl, knowing Nina was tapping into the police social network to organize around the clock support for Evelyn.

'He'll need her to be strong if he pulls through,' said Assistant Commissioner Thaler. 'Now.' He thrust the paper in his hand towards Carl. 'The Commissioner's appointed you acting chief inspector, effective immediately. Congratulations.'

'Thank you, Sir. Will someone be acting in my position?'

'Not at this point in time, Carl.' Assistant Commissioner Thaler leant back in his chair behind his desk. 'Should be a good opportunity for young Fuller to show us what he's made of, don't you think?'

'Yes, Sir.' And for you to see how I handle the role, thought Carl.

'Move into the chief inspector's office so you'll be available to the others,' said Assistant Commissioner Thaler. 'That will be all, Chief Inspector.'

———

By the time Carl made it down to the third floor, the Commissioner's email announcing his appointment as acting chief inspector had hit everyone's inbox.

'Congratulations, Boss,' said Harry.

'Sorry I can't make you acting inspector just yet, Harry. They want to wait and see what happens with the chief.'

Harry shrugged. 'Let's hope it doesn't come to that.'

'You'll need to take ownership of the Clarke case, I'm afraid.'

'No problem, Boss.'

'I'll see if I can find you another detective once I get my head around my new role.'

'Don't stress over it, Boss.'

'Anyway, keep me in the loop, Harry.'

'Right, Boss.'

Carl went into his office to collect the things he'd need, and then made his way to the chief's office on the fifth floor to sort out the required accesses he'd need to operate in the role.

CHAPTER TWENTY-THREE

Harry called the team together to review their progress.

'I'll be assuming control of the Clarke case while the Boss is acting as the chief,' said Harry.

'Are they making you acting inspector?' said Wayne.

'Not at the moment.'

'Lousy bastards.'

'They'll play it by the rules, so let's not get sidetracked, shall we?'

'You've got our support, Sarge,' said Nigel. 'We'll look after you.'

'Thanks,' said Harry. 'Now, where are we? Anything new to report?'

'Got into Swan's phone,' said Nigel. 'Contacts have been wiped.'

'What about her email?'

'Same. No photos either.'

'Someone's playing with us,' said Wayne. 'I reckon that phone was left in her apartment on purpose to make us think we had something.'

'What about the call log, Lisa? Find a number for anyone called Joe?' said Harry.

Lisa looked up and smiled. 'There's a Giuseppe Lombardo at 35 Wisteria Avenue, East Park.'

'Anything on Registrations?'

'He's forty-two and drives a Mercedes, rego number SDRT678.'

'He's got to be our man.'

'We've got a photo from Registrations,' said Lisa.

'Any luck with the dry-cleaning tag, Nigel?' said Harry.

'They had a phone number; 0413 657 213.'

'That's our man,' said Lisa.

'We'll need prints and DNA from Lombardo to see if he's the driver of Clarke's car and the owner of the clothes found in Swan's bin,' said Harry. 'Pay him a visit, Nigel, and bring him in to be tested. Arrest him, if you have to.'

'Right, Sarge. I'll get onto the paperwork.'

'How are we going with the background checks on the three amigos from the casino, Wayne?'

'I spoke to the head gardener at East Park, Sarge. Swan and Thompson were both taken on as part of a local government initiative to employ prisoners on release supported by Councillor Callinan.'

'Oh, what did Thompson do time for?' said Harry.

'Insurance fraud. Set fire to his own premises.'

'Another prison trained horticulturist?' said Lisa.

'Believe so,' said Wayne.

'Wonder if they knew Callinan or he simply supported the program?' said Lisa.

'More likely to be the latter,' said Harry, 'but let's keep an open mind on that until we find out otherwise.'

'Anything on the Swan woman?' said Wayne.

Harry scanned the daily update from Crime Stoppers. 'Nothing. Seems she's vanished without a trace.'

'Either that or she knows how to hide,' said Wayne.

'Or she's dead,' said Nigel.

———

Nigel pulled up in front of 35 Wisteria Avenue, East Park. The house was a stone fronted bungalow with faded terracotta tiles. Nigel thought the front lawn, edged with garden beds planted with rose bushes waiting to explode with color, was overdue for a cut. As he surveyed the overgrown grass, he could hear his father's voice inside his head berating Lombardo for not looking after his lawn properly. Nigel sighed and thanked his lucky stars for guiding him into apartment living and away from gardening.

He waited in the car with Lisa until the patrol car with their support team pulled in behind them.

Accompanied by two uniformed officers, they crunched their way up the gravelled driveway. There was a dark grey Mercedes sedan, registration number SDRT678, parked under the carport.

'Looks like our man is home,' said Lisa.

Nigel directed Lisa and one of the uniformed officers around to the back of the house, then he and the second officer stepped onto the front veranda and approached the front door. Nigel pushed the button for the doorbell. They waited.

Nigel was reaching to push the button again when the door opened.

'Police,' said Nigel, showing his ID. 'We're looking for Giuseppe Lombardo.'

'I'm Joe Lombardo, mate. What do you want me for?'

'Do you know a Gail Swan, Mr Lombardo?'

Joe glanced at the uniformed officer. 'Yeah, I know Gail.'

'When was the last time you saw her?' said Nigel.

'It's been a while.'

'Can you be a little more precise?'

'Three or four weeks, I suppose. Why do you want to know?'

'Would that be after you were last seen with her in Ashcroft?'

Joe leant on the doorframe. 'I haven't been to Ashcroft for months.'

'That's interesting,' said Nigel. 'We have a witness that says she saw you there about four weeks ago.'

'She must be mistaken. The last time I visited Gail's place up there was back in June. I haven't seen much of her since then.'

'Have you visited her apartment in Portside?'

'That's the last place I saw her,' said Joe.

'What's the nature of your relationship?'

'Purely professional,' said Joe. 'I'm a business consultant. I help people start their own business.'

'Is that what you're doing with Gail Swan?'

'Yes, she's planning on starting her own accounting practice,' said Joe. 'I've given her a few ideas to follow up. I'm waiting for her to get back to me.'

Nigel reached into his inside suit coat pocket. 'This is a search warrant, Mr Lombardo.' He handed the warrant to Joe and then turned to the uniformed officer behind him. 'Get the others.'

The constable pressed the button on his radio and spoke to his partner.

Joe looked up from examining the warrant. 'What does this mean?'

'It authorises me to collect a DNA sample and your finger-prints, Mr Lombardo.'

'Why?'

'We're investigating the murder of Doug Clarke, Mr Lombardo.'

'Got nothing to do with me, mate!'

'I didn't say it did,' said Nigel, 'but your friend, Gail Swan, who we understand was trying to buy his business, has disappeared. We're trying to identify the owner of items found in her apartment and her house in Ashcroft.'

'What items?'

'I'm not at liberty to disclose that, Mr Lombardo, but I'll have to ask you to come with us so we can collect the samples.'

'And if I refuse?'

'I'll be obliged to arrest you, Mr Lombardo.'

Joe looked along the veranda as Lisa and the second constable came into view. 'Can I get my keys and my phone?'

'Where are they?' said Nigel.

'In my office.'

Nigel turned to the constable at his side. 'Go with him.'

———

At Police Headquarters, Nigel watched the Duty Sergeant use the fingerprint scanner to record Joe Lombardo's fingerprints and then swab the inside of his cheek to collect the material required to build his DNA profile. When the Duty Sergeant finished, Nigel escorted Joe to an interview room and left him there with an armed constable.

'Won't be long, Mr Lombardo,' said Nigel, opening the door of the room. 'I'll just get the results from the fingerprint analysis and then you should be on your way.'

Nigel returned to the Duty Sergeant's desk.

'Did we get a hit, Sergeant?'

'You're in luck, Detective. Got a match with those prints you asked me to check.'

Nigel looked at the printout of the results. There was no doubt Lombardo had been in Doug Clarke's car, Gail Swan's apartment, and her house in Ashcroft. He pulled out his mobile phone and called DS Fuller.

'Lombardo's prints match with all the samples, Sarge.'

'Better get him to call a lawyer.'

———

Nigel waited for Philip Carol, the lawyer Joe Lombardo had called, to take his seat next to his client, and for Lisa to lead them through the preliminary steps of a formal interview.

'What's the charge?' said Philip, when they had completed the preliminaries.

'Suspicion of involvement in the murder of Doug Clarke,' said Nigel.

'What's your evidence, Detective?'

'We'll get to that in due course, Mr Carol,' said Nigel, turning his attention to Joe Lombardo. 'Where were you on the morning of Saturday, the eighth of September, this year, Mr Lombardo?'

'What's so important about that date?' said Joe.

'That's the day Doug Clarke was killed.'

'Think I was home that morning. I don't work Saturdays.'

'Anybody with you?'

'Don't think so,' said Joe. 'I sleep in on Saturdays. Don't get up until after ten most weekends.'

'So, you didn't by any chance have a meeting with Doug Clarke that morning?'

'Why would I have had a meeting with him?' said Joe. 'Anyway, like I said, I don't work Saturdays.'

'Ever been in Doug Clarke's car, Mr Lombardo?'

'I've never met the man, so why would I have been in his car?'

'Are you sure you didn't drive it up the highway to North Summit and abandon it behind some trees, Mr Lombardo?'

'Are you nuts?'

'Then how do you explain this?' said Nigel, sliding the printout of the fingerprint analysis across the table to Joe.

Joe looked at the paper and then at Nigel. 'What is that supposed to be?'

'This is a fingerprint analysis report,' said Nigel. 'We've compared your fingerprints with some fingerprints found in Doug Clarke's car and several found in Gail Swan's apartment. We already knew the prints from Clarke's car matched some of the prints found in Gail Swan's apartment. Now we know they both match with yours.'

Joe folded his arms. 'I admit being in Gail's apartment. We had several meetings there.'

'You've also been to her house in Ashcroft,' said Nigel. 'That's where that print came from.' He pointed to the bottom set of images on the page.

'Visiting clients at home is not a crime,' said Philip.

'I think Gail Swan was more than a client,' said Nigel. 'I've been told you were in a romantic relationship with her, Mr Lombardo.'

'You've been misled,' said Joe. 'My relationship with Gail is strictly professional. I visited her in Ashcroft to familiarize myself with her current situation, that's all.'

'Did you visit her in Ashcroft on Sunday, the ninth of September?'

'No,' said Joe.

'I have a witness that says you were seen in Ashcroft on the morning of Monday the tenth, driving her car,' said Nigel.

'They must be mistaken,' said Joe. 'I never left the city that weekend.'

'Spend any time with anybody that weekend, Mr Lombardo?' Joe shook his head.

'You need to answer for the recording,' said Lisa.

'No,' said Joe. 'I had a quiet weekend at home.'

'Your evidence is pretty circumstantial,' said Philip.

'My evidence places your client inside Doug Clarke's car

with Clarke's blood on his fingers,' said Nigel, 'and it places him in a house in Ashcroft where clothes stained with Clarke's blood have been found.'

'Still circumstantial,' said Philip.

'We'll have the results back on your client's DNA sample in the next few hours, Mr Carol. If it matches the sample extracted from those bloodstained clothes your circumstantial argument will be meaningless. In the meantime, I'm holding him on suspicion of murder.'

'You're making a mistake,' said Joe. 'I didn't kill him.'

'What did you do?' said Nigel. 'How did your bloodstained prints end up inside his car?'

'Someone's setting me up,' said Joe.

'Who would that be?'

'How would I know?' said Joe. 'You're the detective. You figure it out.'

———

Joe Lombardo was sitting in a holding cell when Nigel got the DNA results showing the comparative analysis of the profiles was negative. Nigel stared at the screen and then printed out the results.

He took the printout into DS Fuller.

'We have a problem, Sarge.'

DS Fuller looked up from his screen. 'What sort of problem?'

'Lombardo's profile doesn't match the profile from the shirt.'

'That's not helpful.'

'What do you want me to do, Sarge?'

'We still have his bloodstained fingerprints in Clarke's car, which implicate him in disposing of the car and perhaps the body. Charge him with being an accessory and let's see if we can get him to talk.'

CHAPTER TWENTY-FOUR

Philip Carol sat at their usual table in the back corner of the restaurant and waited for David Callinan to arrive for their weekly lunch engagement. He perused the menu and decided he'd order the steak.

'Hello, Phil,' said David, pulling out a chair and sitting down. 'Sorry I'm late.'

'I've decided on the steak,' said Philip. 'Fancy a shiraz?'

David ran his finger down the wine list. 'This one from the Hunter is a good drop. Let's have that.'

When the waiter had taken their order, they got down to business.

'Joe's been arrested,' said Philip. 'They're charging him with being an accessory to Doug's murder.'

'On what grounds?'

'Bloodstained fingerprints inside Doug's car.'

'That was a bit careless of him.'

'It gets worse. He dumped the clothes he was wearing in the bin at Gail's place in Ashcroft,' said Philip, 'expecting her to put the bin out before anyone thought to look there, but she hasn't been there since, has she?'

'Have you heard from her?'

'No, but the police claim they have a witness who saw her with Joe in Ashcroft on the Monday morning.'

'Guess that was always going to be a risk.'

The waiter arrived with their steaks and poured them each a glass of shiraz from the bottle they'd ordered.

'Any progress with Joanna?' said David, lifting his glass to sample the wine.

Philip took a sip of his shiraz. 'Good choice.' He took another sip and returned his glass to the table. 'She's decided to accept our offer.'

'Finally,' said David. 'Does that mean we'll be shutting down the casino operation?'

'That's the plan, provided we can get Gail back on track.'

'What if we can't? Do you have a plan B?'

Philip cut his steak and forked a piece into his mouth. 'You're plan B, Dave. I hope your finance broking registration is up to date.'

David put down his utensils. 'I'll have to step down as mayor if we go down that pathway.'

'Being mayor didn't seem to worry Doug,' said Philip.

'Yeah, but he didn't lodge a complaint, did he?'

'Pity he wanted to blow the whistle on us. Would have been a lot easier if he'd just rolled over and taken the money instead of threatening to go to the police.'

'Told you he was a greedy bastard,' said David. 'What I'd like to know, though, is how he found out.'

'No point in arguing over that,' said Philip, 'or what's happened if you want to stay on the payroll.' He lifted his glass and took another sip of his shiraz. 'This really is good.'

David took another sip of his wine. 'We'll need to contact Gail if Joanna's going ahead. Any idea how we're going to do that?'

'Talk to Jack.'

'We'll need to find a way to keep Jack and his mates happy if there's no more money going through the casino.'

'They'll get a bonus, and the standard warning,' said Philip. 'Besides, they can always go back to what they were doing before. There will be good money in it for them if they do.'

David poured himself another glass of shiraz and topped up Philip's glass. 'Fair enough. Do you think we need to worry about Joe?'

'He knows the rules.'

'What if the cops start asking questions? They're bound to run some background checks on him.'

'What are they going to find?'

'He worked for me ten years ago.'

'He left to start his own business, didn't he? What's there to worry about? Ten years is a long time.'

'He called me a few times when they were talking to Doug.'

'Tell the police you were giving him accounting advice. They can only find out he called, not what you talked about.'

'That's what I told them about Gail,' said David. 'I'm not sure they believed me.'

'Who'd you talk to?'

'That West character.'

'Think he's been taken off the case,' said Philip. 'I'm dealing with a Detective Sergeant Fuller.'

'That's a bit unusual, isn't it?'

'I gather he's been promoted to cover for his boss. Anyway, that's not our problem.'

'Do you know where Tony is?' said David.

'With Gail, as far as I know.'

'The police are going to want to talk to her when she surfaces,' said David. 'Are you sure we shouldn't just proceed with plan B.'

'I'm not calling the shots, Dave, but if I was you, I'd get things in place for plan B. I'm not sure certain people will want her talking to the police.'

———

After lunch, David Callinan returned to his office and called Jack Swan.

'Have you heard about Joe?'

'Yeah. How bad is it?'

'Looks like he'll be doing time,' said David, 'but he's got no-one to blame but himself. Should have been more careful.'

'Yeah, well, I can't do anything about that, can I? What do you want me to do?'

David flinched. Dealing with thugs like Jack Swan always made him feel uneasy. He took a slow breath and stuffed his feelings of revulsion down into the void, to a place beyond his awareness.

'We need to get Gail back so we can complete the deal.'

'I don't know where she is,' said Jack.

'Talk to Tony. He's supposed to know where she is.'

'Why don't you call him?'

'Better you talk to him, Jack. He trusts you,' said David, hoping he'd never have to be in the same room with Tony ever again.

'What if he doesn't want to talk?'

'Get back to me. I'll pass the message up the line.'

'Okay. What's happening with me and the boys?'

'We'll have something for you when we've sorted things with Gail and Tony,' said David. 'Get Gail to call me.'

'Yeah, right. You take care, Dave.' Jack ended the call.

David sat and stared through his office window at the trees in the urban forest. He knew Jack and Peter were somewhere within the forest tending to the playing fields. He thought it must be pleasant working out in nature at this time of year, when the approaching summer reached out and suppressed the last gasps of winter.

The silent trees of the forest reminded David of Doug's death. He turned away from the window and wished Doug hadn't been so pigheaded. He'd only wanted to take his business away from him, not his life, even though he'd regarded the man as a complete arsehole ever since the day he'd been elected mayor.

David leant back in his chair and gazed at the ceiling, and wondered how Doug had known where their money was coming from. Had Gail slipped up and disclosed more than she should have? He'd told her seducing him would be risky, but she couldn't help herself once she'd ensnared him. He wondered what Joe had thought of that.

He speculated whether she'd come back to him, seeing Joe would be spending the next few years in prison. Then he caught his reflection in the window pane and laughed at his own vanity. He knew she'd finished with him.

But, he did want to hear her side of the story, and the story she was going to spin to the police about her disappearance.

He sat up with a start. Shit! What if her disappearance hadn't been an act?

If she didn't come back, he'd be the one taking the biggest risk. He knew there was no way of walking away now. If it came to plan B, he'd be rich beyond his wildest dreams, but they'd own him, completely.

And, it wasn't like he could go to the police and explain the mess away. They'd lock him up. And, who knew how safe he'd be inside with the likes of Joe and Tony in there with him?

He opened the credenza next to his desk and lifted out the bottle of cognac he kept there for just these occasions, and poured himself a glass. He lifted the drink to his lips and hoped Gail was still alive.

CHAPTER TWENTY-FIVE

Carl looked up from his desk and beckoned Harry into his office. 'What's happening with Lombardo?'

'His prints match the bloodstained prints found in Clarke's car, Boss. So, it looks like he's been in the car and probably handled the body, given the prints are on the inside of the driver's door.'

'What's he saying about it?'

'Denying everything. Says he's been framed but he doesn't have an alibi for the weekend Clarke was killed. Claims he spent the weekend at home, even though we have a witness claiming she'd seen him in Swan's car in Ashcroft on the Monday after, the same day Clarke's car was found between Ashcroft and North Summit.'

'So, you think Lombardo drove the car up there.'

'Fits with what we know, Boss, especially when you consider Clarke's car is the same make and model as Lombardo's. It's even the same color. He could have hidden it in plain sight in his own driveway. Who would have noticed?'

'Guess he could have switched the plates for the drive up,

which could explain why no-one reported seeing it,' said Carl. 'Get Forensics to go over the plates. There could be signs of tampering, especially if he switched them back in the dark.'

'I'll give Dean a call to follow up on that.'

'What are you doing with Lombardo?'

'I've charged him with being an accessory to murder so we can hold him while we search his place and find out more about him, but his DNA doesn't match the profile from the shirt.'

'Makes me think Swan and someone else must be involved,' said Carl. 'We know from that profile Swan wasn't wearing the shirt but I'll bet she's linked to whoever was.'

'The only other person we can connect to Swan is David Callinan, and he has an alibi for that weekend, and I've verified he was a presenter at that workshop he told us about, and confirmed Swan was there.'

'Even if his story stacks up, Harry, he's still someone with a motive for wanting Clarke out of the way.'

'Can't imagine anyone arranging a murder to become the mayor of East Park, Boss. That doesn't make sense. It's not like there's a financial gain beyond a pretty dismal honorarium.'

'Might not be about the money, Harry.'

'Pretty way out there even for an ego trip, Boss.'

Carl smiled. 'Who's Lombardo's lawyer? Is he going to give us grief about holding his client?'

'Philip Carol,' said Harry. 'The same Philip Carol we met at Joanna Clarke's.'

'That's interesting.'

'Lombardo lives in East Park, Boss. Carol and Associates are one of the better-known firms out there.'

'Could be interesting when this goes to trial,' said Carl. 'I wonder if Carol will represent Lombardo himself.'

'Guess we'll find out soon enough.'

'Making any progress on Richard Clarke's death?'

'I've got Traffic looking at their camera footage between Clarke's office and Appleby Gorge Road,' said Harry. 'We might get lucky if we can pick up Richard's car. And, I've got Wayne doing background checks on the three he played poker with.'

'Focus on Swan,' said Carl. 'It can't be a coincidence that he and his ex were both talking to Richard Clarke. Any sign of her?'

'Nothing, Boss. Not even a call to Crime Stoppers.'

———

Harry read through the statements Uniform had collected from Gail Swan's Portside neighbours. Several people had reported seeing a dark grey Mercedes sedan parked in the street outside her apartment building on numerous occasions but none had recalled seeing who'd parked it there. Now that he knew Lombardo and the victim drove identical cars, Harry wondered who had been the more frequent visitor.

He looked for the statement Nigel had taken from the neighbour who had called Crime Stoppers. The statement had been made by a Mr Rehn, who had identified Swan's visitor as being Doug Clarke. He read Mr Rehn's details. Rehn was a retired public servant living on his own.

Harry decided to interview him again and ask him about who else he remembered visiting Gail Swan.

He read through the statements Sgt Snow's officers had taken from her neighbours in Ashcroft. They hadn't paid much attention to the comings and goings at her house in Carey Road, which didn't surprise him, given the distance between houses in that part of Ashcroft. After reading the statements, he knew they'd been lucky Lori Richmond had seen Lombardo and Swan in her car on the Monday after Clarke's murder.

He leant back in his chair and wondered how far they'd get prosecuting Lombardo with a case depending on that sighting and fingerprints. The most incriminating prints were those found in Clarke's car. The ones found in Swan's residences only verified that Clarke had been inside the Portside apartment and Lombardo had been in both.

The telephone on his desk rang.

'We're on our way,' said Dean Lang.

'Nigel will meet you there,' said Harry.

Harry put down the receiver and looked around. Nigel and Lisa were looking at the footage of Richard Clarke's BMW that Traffic had sent through.

'Anything?' said Harry.

'There!' said Lisa, pointing to the dark colored Mercedes four cars back from the BMW. 'Is that Lombardo's car?'

'Could be,' said Harry.

'Freeze it there, Nigel! Zoom in on the number plate.'

They watched as the software resolved the image into SDRT678.

'That's Lombardo's car,' said Lisa.

'That's the last intersection before Appleby Gorge Road goes into the hills,' said Nigel. 'There are no cameras after this one.'

'Something else to ask Lombardo about,' said Harry, wondering what the connection between Lombardo and Richard Clarke might be.

'This is getting complicated,' said Lisa.

Harry remembered why he'd walked over. 'Forensics are on their way to Lombardo's.'

'We better get going, then,' said Nigel.

———

Harry met with Wayne to see how he was going with his investigation into Jack Swan and his mates.

'Got something interesting here, Sarge. I've been looking at

Swan's bank accounts.' Wayne pointed to his screen. 'See this entry here?'

Harry focused on the entry Wayne was tapping with his finger.

'That's his regular fortnightly pay from East Park Council. Now look at this one.'

Harry shifted his focus.

'This is a direct credit from an account at B and A,' said Wayne. 'There's one every month.'

'That's more than his monthly pay from East Park,' said Harry, doing a quick calculation in his head. 'Whose account is it coming from?'

Wayne opened another file. 'It's an account in the name of the East Park Syndicate.'

'Who are they?'

'They're a group of gamblers, according to the paperwork the bank sent through.'

'Did you get a list of members?'

Wayne scrolled down to the next page in the document and tapped his finger on the screen. 'Our four punters and someone called Anthony Slade.'

Harry wondered who Anthony Slade was and what his role was in the scheme of things. 'How much money is going through that account?'

'Cash deposits of between thirty and forty grand a day,' said Wayne, 'and most of it's then transferred to an account at First National.'

'How are they getting around the reporting on cash deposits over ten grand?'

'It's all described as winnings from the casino and signed off by whoever makes the deposit. Mostly our four punters and occasionally by Slade.'

'Who owns the account at First National?'

'Still waiting on that detail,' said Wayne, 'but what's interesting is there haven't been any deposits into this account since the day after Lisa and I spoke to Jack Swan and his mates at the casino.'

'Do we know who's doing the transfers?'

'According to the bank, Slade's the only one authorized to operate the account electronically.'

'Are the others receiving payments like Swan?'

'Yes,' said Wayne, 'including our mate Richard Clarke, but I wouldn't be surprised if his wife isn't aware of the account. She told us he'd blown all their money. There's close to fifty grand in his account at B and A.'

Harry scratched his head. 'What the hell was he up to?'

'And, that's not all the good news, Sarge,' said Wayne. 'Look at this.' He opened another file showing a First National statement for Gail Swan's account. 'She's getting payments from another of Slade's accounts at B and A.'

A bell went off in Harry's head. He'd heard Lisa say something about Gail receiving monthly payments from an Anthony Slade. 'We need to talk to this Slade character.'

'And, Sarge, there haven't been any payments into her account since Doug Clarke was killed.'

'What about withdrawals?'

'Not since the Monday after Clarke was killed,' said Wayne. 'Looks like she bought petrol in Ashcroft.'

That tallied with what Lori Richmond had told him, thought Harry, so no surprise there. 'Do we have an address for this Anthony Slade?'

'35 Wisteria Avenue, East Park, according to the bank,' said Wayne.

'Hang on,' said Harry, 'that's where Lombardo lives.'

Wayne leant back in his chair. 'Think you'd better give Nigel a call, Sarge.'

CHAPTER TWENTY-SIX

City Hospital was not a place Carl liked visiting. He'd stopped liking the place when his mother died in one of its rooms when he was sixteen. She'd suffered a stroke three years earlier from which she'd never recovered. He shuddered at the memory of her last days as he rode the elevator up to the intensive care ward to visit Chief Inspector Rankin.

When Evelyn had rung Carl to tell him the chief had regained consciousness, and the doctors were conducting tests to determine how badly he'd been affected by the stroke, she'd asked him to drop in to the hospital on his way home.

Carl was worried by the severity of the stroke that had knocked down the chief. Thanks to his mother's experience, he knew more than most people about strokes and their impact. She'd been paralysed down one side of her body and found it difficult to speak after her initial stroke, and had died several days after her second. He hoped the improved rehabilitation techniques he'd read about online would boost the chief's chances of recovery.

He wasn't ready to contemplate life without the chief, who'd been his mentor ever since he'd joined the force. He wanted him to get better. He wanted the chief to be there for Sophie as her surrogate grandfather.

The elevator doors opened. Carl stepped into the ward and walked towards the nurses' station.

The intensive care ward was where he'd come to see Nina after the accident that had nearly taken her from him. His only good memory of the place was taking her home after she'd recovered. Then, he thought of Sophie, who'd been born in City Hospital.

He smiled at the nurse. 'I'm here to see George Rankin.'

The nurse consulted her list. 'Can I have you name, please? Visitors are restricted.'

'I'm Carl West.'

The nurse looked at her list again. 'He's in room three. You can go in, Mr West.'

Carl walked down the corridor to room three. Evelyn was sitting in the chair by the window holding her husband's left hand. The chief lay in the bed with his eyes closed.

Carl knocked softly on the door as he entered the room. Evelyn smiled. The chief did not move.

'How is he?' said Carl, doing his best to ignore the equipment the chief was hooked up to.

Evelyn got out of her chair and hugged Carl. 'Not good,' she whispered in his ear. 'He's awake but he can't speak.' She squeezed the chief's left hand.

The chief opened his eyes. A smile briefly cracked the left side of his face.

'Glad to see you're still with us, Chief,' said Carl.

The chief's eyes rolled up.

Carl smiled. Whatever else had happened, it appeared the chief hadn't lost his sense of humour.

'He's paralysed on the right side,' said Evelyn. 'They don't know yet whether that's permanent or not.'

'There's a lot they can do with rehabilitation these days,' said Carl. 'It's not like it was when my mother had her stroke. Has he been seen by a physiotherapist yet?'

'Booked for tomorrow,' said Evelyn, 'and a speech therapist.'

'And how are you holding up, Evelyn?'

'Never thought it would be so tiring just sitting here,' said Evelyn, resuming her seat.

'Is anyone else coming in?'

'There's only my sister, Lorraine,' said Evelyn. 'She's very supportive.'

Carl knew what it was like being part of a family with few members. 'Now the chief's awake, do you think it would be okay for Nina to bring Sophie in?'

'I don't want to scare her,' said Evelyn.

'I'm sure she'll be okay,' said Carl. 'She loves her Grandpa George.'

'I'll let you and Nina decide,' said Evelyn. 'I'm here all day.'

Carl held the chief's left hand. 'We're all thinking of you, Chief.'

The chief tried to say something and then gave up.

Carl could see the frustration in his eyes. 'Take it easy, Chief. I'll call in again tomorrow.'

Evelyn stood up and walked out into the corridor with Carl.

'The prognosis is not good, Carl. The doctors are saying it was a massive stroke and he might not survive another one.'

'He's like a father to me,' said Carl. 'I want him to pull through.'

Evelyn squeezed his hands. 'I know, Carl. Thanks for coming.'

Carl caught the six-forty train to Morton Sands. He spent most of the journey staring into space, mustering the courage to contemplate the obvious.

He wasn't sure how he'd cope if the chief died. It had been bad enough when his grandfather, who'd been the most significant male figure in his life until George Rankin had taken him under his wing, had died.

Carl hoped the chief would recover but he'd read that stroke survival rates went down with age and severity. The chief was sixty-four and by all accounts he'd suffered a massive stroke, severe enough to render him unconscious for three days and to rob him of his ability to control his body.

As he stepped off the train at Morton Sands, the words Evelyn had said to him in the corridor came back to him.

Bugger the prognosis, thought Carl. The doctors hadn't thought Nina would live when she'd arrived at City Hospital after her accident, and she'd proved them wrong. There was always a chance the chief would pull through and recover, even if it took him months of rehabilitation.

Carl had known the chief a long time, and there was one thing he was certain of: the chief was not a quitter. He would fight until the end.

———

Sophie was waiting for Carl to bath her when he arrived home. On the verge of falling asleep after a big day on the beach chasing seagulls with Nina, she had refused to go to bed until he arrived home.

When he walked into the house, she ran up the passageway to him. 'Daddy! Daddy!'

'How's my little princess?' Carl picked her up and carried her into the kitchen.

'She needs a bath,' said Nina. 'Can you do that while I fix you something?'

'Sure,' said Carl. He kissed Nina on the cheek and took Sophie into her room to undress her for her bath.

After making their usual mess splashing water about in the bathroom, Carl put Sophie to bed and read her a story. She was asleep before he finished the book.

'What did you do today?' said Carl. 'She's already asleep.'

'We spent the afternoon on the beach,' said Nina. 'How's the chief?'

'He's paralysed down his right side,' said Carl. 'He's conscious but he can't speak. He's hanging in there, though. Still got those mischievous eyes.'

'That must be so frustrating,' said Nina. 'How's Evelyn coping?'

'Seems to be holding up. Lorraine's giving her moral support, apparently.'

'Must be tough doing it on her own,' said Nina, placing a bowl of spaghetti in front of him.

'Guess we're the closest they've got to family, apart from Lorraine,' said Carl. 'Are you up to taking Sophie in to see him?'

'Do you think that's wise?'

'I'm sure he'd love to see you and Sophie. You know he thinks the world of you two,' said Carl. 'You don't have to stay long. They probably won't let you anyway.'

'I meant taking Sophie in there.'

'It will be an adventure,' said Carl. 'Evelyn is dying to see you.'

'I hope you don't mean that literally.'

Carl twirled strands of spaghetti on his fork. 'I'm not sure the chief is going to be around much longer, sweetheart. The doctors are saying he probably won't survive another stroke.'

'He's got to survive this one first.'

'All the more reason to go in while he's still with us,' said Carl. 'Seeing Sophie might be just what he needs to hold on.'

'And how are you coping, Carl? I know how much he means to you.' Nina sat beside him and wrapped her arms around him.

'I'm doing okay, but I'm not sure how I'll be if he doesn't come out of this, though.'

Nina rested her head on his shoulder. 'We've been there before.'

'Yeah, and that wasn't exactly a stroll in the park,' said Carl.

'I miss them,' said Nina. 'There's not a day goes by I don't think about them and how they would have loved seeing Sophie grow up.' She kissed Carl on the head and got up from the table. 'Do you want a coffee?'

CHAPTER TWENTY-SEVEN

On Friday morning, Carl decided to attend Harry's team briefing in the squad room on the third floor.

'Morning, Harry,' said Carl. 'Thought I'd sit in on the briefing.'

'How's the chief?'

'He's awake, but he's got a few issues. Don't think he'll be back for a while, if at all.'

'That bad?'

'Paralysed down his right side,' said Carl, 'and he can't talk at the moment.'

'What's that going to mean for us?'

'I've got a meeting with Assistant Commissioner Thaler later today,' said Carl. 'I'll let you know after that.'

'Fair enough.'

'What's happening with the Clarke case?'

'Let's find out, shall we?'

They walked to the area in front of the whiteboard covered with case notes, where the team was waiting.

'Any news on the chief inspector?' said DC Templar.

'I went to see him last night,' said Carl. 'He's awake but he's got a long recovery in front of him, I'm afraid.'

'Give him our regards,' said DC Paterson.

'I'll do that,' said Carl. 'Over to you, Harry.'

'Okay, we have a new person of interest, Anthony Slade,' said Harry, writing the name on the whiteboard. 'He operates the bank account Jack Swan and his mates put their casino winnings into. Makes monthly payments to them from that account as well, including to Richard Clarke. He's also making payments to Gail Swan from another of his accounts.'

'What do we know about this Slade?' said Carl, hoping they had identified a significant player in whatever was going on with Swan.

'Has the same address as Lombardo,' said Harry. 'We searched it yesterday.'

That's interesting, thought Carl. 'Anything turn up?'

'I pulled Slade's photo from Registrations,' said DC Beard. 'One of the neighbours recognized him. Said Slade and Lombardo had lived there for several years.'

'Do we know who owns the house?' said Carl.

'A company called EPS Property. Looks like it's a rental.'

'Any sign Gail Swan has been there?' said Carl.

'No,' said DC Beard, 'but Forensics are running tests on hair samples from the bathroom, and they've got several sets of prints that don't belong to Lombardo.'

Hope they've got enough to get a DNA profile, thought Carl. 'Anything that might help us work out who Lombardo's connected to?'

'A laptop,' said DC Beard, 'but we're still working on access.'

'Does Lombardo have an online presence?' said Carl. 'He's supposed to be a business consultant, isn't he?'

'Looks like he operates from a home office,' said DC Beard, 'He's got a LinkedIn profile.'

'And,' said DC Templar, 'he used to work for David Callinan.'

'How long ago?' said Carl.

'About ten years,' said DC Templar. 'Looks like he left when he set up his consultancy, according to his profile.'

'Anything online about Slade?' said Carl.

'Nothing,' said DC Paterson.

'We're working on their phone records,' said Harry.

'Sounds like you have a few things to follow up,' said Carl. 'Let me know how you get on.'

———

Joe Lombardo sat next to his lawyer with his arms crossed on his chest. DC Beard started the video recorder.

'What's your connection to Anthony Slade?' said Harry.

'Tony works for me,' said Joe.

'Is that in your consulting business or something else?'

'He's my research assistant.'

'Where is he?'

'Don't know,' said Joe. 'Haven't seen him for a couple of weeks.'

'When was the last time you did see him?'

Joe shrugged his shoulders. 'The last Friday in September, I think. He was going for a few weeks holiday.'

'Any idea where?'

Joe shook his head. 'No idea.'

'Do you have a phone number for him?' said Harry. 'I'd like to ask him a few questions.'

'0423 625 184.'

'Thanks.' Harry placed a photograph of Jack Swan on the table in front of Joe. 'Do you know this man?'

'Don't think so. Who is he?'

'His name is Jack Swan. Did Tony ever mention him to you?'

'No,' said Joe.

'What about Gail? He's her ex.'

'She never talks about the past,' said Joe. 'She's only interested in the future.'

'What about this man?' said Harry, showing him a photograph of Peter Thompson.

'No, don't know him,' said Joe.

'What about this one?' said Harry, turning over a photograph of James Weir.

'No,' said Joe. 'Never seen him.'

'And this one?' said Harry, flipping over a photograph of Richard Clarke.

'That's Richard Clarke, isn't it?' said Joe, 'Saw his picture in the paper.'

'Ever meet him?'

'No.'

'Gail ever mention him to you?'

'The only Clarke Gail ever talked about was Doug,' said Joe. 'She admired him for what he'd done for a couple of lads from her home town.'

'Is that why you were helping her negotiate to buy his business?'

'I had nothing to do with that,' said Joe. 'All I did was help her work out how she'd have to set herself up if she wanted to copy his business model.'

'What about your research assistant? Was he helping her?'

Joe looked at Philip Carol and then back at Harry. 'Not to my knowledge.'

'Do you keep in touch with David Callinan?' said Harry.

'He sends me a few leads.'

'Are you aware Tony is part of a gambling syndicate?' said Harry.

'What he does in his own time is none of my business,' said Joe.

'How long has he been living with you?'

'A couple of years,' said Joe. 'Since he and his wife split up.'

'Any chance he'd go back to her?'

'I doubt it,' said Joe. 'She's moved in with another guy.'

'Do you have her contact details?'

'No,' said Joe. 'I only know what Tony tells me.'

'Does she have a name?'

'Patricia,' said Joe, 'but he calls her the bitch these days.'

Harry smiled. 'Where were you on the evening of Monday, the twenty-fourth of September, around six?'

'Don't remember,' said Joe.

'Perhaps this will refresh your memory,' said Harry, showing him the still shot of a Mercedes sedan Nigel had lifted from the traffic video captured by the camera on Appleby Gorge Road.

'Doesn't help.'

Harry placed a print of the enhanced number plate onto the table. 'That's your car on Appleby Gorge Road at twenty minutes past six on the evening of twenty four September, Mr Lombardo.'

'Is it?' said Joe.

'This print is from a traffic video showing your car following Richard Clarke's BMW from East Park onto Appleby Gorge Road.'

'How could my client be following him?' said Philip Carol. 'He's already told you, he didn't know Richard Clarke.'

'But his mate Tony knew him,' said Harry.

'How could you possibly know that?' said Philip. 'You haven't even spoken to him.'

'He and Richard were members of the same gambling syndicate,' said Harry.

'Still doesn't mean my client was following Richard Clarke,' said Philip.

'Maybe not,' said Harry, 'but it makes it a possibility, doesn't it?'

'Coincidence,' said Joe. 'Did you say it was a Monday?'

'Yes, the twenty-fourth was a Monday,' said Harry.

'I think that's the night Tony and I had dinner at Gloria's. It's just outside Appleby.'

'Anyone who can vouch for that?'

'I paid with my credit card,' said Joe.

'Are you accusing my client of involvement in the death of Richard Clarke?' said Philip.

'No, Mr Carol,' said Harry. 'I'm just trying to work out why his car was on the same road as Richard Clarke's on the last night of his life.'

'Well, now you know,' said Joe.

'And, thanks for Tony's phone number,' said Harry.

———

Harry called the number Joe Lombardo had given him for Tony Slade and left a message for Tony to call him.

'Check out Lombardo's story about dining at Gloria's on the evening of the twenty-fourth, Nigel.'

'Do you believe him about it just being a coincidence they were on the road the same time as Clarke?' said Nigel.

'I'm not sure I believe anything he's told us,' said Harry. 'There's too much money swirling about for Slade to be some sort of research assistant, if you ask me.'

'I'll see if I can track down his ex,' said Nigel. 'I'll get onto Births, Deaths and Marriages.'

'See what you can find out about Lombardo while you're at it,' said Harry.

'Wayne's chasing up his LinkedIn connections,' said Nigel.

Harry looked at his watch. 'I've got to go. Lisa and I are interviewing your Mr Rehn again.'

'Why's that?' said Nigel.

'I'm hoping he might be able to tell us who else visited Gail Swan before she disappeared.'

———

Mr Rehn had gone to some trouble preparing for their visit, thought Harry, as he accepted the old man's offer of cake and coffee. He wondered how many visitors Mr Rehn had each week as he watched him serve Lisa a piece of chocolate cake.

'How long have you lived here, Mr Rehn?' said Lisa.

'Moved here after the wife died,' said Mr Rehn, 'so, that'll be three years next month.'

'Where did you live before?' said Lisa.

'We had a house with a big yard a few streets from here. I didn't want to move out of the district. I know where everything is around here.'

'Do you own this apartment?' said Harry.

'Yes,' said Mr Rehn, 'but most of the others belong to a bloke called Slade, so he runs the place. He's got more votes than anybody else on the body corporate, so it's his way or the highway, I'm afraid. Still, it means I only have to pay the quarterly fee and leave all the maintenance to him. He's done a good job so far.'

'Are there many other owners?'

'The only other one like me is Mrs Total, in number three. We bought off the plan, you see. Slade's company bought the rest after I'd signed on.'

'Have you met this Slade fellow?'

'A couple of times,' said Mr Rehn. 'A young bloke to have that much money, I reckon.'

'Maybe it's his Dad's money,' said Lisa.

'Who knows?' said Mr Rehn, 'as long as his tenants behave themselves, I don't really care.'

'Do you have any family?' said Lisa.

'My daughter,' said Mr Rehn. 'She keeps an eye on me, and my grandkids pop over every now and then. They live such busy lives these young people today.'

'Is this Mr Slade?' said Harry, showing him a copy of Tony Slade's driver's licence photograph.

Mr Rehn put on his reading glasses. 'That's him.'

'Ever see him visiting Gail Swan?'

'He has a property manager that looks after his tenants, Sergeant. I only see him for the annual meeting of the body corporate.'

'What about this man?' said Harry, showing him a photograph of Joe Lombardo.

'Don't know his name,' said Mr Rehn, 'but he's been here a few times, and I've seen her leaving with him, all dressed up to the nines. Is that important?'

'This is Joe Lombardo,' said Harry. 'We've been told he's Gail's boyfriend.'

'Lucky fellow,' said Mr Rehn. 'She seems like a nice girl. Always friendly whenever I speak to her.'

Harry placed a photograph of Richard Clarke on the coffee table on top of the others. 'Have you seen this man around here?'

Mr Rehn picked up the photograph. 'Yes, I think so. Drives a BMW.'

'That's Richard Clarke. He's the son of Doug Clarke, the man you told our colleague had been here the weekend before he was killed.'

'Ah, yes, the man with the dark grey Mercedes. I always wanted a Mercedes but never got around to buying one,' said Mr Rehn. 'That Lombardo bloke drives one the same model. How likely is that? That she'd have two visitors driving the same car?'

'Not very,' said Harry, picking up the photograph of Joe Lombardo. 'Do you remember the last time you saw this man here?'

'I reckon he was here the week after that Clarke fellow was killed, before that other detective spoke to me,' said Mr Rehn.

'And, have you seen Gail Swan since that time?' said Harry.

'No.'

CHAPTER TWENTY-EIGHT

Harry sat at his desk preparing for Monday morning's briefing. A pinging sound alerted him to the arrival of a new email. He clicked on the notification banner on his screen and opened the email from Dean Lang. A smile spread across his face as he read the contents.

He picked up his phone and called Acting Chief Inspector West.

'Did you see Dean's email, Boss?'

'Yes,' said Carl. 'At least you know who you're looking for now.'

'Will you speak to the media, Boss, or do you want me to do that?'

'Send me his photograph, Harry. I'll front the media. You concentrate on finding him.'

'Okay, Boss.'

Harry attached the digital image they'd downloaded from Registrations to an email and sent it to Acting Chief Inspector West. Then he called his team together around the whiteboard in the squad room.

'Forensics have matched a DNA profile from Lombardo's place with the DNA from the shirt found in Swan's rubbish bin in Ashcroft,' said Harry.

'Has to be Slade,' said Nigel. 'We know Lombardo's DNA doesn't match.'

'How are we going with tracking him down?' said Harry.

'The manager at Gloria's told me he'd been a regular up until a few weeks ago but she hasn't seen him since the last week in September, when he was there with Lombardo,' said Nigel.

So, Lombardo's story checked out, thought Harry, but it still left him in the vicinity of where Richard Clarke had met his end.

'Did she recognize Swan at all?' said Harry.

'Not Gail but she knew Jack. Said he'd been there a few times with Slade and Weir.'

'We're going to have to pull them in for another chat,' said Harry. 'How did you go with Births, Deaths and Marriages?'

'I've got details on Patricia Slade nee Stenhouse. Turns out she's Howard Stenhouse's daughter. I've got a current address in Appleby.'

Somebody else connected to North Summit, thought Harry. 'Anything on Slade's family?'

'His father is the Right Honourable William Slade, member for Hammond.'

'Doesn't he own half the mid-north?' said Wayne. 'What's his son doing playing with Lombardo?'

'Anthony Robert is the youngest of five sons,' said Nigel. 'Maybe he's too spoilt to be a farmer.'

'More likely there wasn't enough farm to go around,' said Lisa. 'It's not that unusual for younger sons to make their way in the world while their older brothers run the farm.'

'Sounds a bit like the story Doug Clarke's brother told us,' said Harry.

'Who's going to interview the Right Honourable?' said Wayne.

'Guess I'll have to sort that out with the chief inspector,' said Harry. 'Meanwhile, I want you to bring in Swan and Weir.' Harry turned to Nigel. 'And, you and Lisa can have a chat with Patricia Slade.'

'Okay,' said Nigel.

'Is she still going by that name?' said Harry.

'No, she's reverted to Stenhouse, according to Registrations,' said Nigel.

'I wonder if she knows Gail Swan?' said Lisa.

'Don't forget to ask her,' said Harry.

———

Nigel parked in front of the Appleby General Store, where Patricia Stenhouse had agreed to meet him and Lisa in the attached coffee shop. It was late in the afternoon and the streets of the small town nestled in the hills beyond Appleby Gorge were deserted, except for the VW Golf in front of the coffee shop.

They got out of the car and made their way into the coffee shop, where a woman aged in her early forties was chatting with an older woman sitting on a stool behind the counter.

'Patricia Stenhouse?' said Nigel, as he approached the counter.

'That's me,' said the younger woman.

'Would you like coffee?' asked the woman behind the counter.

'Two flat whites,' said Lisa. 'Do you want something, Ms Stenhouse?'

'No, thanks. I've had one while I was waiting.'

Lisa paid for the coffees.

'Take a seat. I'll bring them over.'

'Let's sit by the window,' said Patricia, pointing to a table with four chairs. 'Don't think we'll be disturbed at this time of the day.'

'Noticed it was pretty quiet outside,' said Nigel.

'Most of the tourists head back to the city before it gets dark' said Patricia. 'Not a lot of people like driving back through these hills at night.'

Nigel nodded. It wasn't hard to imagine why the tourists would prefer driving through the twists and turns of Appleby Gorge Road in daylight.

The older woman served their coffees and returned to her stool behind the counter.

'What do you want to speak to me about?' said Patricia.

'We're investigating a murder,' said Nigel, 'and your ex-husband has become a person of interest.'

'What's Tony gone and done now?'

Nigel smiled. 'We're not sure he's done anything but we want to ask him a few questions. Do you know where he is?'

'He moved in with his mate, Joe, down in the city. Have you spoken to him?'

'Yes, but he says he doesn't know where Tony is.'

'Neither do I,' said Patricia. 'I haven't seen him for weeks. I thought he was living in the city.'

'When was the last time you saw him?'

'I do the books at Gloria's,' said Patricia. 'I saw him there with Joe about three weeks ago.'

'Speak to him?'

'Not that night. I was running late for a meeting at the basket-ball club.'

Nigel took a sip of his coffee.

'Any idea where he'd go if he wanted to disappear?' said Lisa.

'Not really. Perhaps you should speak to Mark Riley. Tony used to hang out with him a lot.'

'What sort of work was Tony doing when you were married to him?' said Lisa.

'He was a security guard at some nightclub in the city. A place Mark's father owns,' said Patricia. 'He was never home. That's partly why we split up.'

'Would it surprise you to know he was working as a research assistant to a business consultant?' said Lisa.

'Tony?' Patricia laughed. 'Who told you that?'

'Joe Lombardo. Apparently Tony works for him.'

'Well, he studied accounting at uni for a while. That's where I met him and Joe, but he hated it.'

Nigel showed her a photograph of Jack Swan. 'Do you recognize this man?'

'That's Jack Swan. He used to work with Tony but he went to prison after he threatened some kid. Can't say I was surprised. He was a nasty piece of work.'

'Seen him recently?' said Lisa.

Patricia shook her head.

'Did you know his wife?' said Lisa.

'Gail?' said Patricia. 'She did accounting with us at uni. Never understood what she saw in Jack.'

'When was the last time you saw Gail?' said Nigel.

'We lost touch after she divorced Jack. You know how it is? But I saw her a few months ago. She turned up at Gloria's with some older man.'

'Did you talk to her?' said Lisa.

Patricia shook her head. 'I don't think she recognized me.'

Nigel scrolled through his photographs until he found the one of David Callinan he'd downloaded from the City of East Park's website. 'Is this him?'

'No,' said Patricia. 'It was the man who's been on the TV. You know, that fellow found dead in East Park.'

'Doug Clarke,' said Nigel.

'Yes, him.'

'We're investigating his murder.'

'And you think Tony had something to do with it?'

'We want to speak to him because it looks like Joe Lombardo had something to do with it,' said Nigel.

'I could see Tony doing something stupid like that,' said Patricia, 'but not Joe. He's too sophisticated to be mixed up with killing someone.'

'Why's that?' said Lisa.

'Tony's got a real temper on him. Another reason why I left him.'

'Did he ever hit you?' asked Lisa.

'I never reported him, if that's what you're asking?' said Patricia. 'The first time he hit me, I left him.'

'When was that?'

'Close to three years ago.'

Nigel showed Patricia photographs of James Weir and Peter Thompson. 'Do you recognize either of these men?'

'That one,' said Patricia, pointing at the image of James Weir. 'He was always bringing packages to our place when I was living with Tony.'

'What sort of packages?'

'I don't really know. Tony used to take them to work with him.'

Nigel swiped to the next photograph in his collection: Richard Clarke. 'Do you know who this is?'

'He plays poker with Tony and his mates. I remember seeing him at the casino.' She sucked in a quick breath. 'He's the bloke that drove his car into the gorge, isn't he?'

'Yes,' said Lisa. 'That's Richard Clarke.'

Patricia looked at her watch. 'Are we nearly finished? I have to pick up the kids from basketball.'

'I wasn't aware you had kids,' said Lisa.

'They're my partner's kids,' said Patricia. 'Tony and I never got around to having any. Probably just as well, with the way things turned out.'

'Thank you for your time,' said Nigel.

'I hope it was worth the trip up here for you,' said Patricia.

'Just so you know,' said Nigel, 'we'll be making a public request for information on Tony's whereabouts on tonight's news and in tomorrow's papers.'

'Thanks for letting me know.'

CHAPTER TWENTY-NINE

A young lawyer from Carol and Associates turned up to represent Jack Swan and James Weir.

Harry decided they'd interview Jack Swan first.

'Tell us about Tony Slade,' said Harry.

'That's a name that takes me back a while,' said Jack. 'I used to work with him but that was before I went inside.'

'Where was that?'

'At the Merlin. We did security.'

'Seen him recently?'

'Nah,' said Jack.

'What about Mark Riley? Been in touch with him?'

'Nah,' said Jack. 'I've stayed away from them since I got out. Not interested in going back there.'

'Fair enough,' said Harry. 'How long have you known James Weir?'

Jack shrugged his shoulders. 'I dunno. Maybe five years. I met him at the casino.'

'Tony Slade ever mention him?'

'Not that I recall.'

'Do you socialise with James Weir,' said Harry, 'apart from playing poker with him at the casino?'

'Nah.'

'Ever been to Appleby, Mr Swan?'

Jack looked at his lawyer. 'A couple of times. Tony lives up there. We went up there a few times when I was married to Gail. She knew his wife from uni.'

'What about recently?' said Harry.

'Haven't seen Tony since I got out.'

Harry noted that Jack hadn't answered his question.

'So, you don't know he's split with his wife, then?'

'Hadn't heard.'

'Ever been to a restaurant called Gloria's?' said Harry. 'It's just outside Appleby.'

'Not recently,' said Jack. 'It's too bloody far. Besides, my missus doesn't like driving in the hills at night.'

Harry slipped a piece of paper out of the folder on the table in front of him. 'This is a copy of a statement given to one of my officers by the manager of Gloria's.' Harry looked straight at Jack. 'She says you, James Weir, and Tony Slade have been there several times this year.'

Jack rolled his eyes and looked at his lawyer. 'She's lying.'

'Why would she lie to us?' said Harry.

Jack said nothing.

'Do you understand what obstructing the police means?' said Harry.

Jack looked at his hands. 'If she's not lying, she's made a mistake. I haven't been there for years.'

Harry slipped a second sheet of paper out of his folder. 'This is a print of the call log on your phone from your service provider.'

'What? How did you get that?' Jack turned to his lawyer. 'Is he allowed to do that?'

'If he has a warrant,' said the lawyer.

'I have a warrant,' said Harry. 'You're a person of interest in a suspicious death.'

'Whose death?' said Jack.

'Richard Clarke's,' said Harry, 'and now it looks like you might be connected to the murder of Doug Clarke.'

'You're not pinning that on me.'

'What I'm interested in,' said Harry, pointing to the page in front of him, 'is this call you made to Tony Slade last week.'

'Is that all?' said Jack. 'That was just a social call.'

'That's not the only call you've made to him,' said Harry. 'You talk to him a lot for someone you haven't seen for years.'

'I didn't say I hadn't spoken to him,' said Jack. 'You asked me if I'd seen him. And, like I said, I haven't seen him since I got out.'

'Do you know where he is?'

'He didn't say.'

Harry pulled a third piece of paper out from his folder. 'This is a copy of the transactions on your bank account, Mr Swan. The one's I've highlighted come from an account operated by Tony Slade, and that account's in the name of the East Park Syndicate. Want to tell me about that?'

Jack crossed his arms and nodded towards his lawyer.

Harry knew he'd called his bluff.

'My client will not be answering any more questions,' said the lawyer.

'Your client is being charged with money laundering and obstructing police,' said Harry.

'You can't prove anything,' said Jack.

'Leave the arguing to me, Mr Swan,' said the lawyer. 'I'll have you out of here as soon as possible.'

———

Harry ushered the lawyer into interview room three, where James Weir sat waiting for them with a uniformed constable. He waited for Wayne to activate the recording equipment, then placed a photograph of Tony Slade onto the table in front of Weir. 'Do you know this man?'

Weir looked at the lawyer.

'You don't have to answer any of their questions,' said the lawyer.

'But, it might help you if you do,' said Harry.

'I haven't done anything wrong,' said Weir.

'So, do you know this man? I'm trying to find him.'

'That's Tony Slade.'

'When was the last time you saw him?'

'Couple of weeks ago.'

'Where?' said Harry.

'We had a meeting at Gloria's,' said Weir. 'That's a restaurant up in the hills.'

'I've heard of it,' said Harry. 'What sort of meeting?'

'We're in a gambling syndicate,' said Weir, looking at Wayne.

'Was Richard Clarke in this gambling syndicate?'

'That's what the meeting was about. We were deciding what to do with his share.'

'Who else was at this meeting?'

'Jack,' said Weir. 'Peter couldn't make it.'

'Do you know where Tony is?'

'He lives in East Park.'

Harry smiled. 'I know that but he's not home.'

'Then, I can't help you,' said Weir. 'He calls me when he wants to meet.'

'So, he's in charge, is he?'

'He runs the syndicate, if that's what you mean.'

'You told my colleague here that you play poker with your

own money,' said Harry, pulling out a copy of Wayne's interview notes. 'Do you want me to read out what you said?'

'I remember what I said.'

'So, why do you deposit your winnings into the syndicate's bank account, Mr Weir?'

'It's my money, I can do what I like with it.'

'But, you never take any money out of that account, Mr Weir, so I'm intrigued as to where the money you take to the casino every night might come from,' said Harry.

'I always hold back my kitty,' said Weir. 'It's only the money I win above my kitty that goes into the bank.'

'Oh, what about the nights you lose your kitty?' said Harry.

James Weir crossed his arms on his chest.

'Let me tell you what I think happens,' said Harry. 'You and your mates get a fresh bundle of cash to play with every night, and it doesn't matter who wins because all the money, less the casino's cut for hosting your poker games, goes into the bank as winnings the next morning.'

Harry watched a pale red blush spread across Weir's neck.

'Tony's the source of the money, isn't he? That's why he's the one operating the account and paying you and your mates a fee for washing his cash, isn't it?'

'Pure speculation,' said the lawyer.

'That's not what these accounts show,' said Harry, pulling out several sheets of paper. 'You've been in business with Tony Slade for years, haven't you, Mr Weir?'

'What are you talking about?' said Weir.

'You've been delivering packages for him for more than ten years,' said Harry.

'You've got that wrong. I've delivered stuff to his place but I've never delivered anything for him.'

Harry leant back in his chair. 'Who do you make those deliveries for?'

'I pick them up at the depot,' said Weir. 'I have no idea who sends them to him.'

'What's the name of the depot?'

'Citywide Parcels,' said Weir. 'I get most of my business from them.'

'Does Tony Slade give you the money to play poker with?' said Harry.

Weir looked at his lawyer and then at Harry.

'Like I told your mate, here.' He pointed at Wayne. 'I play with my own money.'

'It'll go better for you if you come clean with me now,' said Harry.

'You have no idea what's going on,' said Weir. 'You don't know any more than I do, and I know nothing.'

'James Weir, I'm charging you with money laundering and obstructing a police inquiry,' said Harry.

Weir turned to his lawyer. 'Why are you letting him do this?'

'Take it easy, Mr Weir,' said the lawyer. 'I'll get you out of here.'

CHAPTER THIRTY

Carl was sitting at his desk in the chief inspector's office reading Harry's update on developments in the Clarke case when his phone rang.

'Carl, it's Evelyn.'

Carl thought she sounded flat.

'Hello, Evelyn. How is he?'

He heard her take a couple of breaths.

'He's gone, Carl. About half an hour ago.'

Carl didn't know what to say. He'd been expecting the chief to recover, even though he'd known it was very unlikely he'd return to work.

'I'm sorry, Evelyn.'

'It's probably for the better, Carl.'

Carl knew she was right. As much as he'd hoped the chief would recover, he hadn't wanted to see him suffer the indignity of a quasi-vegetative state for the rest of his life.

'Where are you?' said Carl.

'I'm still at the hospital, waiting for them to finish the paperwork.'

'Do you want me to come and take you home?'

'Would you?'

'I'm on my way.'

———

Later that night, Carl sat out on the back patio with a glass of wine. He felt like a cigarette but he'd given up smoking when Wally Baker had died of lung cancer. He missed Wally. They'd made a good team.

Thinking of Wally Baker resurfaced the memories of Peter James he'd worked hard to suppress. Peter's death had nearly undone him. He'd been standing next to Peter when he'd been shot through a glass door. He'd shot Peter's killer, which was the only time he'd killed another man in the line of duty. He shuddered at the memory and took a sip of the wine.

The only other close colleague he'd lost on the job had been Steve Wood, who'd been killed in a Special Operations' mission that had gone wrong. Thinking of Steve reminded him he hadn't spoken to Marie, Steve's widow, for a while. He made a mental note to give her a call.

He knew he was going to miss the chief. George Rankin had taken him under his wing when he'd first become a detective, and had been a mentor to him as he'd worked his way up to inspector. Carl knew he owed George a debt he now wouldn't be able to repay.

He took another sip of the wine, and decided he'd followed in George's footsteps by mentoring Harry. Perhaps there'd be other opportunities to pass George's gift forward if he became chief inspector.

Nina came out onto the patio and sat down at the outdoor table beside him. 'You okay?'

Carl poured her a glass of wine. 'I'm going to miss him.'

'Think we're all going to miss him,' said Nina. 'Even Sophie.'

'Robert will now have the grandfather duties to himself,' said Carl, thinking of Nina's uncle and aunt, who'd taken on the role of grandparents in place of her deceased parents. 'Hope he can cope.'

'He'll be fine. He's got Nancy to help him,' said Nina. 'When do you think you'll find out who's going to become the chief inspector?'

'I guess that will happen almost immediately.'

'What will happen to your team?'

'That depends on who gets the job.'

'You should be a shoo-in,' said Nina. 'Who else is there with your level of experience?'

'Thanks for the vote of confidence,' said Carl, giving her a kiss on the cheek. 'There's talk of bringing in Paul Henry from Northern Command.'

'Do you know him?'

'He was one of my detectives when I first made sergeant. I can work with him.'

CHAPTER THIRTY-ONE

Philip Carol shut his eyes and rested his elbows on his desk. He'd just listened to an update from Rodney Williams, the lawyer he'd despatched to represent Jack Swan and James Weir, on what had transpired at Police Headquarters. Rodney's news had not been good.

He opened his eyes and gazed through the window towards the urban forest that dominated the East Park skyline. He wondered how long it would take the police to trace the money to its source, if they got their hands on Tony Slade. He realized that if they identified the source, it wouldn't be long before they knew everything about their operation.

He called David Callinan.

'Dave, they've arrested Swan and Weir for money laundering.'

'What?'

'They pulled Tony's bank accounts and traced the transactions. Looks like they're on to the little game we had going at the casino.'

'I told you sending Joe and Tony after Richard was a mistake.'

'Too late to worry about that,' said Philip. 'Where did Tony put the money from the casino?'

'In the EPS Property account at First National,' said David.

'That could be a problem,' said Philip. 'We transferred money from that account to one of my trust accounts when we bought the apartments at Portside.'

'Your office only did the conveyancing, Phil. You don't ask your clients where they got their money from.'

'We set up EPS Property.'

'Stop worrying,' said David. 'The directors are listed as the members of the syndicate. They can't trace it back to us.'

'Unless someone squeals.'

'They all know the penalty for that.'

'Have you heard from Tony?'

'I was waiting for an update from Jack,' said David. 'Guess that's not going to happen any time soon. Do you think they'll get bail?'

'We'll find that out in the morning.'

'Who's going to tell the others what's going on?'

'I have a meeting with them tonight,' said Philip. 'They'll want to know if you're making any progress with the financing option.'

'I've been in touch with Howard Stenhouse about his current development and I've introduced myself to Barry Yorke. Yorke is interested. They have a development in for approval down at the port and they're looking to raise fifteen million. I said we could help.'

'That sounds promising.'

'We should be able to spread the risk over our portfolio and the clients we're picking up from Doug Clarke,' said David. 'That should make them happy.'

'I'm sure it will if we can pull it off.'

'What about Thompson?' said David. 'Has he been arrested?'

'The police haven't said anything about him,' said Philip. 'Perhaps you'd better warn him.'

'Have you heard the stuff on the radio? They're asking for public assistance to locate Gail and Tony.'

'Let's hope they've heard it and stay where they are. We don't want either of them talking to the police.'

Philip ended the call and wondered if Gail and Tony were still alive. He hoped they were, especially Gail. He liked her. But he was under no illusions. They, like anyone else, would be taken out if they were deemed a risk. He knew that applied to him and David as well.

He swivelled back to face his computer and checked on the progress of his passport renewal application. Status update was: posted. He smiled. That meant he'd have it within the next day or so.

CHAPTER THIRTY-TWO

Mark Riley agreed to meet Harry at the Merlin Nightclub, an imposing grey granite building on North Terrace. The premises had started life as a gentlemen's club, a place where high society men gathered to conduct business in a private space. Its current patrons had little in common with the high society men of that distant era. The Merlin was one of the city's hot nightspots for young people looking for sex and other forms of entertainment.

Harry remembered the car park, the scene of a triple murder he'd investigated with Carl several years ago, was located at the rear of the building. He directed Nigel to the entrance off the lane that ran behind the row of buildings fronting North Terrace.

They rang the bell on the back door of the club and waited. The door was opened by a young woman dressed in black with a mop in her hand.

'We're here to see Mr Riley,' said Harry.

'You the police?'

'Yes,' said Harry.

'Oh, okay. He's in his office. It's the second door on the left down there.' She pointed along the corridor that led away from the door.

'Thanks.'

Before they could move, a man wearing a dark blue suit with an open neck white shirt appeared in the corridor and walked towards them.

'Detective Sergeant Fuller?'

'Yes,' said Harry, producing his ID.

'Mark Riley.' Mark extended his hand.

Harry shook hands with him. 'This is Detective Constable Beard.'

'Come into my office.'

They followed him into his office, a large room occupied by a desk with a computer on it, and several armchairs arranged around a low table.

'What was it you wanted to talk about?' said Mark, as they sat down.

'We're looking for Tony Slade,' said Harry. 'We've been told you know him.'

'Oh, who told you that?'

'His ex-wife. She told us he worked here.'

'He used to work here, up until about six months ago.'

'Is he a friend or simply a former employee?'

'Both, I suppose,' said Mark. 'He and I started here around the same time. He was doing security when I started in the kitchen, washing dishes.'

'You've obviously progressed,' said Harry.

'This club belongs to my father. He made sure I understood every aspect of the business before he let me run the place.'

'Has your father retired?'

'I don't think he'll ever retire,' said Mark. 'Besides, we've got three other clubs, so he's got plenty to keep him occupied.'

'When was the last time you saw Tony Slade?'

'He dropped in to say hello a couple of weeks ago.'

'Do you know what he's doing now?'

'Playing poker, I believe,' said Mark. 'Said he was making squillions at the casino.'

'Does that surprise you?' said Harry. 'Him playing poker for a living.'

'He was always into card games.'

'Did you know he's into property as well?'

'Guess he's got to do something with his money,' said Mark. 'There's not much point putting it in the bank these days, is there?'

Harry couldn't argue with that. 'Do you go to the casino?'

Mark shook his head. 'Not my scene.'

Harry took out his phone and pulled up a photo of Joe Lombardo. 'Do you know who this is?'

Mark looked at the photo and shook his head. 'Don't think so.'

'This is Joe Lombardo. Says he's a business consultant,' said Harry. 'He told us Tony was working for him as a research assistant.'

'News to me. Like I said. Tony told me he was playing poker.'

'Any idea where we might find Tony?'

'Said he was living in East Park someplace.'

'Anybody else here he might still be in contact with?' said Harry.

'Try Ken Lawson. Tony worked with him for years.'

'Do you have his contact details?'

Mark pulled his phone out of his pocket and tapped on its screen. 'You can get him on 0423 788 956.'

'Do you have an address?'

'Give me a minute. I'll have to look that up for you.'

———

Ken Lawson lived in Northfield, several kilometres north of the city centre. It took Nigel fifteen minutes to drive them to the address Mark Riley had given them. There was a silver Mercedes sedan parked under the carport.

Harry surveyed the neat front yard of what looked to be a relatively new house as they walked up the driveway and approached the front door. Harry pushed the button for the doorbell and they waited.

'Nice place,' said Nigel. 'Lily's trying to talk me into buying a house like this.'

'Now's not a bad time to be buying,' said Harry.

'Not sure I want to live in a house. Think I'd rather stay in the apartment.'

The front door opened.

'Can I help you?' said a grey-haired man.

'Police,' said Harry, showing him his ID. 'Are you Ken Lawson?'

'Yeah.'

'I understand you worked with Tony Slade.'

'Ah, you're the coppers Mark called about.'

'Yes,' said Harry, wondering what else Mark might have told him. 'We're looking for Tony.'

'Heard something about that on the radio. What's he done this time?'

'What makes you think he's done anything?'

'He's got a temper on him that one. I'm surprised he lasted as long as he did as a security guard.'

'Did he get fired?' said Harry.

'Nah, he just decided to leave.'

'Any idea why?'

Ken shrugged. 'Reckoned he was making more money playing poker at the casino.'

'When was the last time you saw him?'

Ken scratched his chin. 'I don't think I've seen him since he left work to be honest.'

'Any idea where he might hang out besides the casino?' said Harry.

'He moved in with some woman called Gail when he split with his missus. Talked about her all the time.'

'Ever meet her?' said Harry.

'Couple of times at the club,' said Ken. 'She's a bit of a looker.'

Harry found a picture of Gail Swan on his phone. 'Is this her?'

'Yeah, that's her.'

'Her name's Gail Swan. If you've been listening to the radio, you probably know we're looking for her as well.'

'Oh, yeah, you're right. I heard her name the other night,' said Ken.

'Any other ideas where he might be?'

'He lived up in Appleby before he split up,' said Ken, 'and he told me his old man owned a lot of property up in the mid-north. Plenty of places to hide up there, I reckon.'

'Thanks for your time, Mr Lawson.' Harry handed him a business card. 'If he makes contact, give me a call.'

———

Nigel drove them back towards Police Headquarters. 'Guess we're going to have to talk to the right honourable, Sarge.'

'The chief's working on that,' said Harry.

'Might pay to have a look at his properties with Google Earth,' said Nigel, 'if there are so many places to hide up there.'

'You do that. I'm not sure about Tony living with Gail Swan, though. Mr Rehn didn't say anything about him living there.'

'Didn't he say Slade owned the place?'

'I've got Wayne looking in to that. He reckons the apartments belong to a company called EPS Property Pty Ltd. He's tracing the directors. I'm assuming Slade's one of them or an employee.'

'EPS Property?' said Nigel. 'They own the house Lombardo lives in. What do you think EPS means?'

'Could be anything' said Harry, 'but my guess is East Park Syndicate.'

'Isn't that the name of the bank account Slade was operating?'

'Maybe they're investing the money they're washing through the casino in property.'

'That might explain why Swan was trying to get Doug Clarke to sell her his finance business.'

'Still can't see why they had to kill him because they didn't like his asking price,' said Harry.

'Maybe he worked out where her money was coming from,' said Nigel, 'and was silly enough to tell her.'

'She must have told one of the others, seeing as we have a witness placing her in Ashcroft on the morning he was murdered.'

'Guess we're not going to know for sure until we get to speak to her,' said Nigel.

'We still haven't worked out where the money is coming from,' said Harry. 'Knowing that might help us crack this one.'

Harry's mobile phone rang.

'What's up, Wayne?'

'EPS Property has five shareholders, Sarge. Slade, Shaw, Weir, Thompson, and Richard Clarke. Slade's the managing director. Thompson's the company secretary.'

'Pick up Thompson. Sounds like it might be time to ask him a few questions.'

CHAPTER THIRTY-THREE

On the afternoon of Thursday, the eighteenth of October, the activities of the Major Crimes Section came to an early end. At two pm, the detectives, who had reported to Detective Chief Inspector Rankin, crossed the square to the cathedral opposite Police Headquarters to attend his funeral service. After the service, they retired to the lounge bar of the Criterion, scene of their many case closing celebrations during George Rankin's reign as chief inspector, and celebrated for him one last time.

———

On Friday, the nineteenth of October, Detective Inspector Carl West was promoted to the rank of Detective Chief Inspector and Detective Inspector Paul Henry took command of his old team.

That afternoon, there was another round of drinks in the lounge bar of the Criterion to celebrate the new world order.

Later that night, Harry and Jessika joined Carl and Nina for a quiet dinner at Massimo's to celebrate Carl's promotion, while Sophie spent the evening entertaining Robert and Nancy.

CHAPTER THIRTY-FOUR

Harry waited with Detective Inspector Henry outside the parliamentary office of the member for Hammond.

'Have you spoken to Mr Slade before?' said Inspector Henry.

'No, the chief inspector's office arranged the interview,' said Harry. 'He's been out in his electorate until this morning.'

'Excuse me, gentlemen, Mr Slade can see you now.'

They followed the member's assistant into his office.

'How can I help you?' said William Slade, without inviting them to sit.

'We're trying to contact your son, Anthony,' said Inspector Henry.

'Yes, I heard that on the radio on the drive down last night. What's it in relation to?'

'We're investigating Doug Clarke's murder, Mr Slade, and we think he might be able to help us with our inquiries.'

'I don't know how much you know about my family, Inspector. Probably not much, I suspect, since I've tried to shield them from the glare of the media as much as I can.'

'I understand you have five sons, Mr Slade, and that Anthony is the only one not on the land,' said Inspector Henry. 'What I'm interested in is whether you've seen him or heard from him recently or know of anybody who has.'

'Tony's what you might call the black sheep of the family, Inspector. When he came down to boarding school, he lost all interest in the farm. Then, he dropped out of university. He's been a bit of a disappointment to be honest.'

'When was the last time you had any contact with him?'

William put his hands into his pockets. 'The last time I saw him was in the casino. That would be three or four months ago. He told me he was making heaps of money playing poker. I wished him luck. Wish I could make money that easily.'

'Anybody with him?' said Inspector Henry.

'I have no idea. I bumped into him in the lobby.'

'Does he keep in touch with his brothers at all?'

'No-one's said anything,' said William, 'and I meet with at least one of them every time I go home.'

'Is there anywhere up on the farm where he could hide without anyone knowing he was there?' said Harry.

William Slade smiled. 'We run sheep over five thousand square kilometres, gentlemen. I guess there'd be a lot of places you could hide out there if you wanted to, but I wouldn't recommend it. It's not what you'd call hospitable country, and I don't think Tony would be that stupid. Now, if you have no other questions, I've got things to do.'

'Thank you for your time, Mr Slade,' said Inspector Henry, handing him a business card. 'If you hear from Tony, please ask him to call me.'

———

Peter Thompson said he didn't have a lawyer and accepted the offer of a duty lawyer to sit in on his interview.

Harry waited for Wayne to switch on the recording equipment and step them through the required introductory statements.

'Mr Thompson, I assume you're aware we've charged your associates with money laundering?'

'Yeah, Jack told me,' said Peter. 'Said you'd probably arrest me as well.'

'Is that why we had trouble locating you?'

'No. I went to spend a few days with my mother. She's in a nursing home down at Carrick. They don't think she'll last much longer.'

'Sorry to hear that,' said Harry.

Peter shrugged his shoulders. 'What can you do? We're all going where she's going.'

Harry brought his focus back to the task at hand. 'I'll make you the same offer I made your associates. You help us and we'll put in a good word for you with the prosecutor. What do you say?'

'Will I stay out of prison?'

'I can't guarantee that but it will make it easier for your lawyer to argue for a suspended sentence.'

'I only played poker with someone else's money,' said Peter. 'What's the big deal?'

'Participating in money laundering is a crime,' said Harry, 'even if it's not your money.'

Peter leant back in his chair and crossed his arms. 'What do you want to know?'

'Tell me about EPS Property Pty Ltd.'

'I don't know anything about it.'

'You're named as the company secretary,' said Harry, sliding a copy of the company's registration details across the table to him.

Peter picked up the page and read it. 'Someone's put my name on this but I don't know anything about it, honest.'

'We've traced the money you and your mates win at the casino to an account in the name of the East Park Syndicate,' said Harry, 'and we have copies of declarations signed by you stating your deposits into the account are winnings from the casino.'

'The bank makes me sign them. They have to report it.'

'You get a monthly payment from that account,' said Harry. 'What happens to the rest of the money?'

'I have no idea. As I said, it's not my money.'

'Whose money is it?'

'As far as I know,' said Peter, 'it belongs to Tony.'

'Tony Slade?'

'Yeah.'

'Where does he get his money from?' said Harry.

Peter shrugged. 'Don't know.'

'Let's go back to the beginning, Mr Thompson. How did you get involved in this little scheme?'

'Jack asked me if I'd like to make a bit of extra money,' said Peter. 'It's not like my job with the council pays that much, is it?'

'So, how did you get the money to play with?'

'Jim Weir dropped it off every afternoon we had to play,' said Peter.

'Where?'

'At my place. That way Jack's missus didn't get to see it.'

'When did Richard Clarke join in?'

'Couple of years ago. Tony brought him along one night and said he'd be taking his place for a while.'

'What was Clarke like as a poker player?' said Harry.

'Pretty hopeless, but someone has to lose.' Peter smiled. 'Anyway, he got better and started winning after a while.'

'And, he was playing for the same reason you were?'

'Not exactly,' said Peter. 'I got the impression he owed Tony and had agreed to play with us to work off his debt.'

'So, he knew what you were doing?'

'Yeah. We all knew what we were doing,' said Peter.

'Anybody else involved?' said Harry.

'I took my instructions from Jack,' said Peter. 'I don't know who he got his from. I always assumed it was Tony but I know Jack hasn't heard from him for weeks.'

'Do you know Gail, Jack's ex?' said Harry.

'First time I met her she was with Richard,' said Peter.

'Where was that?'

'One night at the casino. Be about a year ago. She was having dinner with him one night before the game.'

'How did you find out who she was?'

'Jack told us. Said he'd introduced her to Richard. Something about some deal Tony had in mind.'

'Any idea what that deal was?'

'Nah. I learnt not to ask too many questions,' said Peter. 'The less you know, the less trouble you get into.'

'Have you been threatened?'

'I'm not supposed to be talking to you,' said Peter, 'but I've had enough. You don't know what it's like looking over your shoulder all the time.'

'Well, it's over now, Mr Thompson. I'll charge you with being part of a money laundering scheme and we'll hold you in the Watch House overnight. But, we won't oppose bail at your hearing. That way it will look like we're treating you the same way as the others. Happy with that?'

'Yeah, but what happens when we go to trial?' said Peter.

'We'll shift you into the witness protection program,' said Harry. 'You'll need to play along with Jack until then. Think you can do that?'

'Yeah. I guess I can always call you if things look dicey,' said Peter.

Harry gave him his card. 'Call me, any time. If I can't come, I can always send someone.'

'Thanks.'

'And, if anything else comes up you think I need to know about, call me,' said Harry.

CHAPTER THIRTY-FIVE

Carl was returning to his office from a meeting with Assistant Commissioner Thaler when his mobile phone rang.

'Carl, got a minute?' said Mike Jonas.

'Sure, Mike.'

'You aware of the body found in the forest up behind Appleby yesterday?'

'Yes,' said Carl. 'Pretty badly decomposed, isn't it?'

'I think it's your missing woman, Gail Swan. I got a match with a DNA profile from her apartment which Forensics think is hers. I'm just chasing up her dental records.'

'Got any clues as to cause of death?'

'Shot at close quarters would be my guess,' said Mike. 'There's a hole in the back of her skull consistent with a gunshot wound.'

'How long ago?'

'Be at least a month, perhaps a little longer.'

That meant she'd been taken out not long after Doug Clarke's murder, thought Carl. 'Who did the Forensics at the scene?'

'Dean,' said Mike.

'Let me know how you get on with the dental records.' Carl ended the call and continued down to the third floor.

When he stepped out of the elevator, he looked across the squad room to his old office. It was empty. DS Fuller was at his desk.

'Where's DI Henry?'

'Gone for a coffee with Wayne.'

'How's it going?'

'He'll be okay. He's making the effort to build a relationship with everyone,' said Harry. 'What brings you down here, Boss?'

'I wanted to let you know it looks like we've found Gail Swan.'

'Where?'

'She's down in the morgue. At least Mike thinks it her. He's checking for dental records.'

'The body from Appleby?'

'Yes,' said Carl.

'Any sign of foul play?'

'Hole in her skull, according to Mike,' said Carl. 'Get the report from Dean.'

'I was hoping she'd have a few answers for us.'

'Looks like you've got more questions,' said Carl. 'How did the interview with Thompson go?'

'He's decided to talk. Claims the money came from Slade and went back to Slade, but he thinks Richard Clarke was pulled in because he owed Slade money.'

'That's interesting.'

'He also said Jack Swan told him he'd introduced Richard to Gail some time last year.'

'Any idea why?'

'Something about a deal Slade had in mind,' said Harry. 'Backs up what Slade's work colleague told us about Slade knowing Gail Swan.'

'Sounds like Slade could be behind the proposal to buy out Doug Clarke's finance business,' said Carl.

'We still haven't worked out where Slade's getting his money,' said Harry, 'but someone's been funnelling money through his casino scheme.'

'Where's it going from that account you mentioned?'

'I've got Wayne looking into that. You know what's he's like when it comes to finding the money.'

'Like a pig in mud,' said Carl. 'Might be worth having another word with Jack Swan when Mike's confirmed the body is his ex.'

'Another murder to solve.'

'Well, at least we know she didn't kill Doug Clarke.'

'But she probably knew Slade did, and why.'

'Any sign of him?' said Carl.

'I'm wondering whether we're looking in the right place,' said Harry. 'There's a lot of space for him to hide in on his father's station up north.'

'And not many people to report seeing him,' said Carl.

'He hasn't been seen in the casino since Richard Clarke's death,' said Harry. 'But how long can someone hide in the bush? He'd need supplies unless someone was feeding him.'

'Any action on his personal bank accounts?'

Harry flicked through the papers on his desk. 'No transactions since the end of September, when he paid for petrol in Appleby the night Joe Lombardo told us they ate at Gloria's.'

'He's a man with access to a lot of cash,' said Carl, 'so, he could still be out there.'

'I hope you're right, Boss. I don't really want to be searching five thousand square kilometres of saltbush country for him.'

When Mike Jonas rang and confirmed the body recovered from the forest near Appleby was Gail Swan, Harry set up an interview with Jack Swan and his lawyer.

'What's this about?' said Jack, as he and Rodney Williams took their seats opposite Harry and Wayne in interview room two on the ground floor of Police Headquarters.

'Gail,' said Harry. 'She's dead.'

'What?'

'Gail's dead, Jack. Her body was found by a bushwalker in the hills up behind Appleby.'

'When?'

'A few days ago, but she's been dead for some time.'

'What's this got to do with my client?' said Rodney.

'When was the last time you saw you Gail, Jack?' said Harry.

'It's got nothing to do with me,' said Jack. 'I didn't kill her.'

'Who said she was killed?'

'Then, why are we here?' said Jack. 'You blokes don't make social calls.'

'I'm trying to determine her movements in the days leading up to her death,' said Harry. And, to give you something to think about, he thought, as he waited for Jack to answer.

'I haven't seen her for years,' said Jack.

'Are you sure about that?'

Jack looked at Harry.

'Didn't you introduce her to Richard Clarke last year?'

Jack looked at his lawyer and then back at Harry. 'Who told you that?'

'Never mind who told me,' said Harry. 'Are you denying it?'

'Someone's been pulling your leg,' said Jack. 'I haven't seen her since she divorced me.'

'She was shot through the head, Jack,' said Harry.

'Shit! She might have been a bitch but she didn't deserve that.'

'Nobody does,' said Harry. 'I'm sorry you had to find out this way.'

————

DI Henry listened as Wayne explained the money trail to him.

'The money from the casino is deposited into an account at B and A by the poker players. Then, it's transferred to the EPS Property account at First National by Slade or someone using his internet banking login,' said Wayne.

'All of it?' said DI Henry, looking at the two rectangles joined by a line Wayne had drawn on the whiteboard.

'Slade made a monthly payment from the account to each of the poker players, including himself, but the bulk of it went to the EPS Property account,' said Wayne, adding five more rectangles and arrows to his diagram. 'And, Slade was making a payment from his personal account at B and A to Gail Swan.' He added another rectangle and drew a line to it.

'What was going into his personal account?'

Wayne found his list. 'Wages from Rileys, those payments from the gambling account, and a monthly payment described as a management fee from EPS Property.'

'I thought DS Fuller said he'd stopped working at the Merlin six months ago.'

'Did he?' said Wayne, picking up the latest statement from Slade's account. 'They're still paying him according to this, and this is dated last Wednesday.'

'But, he's not drawing from the account, right?'

'Hasn't touched it since the end of September.'

'Is he still making payments to Gail Swan?'

Wayne ran his finger down the list of transactions. 'Last payment sent to her account was on the twelfth of September.'

'Interesting,' said DI Henry. 'Looks like he knew she was dead, or about to be.'

'Or he hasn't had access to a computer,' said Wayne. 'The payments are monthly.'

'Where does the money go from the EPS Property account?'

'There haven't been that many withdrawals,' said Wayne, 'but they go to a Carol and Associates Trust account, presumably to fund property purchases.'

'Any other deposits into that account?'

'Lots,' said Wayne. 'Look like rent payments from a property management company.'

'I guess that figures, if EPS owns an apartment building or two,' said DI Henry.

'What do you want me to do with this?' said Wayne.

DI Henry looked at the rectangles and lines Wayne had drawn on the whiteboard.

'Find out why Rileys are still paying Slade. Something's not right there.'

'Anything else?' said Wayne.

'Carol and Associates are representing Shaw and Weir, aren't they?'

'And Lombardo,' said Wayne.

'Find out about the money transferred to their trust account. Get a search warrant if you have to.'

DI Henry's mobile phone rang. He fished it out of his pocket. 'DI Henry.'

'Operations, Inspector. We've located Slade's vehicle. It's being recovered from the river, about twenty kilometres south of Carrick.'

'Any sign of Slade?'

'Not at this stage, Inspector.'

'Keep me posted,' said DI Henry. He slipped his phone back into his pocket. 'Do we know anybody down at Carrick?'

'We've worked with the locals a couple times,' said Wayne. 'Sgt Whitelaw's the officer in charge down there.'

'Apparently they've found Slade's car in the river. About twenty ks south of the town.'

'That's all scrubland around there,' said Wayne. 'Might pay to get them to search the area if his body isn't in the car.'

CHAPTER THIRTY-SIX

Philip Carol sat with his elbows on the desk and his chin resting on his hands. He listened in silence as Rodney Williams updated him on the interview he'd attended with Jack Swan.

'That's not good news about Gail,' said Philip. 'How did Jack take it?'

'He didn't want to talk about it,' said Rodney.

'What's your assessment of how he's taking it?'

'I'd say it came as a bit of a shock, especially the bit about her being shot.'

'So, definitely not an accident?'

'Not according to the police.'

'Wonder who told them Jack had introduced her to Richard Clarke,' said Philip.

'He was pretty adamant that hadn't happened.'

'Someone had to have introduced them.'

'More likely to have been Tony or Joe,' said Rodney. 'Wasn't she working with Joe on her business idea?'

Philip crossed his arms and leant back in his chair. 'Yes, but I guess she won't be telling them anything about that now.'

Philip waited for Rodney to leave his office before he called David Callinan.

'Dave, have you heard from Jack?'

'No.'

'Gail's dead,' said Philip. 'The police have just told Jack.'

'Shit! What happened?'

'Shot, apparently.'

'So, they keep their word, then.'

'You knew the rules when you signed on, Dave.'

'I know. I'm not complaining. It's just I liked Gail.'

'Well, she slipped up. Just make sure you don't.'

'Have you heard from Tony?' said David.

'No. Have you?'

'Jack says he's not answering his phone. Do you think they've taken him out as well?'

'I haven't heard anything, Dave. Then again, they didn't tell us about Gail either. What do you think?'

'I'm starting to think he could be a liability,' said David. 'They're talking about him on the radio and TV all the time.'

'Leave that to them,' said Philip. 'Best we aren't involved in that side of the business. Speaking of business, have you had any luck with Barry Yorke?'

'I've got a meeting with him in the morning. They're interested in exploring options.'

'Let me know how it goes.'

Philip ended the call and looked out across the urban forest, thankful something was going right for them. If the Yorke Group signed on, they'd be able to forget the casino operation and concentrate on moving their funds into financing property development projects.

Philip's thoughts were interrupted by the ringing of the telephone on his desk.

'Mr Carol, there's a policeman here to see you.'

'What's his name?'

'Detective Paterson. Says he's got a search warrant.'

'Send him in.'

Philip waited, wondering why a detective would show up at his door with a search warrant, while his secretary ushered in a tall man wearing a crumpled grey suit and holding a folder in his left hand.

'Who are you?' said Philip, as the detective walked into his office.

'Detective Constable Paterson,' said the detective, showing him his ID. 'I'm from Major Crimes.'

'What's this about a search warrant?'

'I have one,' said the detective, 'but whether I use it or not depends on you, Mr Carol.'

'Fair enough. Tell me what you're looking for and I'll decide if you'll need to use it.'

The detective sat down and opened his folder. 'I'm investigating the accounts of a company called EPS Property Pty Ltd, which I assume is one of your clients.'

'Oh, what makes you think that?' said Philip, recognizing the name of the vehicle they'd set up for investing the proceeds of the casino operation.

'They've paid quite a lot of money into your trust account, Mr Carol.'

'We have several trust accounts,' said Philip. 'Which one are you talking about?'

The detective handed him a piece of paper. 'This one.'

Philip looked at the account details printed on the page. 'That's the account we use for property settlements.'

'Can you tell me what this money was used for?' The detective pointed at the three transactions listed on the page he'd placed on Philip's desk.

'I might have to talk to my client about that first.'

'If they're property transactions, there shouldn't be any client sensitive information, Mr Carol. All property transactions are listed on the public record at the Land Titles Office,' said the detective. 'Besides, if you need a legal excuse for your client, we can use my warrant.'

'I don't think that will be necessary,' said Philip, deciding it would be better to cooperate than to give the detective an excuse to think he was trying to hide something.

The detective smiled.

'Give me a minute.' Philip turned to his computer and opened the EPS Property account and scrolled to the section on property settlements. 'The first amount you have there was used to buy a house at 35 Wisteria Avenue, East Park.' He clicked the mouse several times and looked at the transaction details again. 'The second amount was used to purchase an apartment building at 23 Highland Street, Portside.' He clicked the mouse again. 'The third amount is still sitting in our trust account. It's earmarked for a settlement next month on a house at 67 Whale Street, Morton Sands.'

'Do you think I could have a print out of that information?'

Philip printed the details of the transactions and handed them to the detective.

'Do you deal with this client personally?' said the detective, as he slipped the pages Philip had given him into his folder.

'No. Property transactions are handled by our conveyancing department.'

'But you do help people set up companies like this, don't you?'

'That's a service we provide,' said Philip.

'Did you set up this company?'

Philip returned to his computer screen. 'It looks like we did.'

'The people behind this company have been charged with money laundering,' said the detective. 'It's possible the Prosecutors Office will move to freeze those funds in your trust account.'

'I hope not,' said Philip. 'That would inconvenience my client and the vendors.'

'They may wait until they have a conviction before they seize any assets,' said the detective. 'I'm not sure of their processes.'

'That would be prudent,' said Philip, 'otherwise we'll be challenging any attempt to freeze those funds in the courts.'

————

Philip sat and brooded. The police had obviously been data mining the bank accounts of the group they'd charged with money laundering. He wondered how many other connections they'd unearthed. He guessed they'd be aware of Slade's links to the poker players and possibly to Gail, but she wouldn't be telling them anything. He hoped the others understood they'd suffer her fate if they said anything out of line.

He decided it would be a setback if the Prosecutors Office seized the properties they'd purchased with the money they'd washed through the casino, but it wouldn't be a major disaster. They'd have to write it off as a cost of doing business but, once they started funnelling the syndicate's money into property development projects across the city, there would be more than enough legitimate money to go around. At least he hoped they'd see it that way.

He worried about Joe Lombardo. He was still in the Remand Centre, unlike the others who had been released on bail. Would he hold himself together while he was awaiting trial? He seemed okay the last time he'd met with him to update him on the progress of his case. He wondered if Joe knew about Gail and assumed he did, given his close association with Tony.

He thought of Peter Thompson and wondered why he'd

chosen someone else to represent him, instead of calling him as he'd been instructed. Then, he remembered something Rodney had said about the police claiming someone had told them Jack had introduced Gail to Richard Clarke. Not many would know about that, and it occurred to him that Peter would be one that did.

Philip picked up his mobile phone and opened his list of contacts. He found the name he wanted and pushed the call button.

'Thompson's talking to the police.'

'What makes you think that?'

'He's not using us as his lawyer, and the police let slip some information in their last interview with Swan.'

'Okay. I'll take care of it.'

CHAPTER THIRTY-SEVEN

Nigel and Lisa walked into Citywide Parcels, expecting to see a hive of activity but there was only one person sitting in the office open to the public. Nigel introduced himself and showed her his ID.

'How does your operation work?' said Nigel.

'We've migrated onto an app,' said the woman. 'Customers log their job. Our drivers bid for the jobs, and then pick up and deliver the ones they get. Payments are all automated through the app.'

'Does anyone drop parcels off here?'

'We still have a few people doing that but all our regulars are on the app.'

'How long has that been the set-up?'

'We switched to the app at the start of the year.'

'Does that mean every job processed through your app can be traced?' said Nigel.

'Sure, does.'

'Does it give you a record of what each driver has done?'

'Yeah.'

'What about before you had the app? Did you keep records of what each driver was doing?'

'Yeah. That's how we worked out how much to pay them,' said the woman. 'Now it's all done by the app, apart from the odd job that gets dropped off here.'

'So, if I were to give you a driver's name, you could give me a list of the jobs he'd done listing the customer and the delivery address?'

The woman smiled. 'If you had a search warrant, I suppose I could do that.'

'James Weir,' said Nigel, placing the search warrant on the counter for her to read.

'How far back do you want to go?' said the woman.

'Can you do five years?'

'I think so,' said the woman. 'We have to keep records that far back for the Tax Office.'

'How long will that take?'

'Maybe ten minutes,' said the woman. 'How would you like the output? I can print it or give it to you as a csv file.'

'I'll take the file,' said Nigel, handing her a thumb drive.

The woman pulled up James Weir's records and exported them to the thumb drive as a comma-separated values file. 'You'll need to import that into your spreadsheet program when you open it.'

'Thanks,' said Nigel.

'Is there anything to stop your drivers picking up and delivering packages that don't come through your system?' said Lisa.

'Some of them work for other companies besides us,' said the woman, 'and there's nothing to stop them doing a job for cash.'

Nigel inserted the thumb drive into the usb port on his computer and imported the csv file. He formatted the contents and saved the file as a spreadsheet. Then, he searched the spreadsheet for Tony Slade's addresses in Appleby and East Park. There was no record of James Weir making a delivery to either address on behalf of Citywide Parcels.

He checked to see if Weir had ever picked up a package from either address. Again, there was no record.

He checked to see if there were any records of Weir making a delivery to Peter Thompson's address. Nothing.

Nigel sorted the data in date order. Then he noticed something. There were no Fridays listed. It looked like Weir worked a four-day week. He wondered whether that had any significance.

Nigel took his findings to DS Fuller.

'Whatever he was delivering to Slade and Thompson wasn't recorded by Citywide, Sarge.'

'Thompson told us it was the money for the poker games,' said DS Fuller.

'If they were playing poker most nights after seven thirty,' said Nigel, 'I wonder what time Slade started at the Merlin.'

'If he started there at all,' said DS Fuller. 'According to Wayne, Rileys are still paying Slade despite telling us he stopped working there six months ago.'

'Maybe he's employed in some other capacity,' said Nigel.

'See what you can find out about the Rileys,' said DS Fuller. 'They wouldn't be the first nightclub operators to be mixed up in a few other activities.'

'Oh, and there was one other thing, Sarge. Looks like Weir works a four-day week. There are no Friday deliveries listed in this data.'

'Guess he can afford it,' said DS Fuller, 'given the amount of money he's been paid for playing poker.'

CHAPTER THIRTY-EIGHT

Harry scrolled through satellite images of Slade Station. It was barren country and he wondered how anyone made a living running sheep in such a desolate place. There didn't appear to be many places a person could hide, unless they liked camping out in the open. He zoomed in on an image of the homestead. The collection of buildings looked more like a small village than a homestead. There were half a dozen houses and as many large sheds grouped around a ring of large water tanks. Harry guessed they'd be using artesian water, supplemented with rainwater whenever it was available, which he knew wasn't that often in that part of the world.

He clicked on the next image, and stopped. He was looking at an airstrip with three small aeroplanes and a helicopter parked in front of a large shed. He zoomed in on each of the aircraft and enhanced their registration numbers.

Harry knew it wasn't uncommon for stations in the north of the state to have airfields or aircraft, and he wasn't overly surprised by what he was looking at, but he wondered why they'd have three twin-engine planes and a helicopter. He knew helicopters were used for mustering but he thought three aeroplanes might be a bit extravagant, unless they belonged to visitors.

Opening another window on his computer, he keyed the first registration number into the Civil Aviation Register. The registration holder was listed as Slade Pastoral Holdings Pty Ltd. He keyed in the other two numbers. Both aircraft were also registered to Slade Pastoral Holdings Pty Ltd.

Must be more money in sheep than I imagined, thought Harry. He looked up the number for Hastings Airfield, which was used by light aircraft flying to and from City. After a few redirects, he reached the person he wanted to talk to and explained his inquiry.

'There's at least one flight a week down and back by one of those aircraft, Sergeant.'

'Is that unusual for property owners in that part of the world?' said Harry.

'Slade Station would be our most frequent visitor from the station country up north.'

'Do they have to submit a flight plan for each flight?' said Harry.

'Yes, but that's all done online these days.'

Harry filed that for future reference. 'When do you expect their next flight?'

'There's usually one Friday morning. Gets in around eleven.'

'Thanks,' said Harry.

He swivelled his chair to face Nigel. 'Got a job for you, Nigel. I want you to be at Hastings Airfield tomorrow morning around eleven. One of these planes from Slade Station is due to land around that time. Take your camera. I want to know who gets off it and who meets them.' He handed Nigel the piece of paper with the aircraft registration numbers written on it. 'Run these through the Civil Aviation Register. It'll give you the aircraft type details.'

Wearing a black leather bomber jacket and jeans, and with his baseball cap on backwards, Nigel positioned himself in front of the terminal building at Hastings, from where he could watch planes land and take off. He opened the camera bag he'd placed at his feet, set up his DSLR camera with its telephoto lens, and snapped shots of each aircraft as it came in to land.

At eleven ten, the plane he was waiting for landed and taxied towards the hanger adjacent to the terminal building. Nigel adjusted his viewing angle. When the plane came to a halt and the pilot shutdown the engines, a white van drove onto the tarmac from the other side of the hanger. He took a clear shot of the registration number of the van, and of James Weir as he climbed out of the van and slid open its side door.

He turned his attention back to the aircraft and took several shots of the pilot, including a close up of his face. Nigel thought the man looked like an older version of Tony Slade and assumed it was one of Slade's brothers. He watched the pilot transfer two suitcases from the hold of the aircraft to James Weir's van. The man's obvious effort with each case caught Nigel's attention and suggested they contained something other than clothing.

As he watched, the two men spoke briefly and then loaded several boxes and two suitcases into the aircraft from the back of the van. The ease with which Weir handled the suitcases suggested to Nigel they had to be empty.

When he finished loading, the pilot climbed back into the aircraft, started the engines, and taxied over to a refuelling point. As the aircraft moved away, James Weir got into his van and drove out of sight around the far side of the hanger.

Nigel packed up his equipment and rushed to his car in the car park behind the terminal building. There was only one way out of the airfield, and it didn't take long for Nigel to spot Weir's van three cars ahead of him on the highway back into City.

He used the hands-free phone button on the steering wheel and called DS Fuller.

'The plane was met by Weir,' said Nigel. 'He's picked up a couple of bags. I'm following him back towards the city.'

'Where are you?' said DS Fuller.

'Main North Road, just gone over Lane Road.'

'Stay with him,' said DS Fuller. 'I'll get you some back up.'

Nigel slipped into tailing mode, keeping several cars between him and the van as Weir drove towards the city centre and then took the ring route, before turning onto East Park Road. Nigel realized he was heading towards his home address. He pushed the call button on the steering wheel and selected DS Fuller's number.

'I think he's going home, Sarge. We're in East Park.'

'Call me if he does,' said DS Fuller. 'I'll get Wayne and Lisa to take over.'

Weir turned into Rose Street, slowed, and then turned into the driveway of his house at number fifteen. Nigel continued up the street and turned right at the next intersection.

He called DS Fuller and waited until Wayne and Lisa pulled up opposite him and started to eat their lunch. He waved and then headed for Police Headquarters.

———

Wayne and Lisa had barely finished their lunch when Weir backed his van out into Rose Street and drove away from them towards East Park Road.

Lisa started the engine and turned into Rose Street.

Wayne picked up the radio handset. 'He's on the move.'

'Looks like he's heading into town,' said Lisa.

'Don't get too close,' said Wayne.

Lisa moved into the left lane and let the car behind her overtake them.

Weir drove into the city and made his way to South Terrace, where he parked alongside a food truck opposite St Catherine's College. Lisa pulled into a parking space several car lengths back from the food truck.

Wayne got out of the car and pretended he was making a purchase from the parking ticket machine on the footpath. Lisa stood next to the car as if she was waiting for Wayne to come back with the parking ticket. They both watched as Weir handed a package to the person inside the food truck and took the envelope that was passed out to him.

Wayne pulled out his mobile phone and called DS Fuller.

'He's delivering packages to food trucks,' said Wayne.

'Find out what he's delivering,' said DS Fuller.

They waited until Weir had driven away and then approached the food truck. The signage advertised kebabs, salads, and ice cream. There were two young men standing inside the truck. One of them was roasting the lamb for the kebabs. The other was closing the door of a cupboard below their cash register.

'Hi! What can we get you?' said the man standing by the cash register.

'I'll have the package that was just delivered,' said Wayne, holding up his ID.

'What?'

'The package,' said Wayne.

The man roasting the lamb turned towards Wayne with a carving knife in his hand.

Wayne undid the button of his jacket so they could see his shoulder holster.

Lisa made a show of taking out her mobile phone. She called Operations and spoke loud enough for the men to hear her. 'We need armed backup outside St Catherine's on South Terrace.' She paused to listen. 'It's a red food truck.'

A siren sounded in the distance. The men looked at each other.

'You're not going anywhere,' said Wayne. 'Hand over the package.'

The sound of the siren got louder and then abruptly ceased. A patrol car with flashing blue lights stopped behind Wayne and two officers got out with their pistols drawn.

The man standing by the cash register opened the cupboard he'd closed as Wayne had walked up to the truck and placed a brown paper envelope on the counter. Wayne pulled on latex gloves and opened the envelope and looked inside.

The envelope was full of small plastic bags of white powder.

'What is this stuff?' said Wayne.

'Crystal meth.'

'Thought so,' said Wayne. 'Step outside, boys.'

'What about our truck?'

'We'll take good care of it,' said Wayne. 'And, boys, keep your hands where we can see them.'

When the men had been taken away, Wayne called Operations and arranged for the truck to be impounded, then he called DS Fuller.

'It's crystal meth, Sarge. Do you want us to follow up Weir?'

'The boss wants the source,' said DS Fuller. 'We know where to find Weir and, besides, he has to report in weekly as part of his bail. We can pick him up anytime.'

CHAPTER THIRTY-NINE

Harry had just finished talking to Wayne when his phone rang again.

'Is that Detective Sergeant Fuller?'

'Yes,' said Harry.

'It's Barry Yorke, Sergeant. You asked me to let you know if anyone approached me to take over what Doug Clarke did for us.'

Harry picked up his pen. 'And, has someone approached you Mr Yorke?'

'I had a meeting this morning with David Callinan. He's an East Park accountant,' said Barry. 'He introduced himself as the new manager of Clarke Finance.'

'Is he working for Mrs Clarke?'

'No. She's sold the business to a group of his clients and they're looking to expand. Apparently, they have access to a lot more money.'

'Did he mention who his clients were, Mr Yorke?'

'We didn't go into that,' said Barry. 'If we do business with them, our contracts will be between us and Clarke Finance. We leave the micro money management to them.'

'What sort of money are they talking about?'

'They're offering to finance our Portside development, and we're looking for fifteen million dollars,' said Barry.

'Thanks for letting me know, Mr Yorke.'

Harry walked over to DI Henry's office.

'I've just had a call from Barry Yorke, Inspector. Appears Doug Clarke's widow has sold her husband's business.'

'Is that a concern?' said DI Henry.

'Not a hundred percent sure,' said Harry, 'but she had been adamant that she wanted to keep it for herself.'

'Was that before or after her son died?'

'Before.'

'Perhaps she changed her mind after he died,' said DI Henry.

'I guess that would have changed things,' said Harry. 'It's just that David Callinan, who reported Doug Clarke to the Local Government Authority when he was mayor, is now the manager of Clarke Finance.'

'Why is that a problem, Harry?'

'Callinan is now the mayor of East Park.'

'What was his beef with Clarke?'

'Conflict of interest. Claimed Clarke was lobbying the development approvals committee on behalf of some of the developers he was financing.'

'I guess that's a problem the council will deal with,' said DI Henry. 'Don't see what it has to do with us.'

'Callinan had advised Gail Swan, Inspector. She was trying to buy Clarke Finance before Doug Clarke was killed. She must have been fronting a group of investors, seeing as she didn't have the money to buy it.'

DI Henry scratched his chin. 'You think this Callinan might be fronting the same group of investors?'

'It's possible,' said Harry.

'Guess it won't hurt to ask Mrs Clarke who bought her business,' said DI Henry.

———

Harry parked in front of 14 Orange Drive, East Park. He hadn't expected to see the sign advertising the house for sale attached to the front fence. He walked up the driveway and rang the doorbell.

Joanna Clarke opened the door. She was accompanied by a young boy with blonde hair.

'Oh, hello, Sergeant. This is my grandson, Dougie.'

'Hello, Dougie,' said Harry.

Dougie smiled and ducked behind his grandmother.

'He won't hurt you,' said Joanna. 'He's a policeman.'

They made their way into the sitting room, opposite the library.

'I suppose you saw the sign,' said Joanna. 'This place has too many memories.'

'Where are you planning to go?'

'I've signed a contract for an apartment on South Terrace. I want to be close enough to help Kathy with Dougie.'

'How is she?' said Harry.

'She's taken over the real estate business so Justin can concentrate on his campaign,' said Joanna, 'and when that's over, we'll probably sell that too.'

'I wanted to ask you who bought your finance business,' said Harry.

'Why do you want to know that?'

'You're aware Gail Swan is dead, aren't you?'

'Yes. I saw that in the paper.'

'Well, she was trying to buy it with someone else's money,' said Harry.

'And, you think they got someone else to buy it for them?' said Joanna.

'That thought did cross my mind.'

'The business was bought by my lawyer and his accountant,' said Joanna.

'I've met your lawyer, Mrs Clarke. Who's his accountant?'

'David Callinan. He was deputy mayor to Doug.'

'Were you surprised he wanted to buy it?'

'Why would I be?' said Joanna.

'David Callinan reported your husband to the Local Government Authority for financing development projects in East Park.'

'Did he? Doug never said anything.'

'Perhaps your husband didn't know,' said Harry.

'Are you any closer to finding?' Joanna looked at Dougie. 'You know what I mean, Sergeant?'

'We think we know who,' said Harry. 'We just have to find him.'

'You will let me know when you do, won't you?'

'Yes,' said Harry. 'Thanks for making time to see me.'

CHAPTER FORTY

Carl joined DI Henry and his team to discuss the latest developments in the Clarke case and to plan their next move.

'What's the latest on Slade?' said Carl.

'We think he's gone north,' said DI Henry. 'There was no sign of him where his car was found down south. Best guess is the car was dumped down there. There was nothing in it.'

'You thinking he flew home on one of those flights DS Fuller found out about?'

'Would explain why no-one's seen him down here,' said DS Fuller. 'And, it's possible he's been a frequent visitor up there despite what his father told us.'

'It's starting to make sense,' said DI Henry, 'now we know those flights are bringing crystal meth down to the city.'

'Explains the money,' said Carl, 'but it's going to create one hell of a headache for the Commissioner if the Right Honourable Member is involved.'

'One step at a time, Chief,' said DI Henry. 'We have to get some facts first. We're going to have to pay the Slades a visit.'

'Is that going to be a problem?'

'It's going to be difficult to arrive unannounced, given the location of their station, Chief. Slade could disappear into the bush before we even get there.'

'How far away is it?'

'Touch over five hundred ks,' said DI Henry.

'Bit far for the helicopters,' said Carl.

'Not if they refuel on the way back,' said DC Beard. 'They could stop at Port Stanley at the top of the gulf. That's only a hundred and fifty ks from the Slade homestead.'

'Let's get Special Operations involved,' said Carl. 'We're going to have to approach from the ground as well as the air, and we don't know how heavily armed these people are.'

'We need to move before they hear about today's arrest,' said DI Henry.

'That might not be possible,' said Carl. 'This is going to take some time to pull together.'

'We can keep those boys for forty-eight hours,' said DI Henry, 'before we have to charge them.'

'Let's do that and keep our fingers crossed. I'll set up a meeting with Special Operations and get this thing on the road. Hopefully, we can execute over the weekend.' Carl stood up. 'Anything else I should know?'

'I had a call from Barry Yorke,' said DS Fuller. 'David Callinan has taken over as manager of Clarke Finance.'

'That's interesting,' said Carl. 'Is he working for Mrs Clarke?'

'No. She sold out to Callinan and Philip Carol.'

'I guess they must have raised the amount she wanted,' said Carl.

'I wonder if Gail Swan was working for them all along,' said DS Fuller.

'Something to think about,' said Carl.

Harry sat in the back of the police helicopter, thankful for the heavy-duty headphones, and watched the red countryside slide by below them. In the distance, he made out the path of a dry watercourse, marked by a snaking line of green trees. Cruising at just over two hundred and fifty kilometres per hour, it had taken them a little over two hours to traverse the distance from the city to the Slade homestead.

The helicopter Harry was travelling in circled above the homestead. The helicopter transporting DI Henry landed in a cloud of red dust next to the airstrip. Harry watched as it disgorged its party of armed officers and then rose back into the air.

The officer sitting in front of him slid open the door of the helicopter and positioned himself with his weapon pointing out through the opening. As they came around for the second time, Harry spotted the vehicles of the ground team heading up the main drive towards the homestead. He looked down and saw people congregating in small groups outside the houses below him.

'We have a runner at ten o'clock,' said the observer sitting next to the pilot.

Harry turned his head and looked out through the left-hand side window. There was a man on a motor bike riding away from the homestead settlement. The helicopter banked to the left and slowed to hover above the fugitive, with its open door facing towards him. The sharpshooter made himself and his weapon visible in the open doorway. The motor bike rider looked up at the helicopter and then turned away.

'Police! Stop!'

Harry heard the command boom from the loud hailer attached to the underside of the helicopter. The man on the motor bike kept going, kicking up a cloud of red dust behind him.

The pilot lowered the helicopter closer to the ground. Red

dust swirled around the man on the motor bike caught in the downwash from the helicopter's rotors. The motor bike rider stopped and looked away from the helicopter.

The observer spoke into the microphone connected to the loudhailer. 'Go back to the homestead!'

The pilot increased altitude but maintained station adjacent to the motor bike. The man turned the motor bike around and rode back towards the homestead.

Harry watched until the man was intercepted by an officer on the ground, then the pilot swung the machine back towards the station's airfield and they landed.

As the vehicles of the ground party arrived and officers swarmed over the buildings of the homestead, the second helicopter landed on the airstrip, blocking any possibility of someone attempting to leave by plane.

It took around ten minutes for the Special Operations officers to round up the dozen or so people living in the various buildings of the homestead complex and gather them into the common space between the buildings.

When the man who had attempted to flee on the motor bike was identified as Tony Slade, he was arrested and placed in the rear of one of the police vehicles.

'Which one of you is Angus Slade?' said DI Henry.

'Me,' said a man, pushing his hat back on his head. 'I'm Angus.'

'I have a search warrant,' said DI Henry, handing the warrant to Angus.

Angus passed the warrant to his wife. 'What does this say?'

'It's a search warrant. Says they're looking for drugs.' She handed the paper back to DI Henry.

'You've come a long way to find nothing,' said Angus.

'We'll see,' said DI Henry. 'I'd like everybody to stay here while we search.'

'Can we sit on the veranda of the main house?' said Angus. 'It's going to take you a while to look around.'

'After we've searched the house,' said DI Henry, turning to the Special Operations Inspector. 'Get the dogs.'

They waited in the mid-morning sun as one dog handler and his dog searched the main house and the other started on the nearest shed.

Twenty minutes later, DI Henry allowed the Slades to move out of the sun and onto the veranda of the house.

Harry stayed with the Special Operations Inspector.

After thirty-five minutes, one of the Special Operations officers walked up to his inspector.

'In that shed over there, Inspector.' He pointed to the shed nearest to the airstrip and furthest from the main house.

Harry accompanied the inspector to the shed. When they entered the building, the first thing Harry noticed was a smell that reminded him of the fertilizer his father had used on his vegetable garden.

'Meth lab in the far corner, Inspector,' said the dog handler. 'Biggest one I've seen.'

'Okay, get Forensics in,' said the inspector. He turned to Harry. 'Looks like your lucky day, Sergeant.'

———

In addition to the meth lab, the search uncovered a small arsenal of rifles and shotguns locked in gun cabinets in each house. DI Henry assumed the Slades must have believed they were protected by distance and hadn't thought about being raided by the police.

Special Operations copied the hard drives of every computer and mobile phone they could find, and collected fingerprints from every adult member of the homestead community.

DI Henry approached Angus Slade. 'What's going on here, Mr Slade?'

'I'm not answering any questions until I've spoken to my lawyer,' said Angus.

'Does your father live here when he's not in parliament?' said DI Henry.

'My parents live in Port Stanley,' said Angus. 'I've been running the place for the last twenty years, ever since Dad was elected.'

'Does he know what you're up to?' said DI Henry.

'Like I said, mate. I'm not answering any of your questions until I've seen my lawyer.'

'Is this lawyer in Port Stanley or somewhere else?' said DI Henry.

'He's down in the city,' said Angus. 'Perhaps you've heard of him. His name's Philip Carol.'

'Well, I hope he'll come up to Port Stanley for you,' said DI Henry. 'The only one of you going down to the city is Tony, since he's wanted for murder.'

'You do what you have to do, mate,' said Angus. 'As long as someone gets to stay here to look after the animals.'

'We'll be taking everyone to Port Stanley,' said DI Henry. 'You'll have to get someone out here to look after your animals.'

'That might not be possible,' said Angus.

'Well, I can't leave unaccompanied minors here,' said DI Henry. 'Besides, you'll probably be out on bail within a couple days.'

Special Operations herded the Slades into a collection of farm and police vehicles and the convoy set off for Port Stanley.

———

DI Henry and DS Fuller travelled to Port Stanley by helicopter and set up office in the police station, from where DI Henry called Chief Inspector West.

'I'm sending Tony Slade back with the helicopters, Chief. Harry and I will stay here to oversee the processing of the people associated with the meth lab.'

'How many have you got, Paul?'

'Ten adults and four kids, Chief. The kids are waiting for their grandmother to come and collect them.'

'Are they cooperating?'

'They won't talk without their lawyer,' said DI Henry, 'and, get this. Their lawyer is Philip Carol.'

'Guess you'll be seeing one of his associates, Paul. Can't imagine him travelling to Port Stanley.'

'Might depend on how important the Slades are to him as clients.'

'Any sign the Right Honourable Member is involved?'

'He's lived off the station in Port Stanley for the last twenty years,' said DI Henry, 'but we'll have to wait and see what comes out in the wash.'

'What's it like up there, Paul? I haven't been up there for years.'

'It's still hot and dusty, but there's a new motel a couple of blocks from the station. Hopefully, there'll be something decent to eat up here.'

'I'm sure there'll be something.'

'I'll give you a call tomorrow, Chief.'

DI Henry ended the call and pictured Carl West sitting at home enjoying his Sunday afternoon, while he was sitting in a room with a noisy air conditioner and a desk covered in fine red dust. He hoped the new motel had better room service than the police station.

CHAPTER FORTY-ONE

Nigel turned into Rose Street behind the patrol cars. The street was deserted, which didn't surprise him. It was, after all, five minutes to six on a Sunday morning when most people were still in their beds. He waited beside his car as the four arresting officers entered the driveway of number fifteen. Two of them, pistols drawn, disappeared around the back of the house.

They had no idea if Weir was armed or not. Nigel hoped he wouldn't do anything stupid.

A loud banging shattered the early morning silence, as the officers at the front of the house thumped on the wooden door.

'Police! Open up!'

A gap appeared in the venetian blind of one of the front windows.

'Police!' The officer banged on the door again. 'Open up or I'll knock it down!'

The gap in the blind disappeared and a few moments later the front door opened. James Weir, dressed in a white tee shirt and red boxer shorts, stood with the door in his left hand and stared at the officers standing on his doorstep.

'Hands on your head!'

Weir complied. The officer patted him down.

'James Weir?' said the officer.

'Yeah.'

'You're under arrest.'

'What for?'

'Drugs,' said the officer, grabbing Weir's arm, before turning him around and handcuffing him.

'Where are your keys?' said the officer.

'On the bench in the kitchen.'

The officer led Weir to his patrol car and locked him in the back, while his colleague retrieved Weir's keys.

'All yours,' said the second officer, handing Weir's keys to Nigel. 'We'll take him in and book him.'

The two officers who had covered the rear exit emerged from behind the house and set about sealing off the entrance to the property with crime scene tape.

As the patrol car transporting Weir departed, a white van pulled in behind Nigel's silver Ford and three crime scene investigators climbed out.

Nigel handed the senior constable leading the team Weir's keys. 'The house and his vehicle.'

'Leave it with me, Nigel. I'll send you the report.'

Nigel turned towards the small gathering of neighbours who had been roused from their sleep. 'Nothing to see here, folks. Nothing to worry about.'

CHAPTER FORTY-TWO

It was dark when Peter Thompson returned home from visiting his elderly mother in the Carrick Nursing Home. It had been another upsetting visit. She hadn't remembered who he was and had kept asking for her husband, who had been dead for eleven years.

Peter wasn't sure how many more visits he'd be able to sit through. He thought about what his sister had said about it all being a waste of time after she'd stopped going. He didn't think he could do that. As far as he was concerned, it wasn't right for someone stuck in a nursing home not to have any visitors, even if she didn't remember who her visitors were.

He didn't want to abandon his mother. After all, she hadn't abandoned him when he'd been stuck in prison. She'd been his only visitor during those five long years of shame. He consoled himself with the thought that at least she wouldn't know anything about it this time, if he was sent to prison again.

He pulled into his driveway and parked under the carport. The automatic light didn't come on. Peter thought the heat activated switch had failed again or that perhaps the globe had blown and made a mental note to check it after he'd had something to eat. He switched off the engine, killed the headlights, and climbed out of the car. As he closed the door, he felt two strong hands grab his shoulders. Then his head slammed into the roof of the car. His legs buckled and he collapsed onto the ground next to the car.

He felt a sharp pain in his ribs, and realized his assailant had kicked him.

He felt the weight of his attacker drop onto his belly. He gasped for air.

He felt a fire in his guts. Then the scene was flooded in light, as the faulty automatic light switch activated the one-hundred-and-fifty-watt globe in the carport. Peter blinked and looked up at the man standing over him with a knife in his hand. He thought he recognized his assailant. Then everything went black.

———

Peter opened his eyes and shut them again. There was a bright light shining straight at him from the far corner of the carport. He didn't know how long he'd been lying on the concrete. He opened his eyes again and looked away from the light. His head hurt. His guts hurt. He moved his right hand to his belly. He felt something wet and sticky as he touched his abdomen. He lifted his hand. It was covered in blood.

The memory of the attack came back to him and he remembered being stabbed. He tried to sit up but the effort was too much for him. He slumped back onto the concrete. He realized he needed help.

Keeping his eyes away from the light, he wiped his hand on his trousers, and felt inside his pocket for his mobile phone. He looked at the phone, pressed the home button, and waited for the screen to light up. He felt an immediate sense of relief when it did.

He pushed zero three times and waited.

'Emergency. Which service do you require?'

'I need an ambulance! I've been stabbed!'

CHAPTER FORTY-THREE

With DI Henry and DS Fuller in Port Stanley, Carl decided to interview Tony Slade with DC Paterson. When he arrived at the interview suite, Philip Carol was sitting next to Slade across the table from DC Paterson.

'What are you charging my client with, Chief Inspector?'

'Murder.'

'That's a serious charge to make,' said Philip. 'Who is he supposed to have killed?'

'Doug Clarke,' said Carl.

'That's ridiculous,' said Philip. 'He has an alibi for the day Clarke was killed.'

Carl placed the report he'd received from Forensics onto the table between them. 'Not according to this.' He turned it around so Philip could read it. 'This is a comparison of your client's DNA profile with a DNA profile extracted from a shirt covered in Doug Clarke's blood.'

'Where is this shirt?' said Philip.

Carl lifted the evidence bag he'd brought with him onto the

table. 'This was recovered from a rubbish bin at Gail Swan's home in Ashcroft.'

'I've never been to Ashcroft,' said Tony.

'That may be so,' said Carl, 'but your mate Joe Lombardo's been there.'

'Joe's been a lot of places.'

'But he didn't drive Doug Clarke's car to many of them.'

'I didn't know he'd driven Doug's car anywhere,' said Tony.

'Your problem, Mr Slade, is someone killed Gail Swan before she got around to putting her bin out for collection.'

'It wasn't me. I liked Gail.'

'How about we go back to the beginning?' said Carl. 'Tell me where you were on the morning of Saturday, the eighth of September.'

'Home,' said Tony.

'Home in East Park or up on the station?'

'East Park. Joe was there. We didn't go out until after lunch.'

'Is there anybody else who could vouch for you?' said Carl. 'Joe's been charged with being an accomplice, so he's not exactly a reliable alibi.'

'Maybe one of the neighbours. I always park in the street. They would have seen my car.'

'Ever go out in Joe's car?' said Carl.

'Yeah.'

'And where would your car have been when you were out with Joe?'

'Oh, but his car would have been there that morning too.'

Carl smiled. 'Where were you on the evening of Monday, the twenty-fourth of September, around six?'

'I went to Gloria's with Joe that night, I think,' said Tony.

'Do you remember following Richard Clarke's car that evening?'

'I wasn't driving. We went in Joe's car.'

'I gather you're quite a regular at Gloria's,' said Carl.

'I lived up there when I was married. Gloria's is still my favourite place to eat.'

'When was the last time you were there?'

'The night you mentioned,' said Tony. 'I went up to the station after that.'

'Did you see your father while you were up there?'

'I didn't go into Port Stanley,' said Tony. 'Too many people know me.'

'Tell me about your relationship with Mark Riley.'

'I worked for him in security,' said Tony. 'I quit about six months ago.'

'Why is he still paying you?'

'Is he?' said Tony.

'We traced the funds going into your account at B and A.'

'You'll have to ask him. It must be some mistake.'

'Tell me about the East Park Syndicate,' said Carl. 'How did you get together with the others?'

'We met at the casino,' said Tony, 'and Richard persuaded us to invest our winnings in real estate. We've already bought a couple of places.'

'So I hear,' said Carl, 'but what I'd like to know is where the money comes from.'

'What money?'

'The cash you take to the casino each night you play.'

Tony looked down at the floor. 'I think you know.'

'I want you to tell me,' said Carl.

'You don't have to tell him anything,' said Philip.

'Bit hard to deny it now, don't you think? They raided the station yesterday. They'll know everything soon.'

'Who's in charge of the distribution network?' said Carl.

'I can't tell you that,' said Tony.

'Can't or won't?'

'I don't know who it is,' said Tony.

'What was your role?'

'Investing the money.'

'Were you behind Gail's attempt to buy Clarke Finance?'

'I offered to finance her,' said Tony, 'but he wouldn't sell.'

'Is that why you killed him?'

'I didn't kill him,' said Tony.

'The evidence points to you,' said Carl. 'You stabbed him and Joe dumped the body and disposed of the car.'

'Wasn't me,' said Tony.

'How do you explain the shirt?' said Carl.

'Maybe Joe wore it over his clothes.'

Carl leant back and studied Tony's face. 'Are you telling me Joe Lombardo killed Doug Clarke wearing your clothes?'

'You don't have to answer that,' said Philip Carol.

'I'll take the rap for what I've done,' said Tony, 'but I'm not going down for murder.' He looked directly at Carl. 'I didn't kill anyone.'

'So, you don't deny being involved in money laundering?'

'No.'

'What was your role in manufacturing and distributing the drugs?'

'I knew where the money was coming from,' said Tony, 'but I had nothing to do with that side of the business.'

'Whose idea was EPS Property Pty Ltd?'

'Richard's,' said Tony. 'He introduced us to Mr Carol, who helped us set it up.'

'Is that correct, Mr Carol?' said Carl.

'We've been the Clarke's lawyers for years,' said Philip. 'It was only natural that Richard would recommend us to his partners but I had no idea the money was coming from drugs.'

'What makes you think Joe killed Doug Clarke, Mr Slade?' said Carl.

'He found out Gail was screwing Doug,' said Tony, 'and, he's one jealous bastard.'

'Why would he frame you for it?'

'That's a good question. Perhaps he didn't mean to if he'd thrown the shirt out.'

Carl picked up the evidence bag with the shirt in it. 'When was the last time you saw this shirt?'

'I remember wearing it to golf,' said Tony. 'I would have put it out to be washed after that.'

'Who does your laundry?'

'We have a girl come in who does that sort of stuff. Anna someone.' He smiled. 'Ask Joe. He pays her.'

'So, if I've understood you correctly, Mr Slade, you're telling me Joe wasn't home on the morning of the eighth of September?' said Carl.

'That's right. He wasn't home,' said Tony.

'That blows your alibi,' said Carl.

Tony shrugged. 'You didn't believe me anyway.'

'When did you find out Joe had killed Doug?'

'When I got home that Saturday. Doug's car was parked in the driveway behind Joe's.'

'How did Joe explain it being there?'

'He said Clarke had worked out where Gail's money was coming from and threatened to blackmail us, so he'd taken him out to protect us.'

Carl scratched his chin and wondered whether Tony was spinning him a tale or telling him the truth. 'What was Joe's role?'

'It was all his idea,' said Tony. 'He's our connection to the distributors and the people who supply the raw material for making the stuff.'

Carl looked across the table at Philip Carol. 'Are you alright, Mr Carol?'

'It's a bit stuffy in here,' said Philip.

Carl turned back to Tony Slade. 'You might want to consider engaging another lawyer, Mr Slade, seeing Mr Carol is also representing Joe.'

'Yeah. I thought that might be a problem.'

———

Carl sat at his desk pondering what he'd just learnt. He'd have to interview Joe Lombardo again and deny him access to his lawyer until he did. He picked up his telephone and called the Remand Centre to put that arrangement in place.

The look he'd seen on Philip Carol's face, when Tony Slade had confessed and told them Joe Lombardo had killed Doug Clarke, bothered him. It was more than a look of shock. It reminded Carl of the expressions of fear he'd seen on officers' faces before a raid.

He wondered what the lawyer might be afraid of. Maybe there was more to Tony's story than he had let on. Then he remembered what Harry had told him last Friday about Philip Carol and David Callinan buying out Clarke Finance and wondered where they'd raised the money.

The telephone on his desk rang.

'Chief Inspector West.'

'Operations, Chief. We've just had a call from City Hospital. They admitted a patient with a stab wound last night. He's stable, but he wants to talk to DS Fuller.'

'What's his name?'

'Peter Thompson. We've got him under guard in the IC unit. Claims he was attacked in his own driveway.'

'I'll get one of my people down there,' said Carl.

He called DC Paterson.

'Wayne, someone's got to Peter Thompson. He's in City

Hospital. Have a word with him and get him into witness protection.'

———

Nigel read the report from Forensics. They'd found traces of crystal meth in Weir's van and several kilograms of the drug in the second bedroom of his house, which Weir had turned into a packing room. In addition to the drugs, they'd found thirty thousand dollars in cash inside a suitcase, a mobile phone, and a laptop.

The report included a copy of a spreadsheet downloaded from the laptop, which detailed the places Weir delivered to and amounts he'd collected each week for the last two years.

Nigel smiled. The list would keep Uniform busy for a while when they passed it on to Operations.

He pulled up the latest call log they'd received for Weir's mobile phone and scrolled through the listings. Then he looked at the list of contacts Forensics had extracted from Weir's laptop. The first entry that caught his attention was the name Mark Riley. He ran his eyes down the list of contacts. There was no entry for the Merlin. He chuckled to himself. It didn't seem likely to Nigel that a delivery driver would have the manager's number and not the nightclub's number. He wondered what Weir would have to say about that little discrepancy.

He checked the call log again. Weir had called Mark Riley every Friday afternoon for as far back as the log went.

He searched the list of contacts looking for a Slade. There were two entries. One for Tony and another for Angus, and the call log revealed Weir had spoken to Angus every Thursday evening and to Tony every day right up until the end of September.

Nigel wondered how his predecessors had tracked down

criminals without access to their digital footprints. He knew it certainly would have taken them a lot longer to join the dots, and was thankful for what modern technology had gifted to his generation of investigators.

He looked across the desk at Lisa.

'Ready?'

'His lawyer won't be here for another ten minutes,' said Lisa.

'Well, take a look at this.'

Lisa studied the spreadsheet. 'Looks like he was making two types of deliveries going by the amount of money he collected.'

'What do you mean?' said Nigel.

Lisa inserted a column and used it to total the amounts in the rows next to each delivery address. Then she sorted the data using descending amount in the total column as the criteria. 'Most of the money is coming from those two places.'

'Let me check the addresses,' said Nigel. He keyed the first address into Google Maps. 'That's a house in Morton Sands.' He keyed in the second address. 'That looks like a warehouse in Northfield.'

'Let me look them up on Land Titles,' said Lisa. She opened another window on her computer and logged into the Land Titles system and keyed in the first address. 'The place in Northfield belongs to a Michael Riley.'

'That could be interesting.'

Lisa printed the record and keyed in the second address. 'The place in Morton Sands belongs to a Helen Carol.'

'I wonder if she's related to Philip Carol.'

Lisa looked at the details describing the owner of 67 Whale Street, Morton Sands. 'She'd be about his age.'

'Run a check with Births, Deaths, and Marriages,' said Nigel.

'That could take a while,' said Lisa.

Nigel looked at his watch. 'We can do that after the interview.'

As he took his seat opposite James Weir and his lawyer, Rodney Williams, Nigel thought Weir looked like a man who knew his story had been exposed for the lie it was. Lisa activated the recorder and stepped them through the preliminaries.

'My client wants it on the record that he's willing to cooperate,' said Rodney.

'Okay,' said Nigel, as he opened his folder and picked up one of the photographs he'd taken at Hastings Airfield. He placed the print where Weir could see it. 'Who were you meeting at Hastings last Friday morning, Mr Weir?'

'That's Charlie Slade.'

'And, what was in the suitcases he transferred into your van?'

'I think you know what was in them, otherwise we wouldn't be here, would we?'

Nigel slid the report from Forensics out of his folder and passed it to Weir, who handed it to his lawyer.

'Methamphetamine, according to our analysis of the cases and what was found in your house,' said Nigel. 'You are aware that's an illicit substance, aren't you, Mr Weir?'

'Yeah.'

'So, what were you doing with it?'

Weir twisted his hands together. 'I was paid to collect it from Hastings and deliver it.'

'Who to?'

'I don't know,' said Weir. 'I only have a list of addresses. I don't have any names.'

'You were followed to a food truck on South Terrace last Friday, Mr Weir, and I have a statement here from an Angelo Carletto, the operator of that food truck, admitting to giving you a cash payment for an amount of crystal meth.'

Weir shrugged his shoulders.

'I gather from your record keeping, and the amount of cash in your house, that your deliveries were cash on delivery. Is that right?'

'Yeah.'

'Was this the source of the money you used for playing poker at the casino?'

'We used some of it for poker.'

'What happened to the rest?'

'I gave it to Charlie when we met at Hastings.'

'What else did you give him?'

'Whatever he'd ordered,' said Weir. 'I only took it to the airport. I've got no idea what it was.'

'Where did you pick it up from?'

'Someone dropped the stuff off at my place Friday morning before I went to Hastings.'

'Do you know who dropped it off?'

'I never saw him,' said Weir. 'The stuff was always on my back veranda when I got up.' He looked at Nigel. 'You know how it is, mate. What you don't know you can't talk about.'

'How many food trucks were you running?'

'I wasn't running any.'

'That's not what Angelo Carletto told us,' said Nigel. 'According to his statement, he was dealing for you.'

'No-one was dealing for me,' said Weir. 'I was only the delivery boy.'

'Jack Swan in on this?'

'I only know Jack through poker,' said Weir.

'What about Peter Thompson?'

'I met him through Jack,' said Weir.

'What about Tony Slade?'

'I was working for him,' said Weir, 'and making good money until you lot came along.'

'And, who was he working for?'

'His brothers, as far as I know.'

Nigel turned to Rodney Williams. 'We'll be adding to the charge sheet and opposing bail, Mr Williams.'

'My client wants protective custody,' said Rodney. 'He's been threatened.'

'By who?' said Nigel.

'Tony Slade,' said Weir.

'I don't think you'll have to worry about that,' said Nigel. 'We'll hold you in different facilities.'

'What?'

'Tony was arrested, yesterday,' said Nigel.

CHAPTER FORTY-FOUR

It was mid-afternoon on Monday when Simon Winter, a lawyer from Carol and Associates, arrived at the Port Stanley Police Station.

By the time of his arrival, DI Henry had been briefed by DCI West on his interview with Tony Slade and on the findings of the search of James Weir's house. He had also read the preliminary report from Forensics summarising what they'd uncovered in the drug lab on the station.

DI Henry was closing his folder when DS Fuller came into the office they were sharing. 'We're ready to start, Inspector.'

Angus Slade was sitting in silence beside the young lawyer representing him when DI Henry and DS Fuller entered the interview room. The constable that had been guarding the prisoner stepped out of the room and closed the door.

DS Fuller activated the recorder and asked everyone to state their name for the record.

'How did you get mixed up in this business, Mr Slade?' said DI Henry.

Angus leant forward and settled his arms on the table. 'The

drought. If it hadn't been for the drought, I doubt we'd ever gotten into this mess.'

'You would have had a good year last year, wouldn't have you?'

'It rained a bit,' said Angus, 'a fair bit, to be honest, but you can't recover from five years of drought in one good season. Takes time to rebuild your herd, and breeding stock costs a fortune after a dry spell, especially when everyone's destocked.'

'But why go into manufacturing illicit drugs?'

'Couldn't get anything from the bank,' said Angus. 'If Tony hadn't come to us with this crazy idea we would have lost the station. It's only the proceeds from that operation that's keeping us afloat, and...' He smiled. 'It's drought proof. Silly buggers down in the city want the stuff all the time.'

'You know what this stuff does to kids, don't you?'

'I'm not selling it to kids,' said Angus, 'and, besides, I'm not forcing them to use it, am I?'

'Who are you selling it to?'

'This young fellow says I shouldn't be telling you that,' said Angus, nodding towards Simon Winter.

'You're under no obligation to answer any of our questions,' said DI Henry, 'but it always goes down better with the magistrates if you do.'

'Charlie flies it down to Hastings,' said Angus. 'Some fellow takes it from him and hands over the cash. We make the stuff for a fellow called Lombardo, and he sends the ingredients to Port Stanley on the train. I don't know where he gets it from but there are no checks on goods that come up from the city, are there?'

'So, who actually makes the stuff?'

'We've all had a go,' said Angus, 'but the stuff gets to you after a while. We had to stop Charlie from making it. You need a clear head to fly.'

'Why three planes?'

'Too many of us for one,' said Angus.

'Who else has a pilot's licence beside Charlie?'

'Me, my wife, and Charlie's son, Shaun. He flies the helicopter.'

'How did you find out how to make the stuff?'

'Lombardo sent up this fellow called Vito. He set up the equipment and showed us how to use it. He was here for a couple of months in the beginning, but we've been running it on our own for the last three years or so.'

'How much have you made?'

'Hard to say,' said Angus.

'How much money have you made?'

'Enough to keep the place running and keep the kids at school down in the city.'

'Does your father know anything about this?' said DI Henry.

'I certainly haven't told him.'

'What have you told your kids?'

'We're doing what we can to keep the station,' said Angus. 'They know not to discuss family business. That's how it's always been for the Slade family. That's how we've survived living out here.'

'This might make it a bit tougher for them,' said DI Henry. 'Ever think of that?'

'Guess you think you're never going to get caught,' said Angus. 'What tipped you off?'

'Doug Clarke's murder.'

'Dad always said he'd be trouble.'

––––––

When he'd interviewed the remaining members of the Slade family in custody, DI Henry charged Angus Slade with the manufacture and distribution of an illicit substance and named the others as accomplices.

By the time he'd completed the paperwork, Forensics' crime scene investigators had arrived back in Port Stanley with the remains of the dismantled meth lab, several kilograms of methamphetamine, and a trailer load of the chemicals and pharmaceuticals used to produce crystal meth.

On Tuesday morning, the family members were arraigned before a local magistrate and released on bail to appear at a later date.

After the court appearance, DI Henry handed the case over to the locals and he and DS Fuller caught the last flight back to the city.

CHAPTER FORTY-FIVE

Wayne showed his ID to the constable guarding Peter Thompson's room in the intensive care ward of City Hospital.

'Any sign of trouble?' said Wayne.

'Nothing,' said the constable.

Wayne opened the door and went into the room, where Thompson, with a bandage around his head, was hooked up to an IV drip and several machines monitoring his vital signs. Peter appeared to be sleeping but opened his eyes when Wayne closed the door.

'I remember you,' said Peter.

'How are you feeling?' said Wayne.

'Like shit,' said Peter. 'Where's Sergeant Fuller?'

'He's up north. Asked me to come and see you,' said Wayne. 'What happened?'

'Jack Swan tried to shut me up.'

'You sure it was Swan?'

'I've got a faulty security light in my driveway,' said Peter. 'Doesn't come on half the time and then comes on whenever it likes. Been meaning to get it fixed. Glad I didn't.'

Wayne wondered what he was rambling about but knew better than to interrupt a story once it got going.

'Bastard jumped me when I got home from visiting Mum, Sunday night. It was dark. Smacked my head on the car, kicked me in the ribs, and then he stabbed me in the guts. Bloody light came on after he stabbed me.' Peter raised his right arm and pointed at Wayne. 'It was bloody Jack Swan standing there with a bloody big knife in his hand. I passed out after that. He must have thought I was dead. He wasn't there when I woke up and called the ambulance.'

'Nice friends you have, Pete,' said Wayne. 'What are the doctors saying?'

'I'll live. They've stitched me guts back together. At least I'll be able to shit out my arse and not into a bag.'

'There's a guard outside and you won't be going home,' said Wayne. 'We're putting you into witness protection.'

'What I want to know is how the bastards found out I was talking to you.'

'Would help if we knew who the bastards were,' said Wayne.

'Jack gets his orders from Tony Slade.'

'We took Slade out of circulation Sunday morning,' said Wayne, 'and he's been offline for weeks.'

'Guess you'd better ask Jack when you arrest him, then.'

———

Through the trees, Jack Swan saw several police cars approaching along the road that led to the playing fields. He swung the mower around the cypress pine next to the tennis courts and started to cut the grass along the edge of the path between the courts and the oval. He knew there were no events scheduled for the playing fields. He watched the cars out of the corner of his eye and wondered what the police were doing driving around in the urban forest on a Tuesday morning.

When he reached the oval, he turned the mower around and headed back towards the tennis courts. There was a police car on the path by the courts blocking his way.

He stopped the mower and killed its engine. Two police officers got out of the patrol car. One of them was a slightly built Asian woman wearing body armour. Her partner was a tall athletic young man Jack knew he'd never outrun if it came to a chase.

Jack dismounted the mower and removed his safety helmet and earmuffs, leaving them on his seat. 'Can I help you?'

'Are you Jack Swan?' said the policewoman. 'Your supervisor said we'd find you here.'

Jack felt his breakfast churn. 'Yeah, I'm Swan. What do you want?'

'I'd like you to put your hands on your head,' said the policewoman, placing her right hand on her holster.

'What's going on?' said Jack, placing his hands on his head.

The policeman walked up behind Jack and patted him down. 'You can lower your arms, Mr Swan.' He waited for Jack to lower his arms and then handcuffed him.

'You're under arrest for the attempted murder of Peter Thompson,' said the policewoman. 'You don't have to say anything but whatever you do say may be used as evidence against you.'

'There must be some mistake,' said Jack.

'Tell that to the detectives,' said the policewoman.

'Watch your head,' said the policeman, as he directed Jack into the back of the patrol car.

Jack looked out through the window of the patrol car at the playing fields. He'd enjoyed working in the urban forest. He wasn't looking forward to another stretch in prison. He'd hated it the last time he'd been inside. He turned away from the trees and wished he'd taken the time to check Thompson was dead, instead of running off like a scared rabbit when his security light had come on.

———

Wayne went in with Nigel to interview Jack Swan after they allowed him a few minutes with his lawyer, Rodney Williams.

'Morning, Mr Williams,' said Wayne. 'Jack tell you why we've arrested him this time?'

'Says you're charging him with attempted murder of a work colleague. Is that right?'

'I would have thought Peter was more than a work colleague,' said Wayne, 'more like a partner in crime.'

'My client has denied that accusation,' said Rodney, 'and he's denying he had anything to do with whatever happened to Peter Thompson.'

'Where were you Sunday night around seven, Jack?' said Wayne.

'Home with the wife and kids.'

'Really?' said Wayne. 'Peter says you were at his place, belting the shit out of him.'

'He's full of shit.'

'Is that why you stuck the knife into him?'

'I didn't touch him,' said Jack. 'I wasn't there.'

'We've had people out talking to your neighbours, Jack. Want to guess what they told us?'

Jack crossed his arms on his chest.

'They said you went out around six and didn't come back until after eight. Want to tell me where you were again?'

'Whoever told you that is a liar,' said Jack. 'I was home.'

'Not according to your wife,' said Wayne. 'Want to read her

statement?'

'I do,' said Rodney.

Wayne passed the statement to the lawyer and waited while he read it.

'She's not giving you an alibi,' said Rodney, 'and, she's retracted her alibi for you being home the morning Doug Clarke was killed.'

Jack slumped in his chair.

'Did she find out you were seeing Gail?' said Wayne.

Jack sighed. 'She found out about the money, thanks to you lot.'

'Oh, I thought you were denying that.'

'That's going to be a bit hard now, isn't it?'

'Where were you the morning Doug Clarke was killed?' said Wayne.

'I was with Joe,' said Jack.

'Lombardo?'

'Yeah.'

'Doing what?'

'Taking care of Doug Clarke.'

'Want to step us through that?'

'Are you sure you want to do that?' said Rodney.

Jack looked at his lawyer. 'I've got to get this off my chest. Living with it is a lot harder than I thought it would be, especially the last one.'

'Peter?' said Wayne.

'No, Gail.'

'Start with Doug Clarke,' said Wayne. 'Where was he killed?'

'In the car park behind Gail's apartment. He thought he was meeting Gail but we were waiting for him.'

'Who stabbed him?'

'Me. Joe didn't have the balls.'

'What were you wearing?' said Wayne.

'I ditched the clothes,' said Jack. 'Got blood on them when we dumped the body.'

'What about Joe? What was he wearing?'

'Jeans and some fancy blue shirt. I wiped the knife on it.' Jack sneered. 'You should have seen the look on his face.'

'Where's the knife?' said Wayne.

'In the back of my car, in the wheel well.'

'Okay, you killed him at Portside, why dump the body in East Park?'

'That was Joe's idea.'

'Why kill him at all?' said Wayne.

'Bloody Gail couldn't keep her big mouth shut,' said Jack. 'She told him Tony was funding her business but Clarke knew about the poker game. He tried to blackmail us to get his son off the hook.'

'Richard?'

'Yeah. He owed Tony a shitload of money.'

'So, who ordered the hit? Tony?'

Jack laughed. 'Tony? No-one takes orders from Tony. He's a lackey, like the rest of us.'

'So, who?'

'Follow the money. I'm sure if you dig around in his accounts like you have in mine you'll find the answer.'

'So, you don't know who you were working for?'

'Look, we got paid. I didn't ask too many questions, but I'd say drugs were involved given what Jimmy Weir was doing.'

'What happened with Gail?'

'Ask Tony. All I know is he took her up into the hills and now she's dead.'

Wayne gathered up his papers and closed his folder.

'You used to work for the Rileys. They involved in this?'

'You're not getting anything out of me about the Rileys,' said Jack. 'That's a closed book.'

CHAPTER FORTY-SIX

Carl called a briefing on Wednesday morning with DI Henry and his team.

'Operations are putting together a task force to follow up Weir's distribution list,' said Carl. 'The plan is to hit the two big ones in the morning and then round up the rest. They're currently working out who is associated with each address, apart from the first two on the list. I'll get Nigel to tell you what we know so far.'

'Weir delivered most of the stuff to two addresses,' said DC Beard. 'Lisa did the maths. They represent eighty percent of the money.'

'Where are these places?' said DI Henry.

'One is a warehouse in Northfield. Used to belong to Arthur Redmond. The current owner is Michael Riley, the same Michael Riley that owns half the nightclubs in the city.'

'That's interesting,' said DI Henry. 'What about the other place?'

'His other big delivery is to a house in Morton Sands that

belongs to Helen Carol. She's David Callinan's first wife, but now she's married to Philip Carol's brother, Stephen.'

'What's the address of the place in Morton Sands?' said Carl, hoping it wasn't too close to where he lived.

DC Beard looked at his notes. '67 Whale Street.'

'That rings a bell,' said DC Paterson. 'I'm pretty sure that's the place Philip Carol told me EPS Property was buying.' He flipped through his notebook. 'Here it is. Settlement's set for Thursday, the fifteenth.'

'This is all getting a bit cosy,' said DI Henry, 'a bit too cosy, if you ask me.'

'Let's see how this fits together,' said Carl. 'Tony Slade's admitted he offered to finance Gail Swan's purchase of Clarke Finance before Clarke was killed, and we know now where that money was coming from. After she disappeared, Carol and Callinan bought Clarke Finance. I'd like to know where they got the money from. Was it the same place?'

'We'll need access to their trust accounts,' said DS Fuller.

'We could narrow that down by asking Mrs Clarke for details of the payment,' said DI Henry.

'We've got access to Slade's accounts,' said DC Paterson, 'and, apart from the transfers to Carol's trust account for three property purchases, there's nothing going to either of them.'

'We're assuming they're mixed up with Slade,' said DC Templar. 'What if they're mixed up with Lombardo or the Rileys?'

'Have we looked at Lombardo's accounts?' said Carl.

'No,' said DS Fuller. 'We didn't think he was involved in the money laundering.'

'Slade told me Lombardo was their connection to the distributors, I think that puts him squarely in the Riley camp,' said Carl, 'and I wouldn't be surprised if all those little dealers are Slade's or even Weir's network.'

'I wonder who's living in that house at Morton Sands,' said DS Fuller.

'Guess we'll know tomorrow,' said Carl.

———

There was a large sold sticker on the sign when Harry pulled up in front of Joanna Clarke's house.

That didn't take long, thought Harry, as he walked up the driveway to ring the doorbell.

'I won't keep you long, Mrs Clarke,' said Harry.

'Don't be silly,' said Joanna. 'Come in for a coffee and tell me what you've found out.'

Harry followed Joanna into the kitchen, where she made them both a coffee.

'We've had a confession from a man called Jack Swan,' said Harry.

'Any relation to Gail?'

'Her ex.'

'Bit late for her ex to be getting jealous, isn't it?'

'Wasn't related to that, I'm afraid,' said Harry. 'It had to do with Gail's plan to buy your business.'

'Doug told me he didn't think she had the money.'

'She didn't, but apparently she had some friends that did.'

'So why didn't she?'

'Those friends were the people Richard was playing poker with,' said Harry. 'Their money was coming from the sale of drugs, and it appears Richard was helping them launder it through the casino.'

'Richard?'

'He'd gotten himself into debt to a man named Tony Slade.'

Joanna put down her coffee cup. 'Poor Kathy. She told me

Richard had gambled away all their savings. Is that why he owed this fellow money?'

'Possibly,' said Harry. 'The point is, though, Richard must have told your husband.'

'Doug didn't say anything to me.'

'It appears your husband found out where Gail's money was coming from and threatened to report them if they didn't let Richard off the hook.'

'I can see how that would have been a mistake,' said Joanna, 'but he always thought he was a law unto himself.'

'They killed him to keep him quiet.'

'And, did they kill Richard as well, Sergeant?'

Harry shook his head. 'Don't know. Everything points to his death being a tragic accident brought on by speed.'

'He was such a careful driver,' said Joanna.

'The marks left on the road suggest he was going too fast coming into that corner,' said Harry. 'Perhaps he was being chased, we just don't know.'

'Will there be a trial?' said Joanna.

'Several, I'm afraid,' said Harry, 'so, you'd better prepare yourself for some negative publicity.'

'I hope this doesn't hurt Justin's chances of being elected.'

'I think the election will be over before the trials start,' said Harry. 'Now, there's one question I'd like to ask you.'

'What's that?'

'When you sold the business, where did the money come from? I mean, whose account did it come out of?'

'They did it electronically,' said Joanna. 'Philip said they were acting on behalf of a group of investors, so I knew it wasn't their money.'

'Did it come through his trust account?'

'No, I'm pretty sure he only did the paperwork. The money came from David's trust account, I think.'

'Can you check for me?'

Harry waited while Joanna went to her study and logged into her bank to review the account she'd used for Clarke Finance.

When she came back into the kitchen, Joanna handed him a piece of paper with an account number written on it. 'The money came from that account at First National. It's David Callinan's trust account.'

———

It was late on Wednesday afternoon when Harry and Wayne sat down with Tony Slade and Philip Carol.

'Jack Swan has confessed to killing Doug Clarke,' said Harry, 'and he says you weren't directly involved, Mr Slade.'

'I told your inspector mate I didn't have anything to do with it,' said Tony.

'Are you withdrawing the murder charge?' said Philip.

'Jack had a fair bit to say about why Doug Clarke was killed,' said Harry, 'and I'm afraid that implicates your client.'

'What are you talking about?' said Philip.

'Haven't you caught up with your associate since yesterday, Mr Carol?'

'We're a bit stretched at the moment,' said Philip.

'According to Jack, the reason Clarke was killed is because he threatened to blow the lid on your client's money laundering activities.'

'How would Doug have known anything about that?' said Philip. 'Even I hadn't heard about it until weeks after his death.'

'Richard,' said Tony. 'He was desperate for money. That's how I got him into the game, but I made a mistake. He didn't bank one of his big wins. I told him I wanted the money back. He told his Dad about what he was doing.' Tony leant back in his seat. 'His old man threatened to expose us if we didn't forgive the debt and pay twice what his business was worth.'

'Why didn't you pay?' said Harry.

'What? And open a tap to never-ending blackmail.'

'So, you decided to kill him?'

'Not me,' said Tony. 'I wasn't running the show.'

'Who is, then?'

'Ask Joe. I took my orders from him.'

'Then there's the death of Gail Swan,' said Harry. 'Jack's saying you killed her.'

'Wasn't me,' said Tony, 'and it wasn't Jack, either.'

'How do you know that?'

'She was shot, wasn't she?'

'How do you know that?' said Harry. 'That's not public knowledge.'

'But you told Jack,' said Philip, 'and I passed it on.'

'Point is, I don't have a pistol and Jack prefers a knife.'

'Your prints are in her apartment,' said Harry.

'She was a very attractive woman,' said Tony. 'I'm going to miss her.'

'Do you have any idea who would have wanted her dead?'

'I suggest you take a look under the floorboards in Joe's office.'

CHAPTER FORTY-SEVEN

Paul Henry wasn't surprised when Margaret Yates, from Knight and Richards, turned up to represent Joe Lombardo. He waited for DC Templar to switch on the recorder.

'We're here to discuss a few new developments,' said Paul.

'You mean something beyond my client being suspected as an accomplice to murder?' said Margaret. 'Which I understand he's denied.'

'You've had the opportunity to read the transcripts of your client's previous interviews, Ms Yates?'

'Yes, thank you, Inspector.'

'We've had a confession from a man named Jack Swan,' said Paul.

'So, that clears my client, then?'

'No,' said Paul. 'It implicates your client further. Swan claims your client was with him when he stabbed Doug Clarke and helped him dump the body in East Park, before disposing of Clarke's car.'

'Jack's full of shit,' said Joe.

'He's also confessed to trying to kill Peter Thompson,' said Paul, 'and Peter has verified that for us.'

'I don't know anything about that either,' said Joe. 'I've been in here cut off from everything.'

'We've also arrested Tony Slade, and he's blown your alibi for the morning Doug Clarke was killed.'

'All that means is he wasn't home,' said Joe.

'He told us you had Doug Clarke's car at your place that afternoon.'

Joe shrugged his shoulders. 'He's spinning you a yarn.'

'Jack told us you were wearing a blue shirt, which he wiped the knife on,' said Paul, 'which I suspect is the same shirt we pulled out of a bin at Gail Swan's place in Ashcroft.'

'Anyone could have put that shirt there.'

'Tony's identified the shirt as being his,' said Paul, 'and the DNA we extracted from the shirt confirms that. But, he claims he put it out to be washed a couple of days before Doug Clarke was killed.'

'More like he wore it and helped Jack.'

'Do you know Angus Slade, Mr Lombardo?'

'He's one of Tony's brothers, isn't he?'

'He says he knows you, Mr Lombardo, and that you introduced him to the world of crystal meth production.'

'I don't know anything about crystal meth,' said Joe.

'That's not what Tony told us.'

'That doesn't make it true.'

'What were you and Tony doing if it wasn't organising the production and distribution of crystal meth and washing the proceeds through the casino?'

'I told you. I'm a business consultant.'

'So, are you the one who advised Gail Swan to use Tony's money to buy out Doug Clarke?'

'She wasn't using Tony's money. He was putting all his winnings into property.'

'So, whose money was she going to use?'

'Callinan was financing her. He has a stack of investors on his books. Look, I used to work for him. We were always looking for ways to invest people's money.'

'So, you're denying any involvement with the Slades' crystal meth business?'

'Yes,' said Joe, turning to Margaret. 'Did you get that? I have nothing to do with drugs.'

'Do you know Michael Riley? You know, the guy who owns half a dozen nightclubs in the city.'

'He's one of my clients,' said Joe. 'I help him with the financial management of his nightclubs.'

'You must be good, Mr Lombardo. I see he's paying you a small fortune for your services.'

Joe smiled.

'We arrested him this morning during a drugs raid,' said Paul. 'I wonder what he'll have to say about the quality of your services.'

'I'm sure he'll recommend me,' said Joe.

'Oh, and there's one other thing, Mr Lombardo.' Paul reached down, opened his briefcase, and lifted out an evidence bag containing a pistol. 'We found this under the floor in your office. Do you have a licence for it?'

'Who says it's mine?'

'It's got your prints on it, Mr Lombardo.'

'All that means is I touched it.'

'It's the same calibre as a bullet found in the wreckage of Richard Clarke's car,' said Paul.

'What is it? Nine mill?' Joe leant forward and examined the pistol. 'They're as common as shit.'

'High probability this is the weapon that killed Gail Swan,' said Paul.

'But that's got nothing to do with me,' said Joe.

'I'm not so sure about that, Mr Lombardo. I think you had a reason to kill her, and the opportunity.'

'What opportunity?'

'I don't think Gail ever got back from Ashcroft, Mr Lombardo, and that would make you the last person seen with her on the Monday morning after Doug Clarke was killed.'

'I wasn't in Ashcroft that weekend.'

'You're forgetting those fingerprints you left in Doug Clarke's car, Mr Lombardo.'

'And you're dreaming, Inspector.'

'I don't think so, Mr Lombardo. You should have switched off your phone and picked up after yourself,' said Paul, holding up a second evidence bag with a nine-millimetre shell casing inside it.

CHAPTER FORTY-EIGHT

David Callinan welcomed Harry and Wayne into his office.

'Now, what exactly do you want to know about the purchase of Clarke Finance?'

'You told Mrs Clarke you were buying her business on behalf of a group of investors. Is that correct?'

'Yes, I'm the managing agent,' said David.

'What's in it for you?' said Harry.

'I charge a fee for managing their investment.'

'Just like Doug Clarke did for his investors?'

'We'll continue to service his investors,' said David. 'That was one of the conditions Joanna insisted on.'

'Fair enough,' said Harry. 'That makes sense to me. What I want to know is the names of the investors who funded the purchase?'

'I'm afraid that's confidential.'

'It might be confidential,' said Harry, 'but it's not privileged client advice, Mr Callinan.'

A sheen appeared on Callinan's brow, despite the air-conditioned atmosphere of the office they were in. Harry knew he was on to something.

'You'll need a court order before I can divulge that information,' said David.

Harry put his hand into the inside pocket of his suit coat. 'Thought you might say that.' He handed the search warrant to David.

'Why do you want a copy of my trust account transactions?'

'You paid Mrs Clarke out of that account,' Mr Callinan. 'I want to know where the money came from.'

'All sorts of transactions go through that account, Sergeant. That's my practice's clearing account.'

'Well, you could make it easy by telling me who put up the money to buy out Mrs Clarke?'

David leant back in his chair and closed his eyes. Harry wondered if he'd cooperate or make him search through the account.

'The bulk of the money came from Michael Riley and Stephen Carol. They're my biggest client,' said David. 'You might have heard of them, they own several successful nightclubs in the city.'

'I've heard of Michael Riley,' said Harry. 'Who are the others?'

'Philip Carol and I are the other investors.'

'How long have you been doing business with Michael Riley?' said Harry.

'Be around ten years,' said David. 'Philip introduced him to me when his brother went into partnership with Michael. That was when they bought half a dozen new clubs.'

'Did you introduce Joe Lombardo to them?'

'They poached him,' said David. 'He was working for me as an auditor when they came on board. They engaged us to set up a financial management system across all their sites.' David smiled. 'I sent Joe to them. He didn't come back.'

'So, your firm does the accounts for Michael Riley?'

'We do the tax reporting and the company filings,' said David. 'Is there anything else you want to know, Sergeant.'

Harry stood up. 'No, I think we're done.'

'Why the interest?' said David.

'Well, the person who wanted to buy Clarke Finance ended up dead, but you told us she didn't have the money in any case. I wanted to know who did.'

'Do you think we were behind Gail's proposal?'

'The thought did cross my mind.'

'I assure you, Sergeant, we only made our offer when Joanna told Philip she wanted to sell after Richard died in that dreadful accident,' said David. 'I had nothing to do with Gail's plans, apart from the advice I gave her on how to set up her business.'

'Before we go,' said Harry, 'you might want to put a hold on any money you're holding for Michael Riley and Stephen Carol.'

'Why's that, Sergeant?'

'They've been arrested, and I suspect they may have been planning to launder funds through Clarke Finance.'

The color drained from David's face and Harry wondered what it would feel like to realize you'd been duped by one of your biggest clients. He glanced at Wayne, standing poker faced beside him, and hoped his own face wasn't betraying his thoughts.

'Really?' said David. 'If news of that gets out it could ruin my reputation. I've spent my whole life building this business.'

'You should have nothing to worry about,' said Harry, 'unless you were aware of their plans and the source of their money.'

The color returned to David's face. 'I assure you, Sergeant. We do everything above board and according to the law here.'

'I'm sure you do, Mr Callinan,' said Harry. 'Are you aware if you are holding any of their funds in your trust account?'

'No, they were waiting for me to strike an agreement with the Yorke Group,' said David. 'No-one moves money these days unless there's a reward for doing so, and I certainly don't pay interest on funds sitting in my trust account.'

'Might be prudent to use funds from some of your other investors for your current projects,' said Harry. 'This could take a while to sort out.'

———

When the detectives had gone, David opened the credenza and poured himself a cognac. He sipped his drink and wondered if the detectives had believed his story about being nothing more than a service provider. He wasn't worried about the younger one that had done the talking. He thought he'd believed him, but he wasn't so sure about the older detective with an impenetrable face who hadn't said a word.

He put down his glass, picked up his mobile phone, and called Philip. He heard the call being diverted.

'Carol and Associates.'

'Amanda, it's David Callinan. Is Philip about?'

'He was called out, David. Can I take a message?'

'Ask him to give me a call when he gets back in.'

David ended the call, assuming Philip had been called in to represent Michael and Stephen while they were being interrogated by the police.

———

Philip Carol sat in his car thinking, after spending the afternoon inside Police Headquarters. He realized that the delivery driver's records, the confession of the Slades, and the amount of drugs seized at the Northfield warehouse and the house in Morton Sands, gave the police a strong case against Michael and Stephen. He wasn't sure the police would be able to link them to the deaths of Doug Clarke and Gail Swan, but he suspected they'd try. After all, Jack Swan had confessed to killing Doug Clarke on behalf of Tony Slade, although Tony had blamed Joe.

He didn't know what Joe would do now that he'd been charged with killing Gail, or how much Peter Thompson actually knew about the operation, since he'd only been involved in the poker game. That meant his knowledge was limited to Tony's part of the operation, and he'd already confessed. Too bad Jack had failed to silence Thompson.

As he drove back to his office in East Park, Philip wondered how long it would take the police to find out he and David had invested in the nightclubs when Michael and Stephen had joined forces, and whether he'd be able to convince them he was only a passive investor with no active role in the operations of the business. He knew there were no records of their interactions, apart from contracts he'd drawn up for them and court cases he'd been involved in on their behalf, and thought he'd be able to explain any phone calls they found out about as either private conversations with his brother or discussions with them as clients.

When he got back to the office, his receptionist passed him the message from David.

'What's up, Dave?'

'Had the police here again today asking me about who funded the purchase of Clarke Finance.'

'What did you tell them?'

'The truth.'

'How did that go down?'

'They warned me not to use any more money from Michael and Stephen. Said something about them being arrested.'

'That would be good advice to follow,' said Philip. 'It looks like Michael and Stephen are in serious trouble for drug dealing.'

'What else did you hear?' said David.

'They've charged Joe with Gail's murder.'

'Joe?'

'Yes. Caught me by surprise, too.'

'What do we do now?'

'Sit tight and stick to the script. You're their accountant, not their business manager. That's Joe.'

'What if the boys talk about being recruited to the poker game?'

'You only spoke to Jack. He knows the rules, and he knows he's no safer inside than out.'

There was a silence and Philip imagined he could hear David's mind ticking over.

'What about our investment in the nightclubs? How do we explain that?'

'Keep it simple, Dave. We invested in a nightclub business, not a drug dealing operation.'

'Do you think they'll believe us?'

'Can't see why not,' said Philip. 'Look, I have to go. I've got a lot to do before tomorrow morning.'

Philip ended the call and opened his briefcase. He had to be in court in the morning, and he wanted to be prepared.

CHAPTER FORTY-NINE

On the Friday afternoon after the court appearance of Michael Riley and Stephen Carol, Carl called a meeting with DI Henry and his team.

When the team had assembled and settled, Carl stood in front of the whiteboard covered with photographs and notes outside his old office.

'The Commissioner is moving the investigation into the network distributing the crystal meth manufactured by the Slades to the Drugs Taskforce. He asked me to pass on his congratulations for a job well done,' said Carl. 'I want DI Henry to focus on securing convictions for the murders of Doug Clarke and Gail Swan, and the attempted murder of Peter Thompson.'

'What about the death of Richard Clarke?' said DS Fuller.

'Unless someone confesses or comes forward with new evidence, I don't think we have enough to bring a charge, although I wouldn't be surprised if Lombardo or Slade were involved.'

'What about the money laundering through the casino?' said DC Paterson.

'I think we have enough to proceed with that, thanks to Peter Thompson and the confession we've got from Tony Slade.'

'Do you reckon that smart-arse lawyer is involved in that,' said DC Paterson. 'He put their company together.'

'Unless we can find a direct link, that's going to be hard to prove,' said Carl. 'After all, that's what lawyers do, isn't it?'

'His brother's involved,' said DC Beard.

'That still doesn't make him a criminal,' said Carl. 'We'd need to show criminal intent and that he was getting something from their property transactions apart from his normal fees to go there.'

'Still, it's a bit strange they all used the same legal firm for their defence,' said DI Henry.

'Yes, but not conclusive,' said Carl. 'They had, after all, used the firm for their paperwork and Carol and Associates does a lot of criminal work.'

'What about that accountant?' said DC Paterson. 'I didn't get a good feeling about him.'

'Me neither,' said DS Fuller.

'You're going to need something besides gut feeling to convince me,' said Carl. 'His story holds water for now.'

'He took advantage of Swan's death,' said DS Fuller. 'Makes me think he knows more about what she was up to than he's let on.'

'Proving that is going to be a problem, Harry.'

'What about the Right Honourable Member?' said DI Henry.

'The Commissioner wants him left out of it unless something comes up when his sons go to trial.'

'Is there anything else, Chief?' said DI Henry.

'First round is on me,' said Carl.

CHAPTER FIFTY

It was after eight when Carl got home. Too late to take Sophie for a walk down to the playground but not late enough to miss out on giving her a bath before she went to bed.

'You sure you're okay to bath her?' said Nina.

'I've only had a couple of beers,' said Carl. 'Chief inspectors have to lead by example.'

'That would be a change,' said Nina. 'I don't recall it stopping you when you were an inspector.'

'Times are changing,' said Carl. 'Now, come on, Sophie, let's get you organized for your bath.'

After he'd bathed Sophie and put her to bed, Carl sat in the kitchen with Nina.

'Are you glad you got the promotion?' said Nina.

Carl picked up the coffee she'd made for him. 'It's not quite what I'd expected. It's a bit of a challenge standing back and letting others do the work.'

'But it will keep you out of harm's way,' said Nina. 'I didn't like it when I was waiting up for you to get home or when you were called out in the middle of the night.'

Carl reached across the table and touched her hands. 'Those days are over. Now it's all supervising the troops and protecting them from the politics upstairs.'

'Do you think we should think about a little playmate for Sophie before she gets much older?'

Carl finished his coffee. 'Are you propositioning me, Mrs West?'

Nina smiled. 'I'll take that as a yes.'

A NOTE FROM PETER

If you enjoyed *The East Park Syndicate,* you can help other readers share your enjoyment by telling them about the book and writing a review.

Drop by at **www.petermulraney.com** and join my **Crime Readers Group** to download a free copy of *Deadly Sands,* and be one of the first to know when my next book will be released.

ACKNOWLEDGMENTS

A book is a community project. I'd like to acknowledge the emotional support I received from Toni during the writing of *The East Park Syndicate*, and the editorial assistance provided by Francesco during the massaging of the original manuscript into the final book.

This book has also received assistance from the members of my Street Team, who act as beta readers and provide feedback that always improves the quality of the final product.

It's also great to have readers who write reviews and spread the work among their friends.

A big thank you to you all.

ALSO BY PETER MULRANEY

Inspector West series

After

The Holiday

Holy Death

Whistleblower

Twisted Justice

Inspector West Collection One

Inspector West Collection Two

Stella Bruno Investigates series

The Identity Thief

A Gun of Many Parts

Bones in the Forest

A Deadly Game of Hangman

Taken

Fallout

Stella Bruno Investigates: Books 1 to 6

The Identity Thief Collection

The Fallout Collection

Ryan Holiday PI Short Stories

Rosie

Framed

Living Alone series

After She's Gone

Cooking 4 One

Sanity Savers

Living Alone (Collection)

Living Alone Journal

Novella

The New Girlfriend

Everyday Business Skills

Everyday Project Management

Everyday Productivity

Everyday Money Management

Writings of the Mystic

Sharing the Journey: Reflections of a Reluctant Mystic.

A Question of Perspective

My Life is My Responsibility: Insights for Conscious Living

My Life is My Responsibility Workbook

I Am Affirmations: The Power of Words

Beyond the Words: Reflections on I Am Affirmations

Mystical Journey: A Handbook for Modern Mystics

Sharing the Journey Coloring Books

Mandalas

Mandalas by 3

Sharing the Journey Coloring Journals

Sharing the Journey Coloring Journal

Sharing the Journey Coloring Journal ~Discovery

Sharing the Journey Coloring Journal ~ Reflection